DROWNING IN THE DESERT

WESTERN LITERATURE AND FICTION SERIES

Like the iconic physical landscape and diverse cultures that inspire it, the literature of the American West is imbued with power and beauty. The Western Literature and Fiction Series invites scholarship reflecting on the authors and works that define the creative expression of the past and present while championing the literary fiction that propels us forward.

Drowning in the Desert

A Nevada Noir Novel

BERNARD SCHOPEN

UNIVERSITY OF NEVADA PRESS | *Reno & Las Vegas*

University of Nevada Press | Reno, Nevada 89557 USA
www.unpress.nevada.edu
Copyright © 2023 by Bernard Schopen
All rights reserved
Manufactured in the United States of America

First Printing

Cover design by Martyn Schmoll
Cover photograph © Alex Diaz

Library of Congress Cataloging-in-Publication Data
Names: Schopen, Bernard, author.
Title: Drowning in the desert : a Nevada noir novel / Bernard Schopen.
Other titles: Western literature and fiction series.
Description: Reno : University of Nevada Press, [2023] | Series: Western literature and fiction
    series | Summary: "This is a tale about water, money, politics, and corruption in Nevada,
    in both the clamor of Las Vegas and the still of the desert. It's also about the struggle of
    men and women to find in this inhospitable world, and in one another, the means to make
    a life."—Provided by publisher.
Identifiers: LCCN 2023003140 | ISBN 9781647791186 (paperback) | ISBN 9781647791193
    (ebook)
Subjects: LCSH: Nevada—Fiction. | West (U.S.)—Fiction.
Classification: LCC PS3569.C52814 D76 2023 | DDC 377.419576—dc24
LC record available at https://lccn.loc.gov/2023003140

To Greg and Alice and Verne and Annie and Barb

Acknowledgments

As this novel took shape, several people offered helpful comments. I would like to thank for their interest and efforts Phil Boardman, Mike Croft, Christine Kelly, Robert Merrill, Gaye Nickols, John Petty, Verne Smith, Danilo John Thomas, and Curtis Vickers.

I also here lament the passing of the two careful readers whose intelligent criticism and constant encouragement over the years kept me on task—Margaret Dalrymple and Michael Binard.

DROWNING IN THE DESERT

1

Water came now in a weak but steady stream. The flow drained from an old iron pipe into a battered galvanized-steel stock tank, then spilled over to soak back into the mountain or to evaporate in the dry thin air.

The spring greened a wide bench near the tree line. Beyond a pine-pole corral, on the slope a few shrubs rooted in rocky creases. Above these there was only granite, boulder and talus and scree trailing from gray crags, and, higher, even in mid-August, bright white snow.

The sun said it was well past midday. The wind soughed. A jay fussed. Near the corral, a young bay mare cropped the sparse mountain foliage. Beside the water tank stood Fats Rangle, squat, still.

His boots were muddy, as were the knees of his jeans, and his work shirt was patched darkly, his Stetson stained with sweat. He'd ridden all morning to get up here, and after unsaddling, brushing, and hobbling the horse, he'd worked on the spring, snaking the pipe clear of a clog of corrosion and rust and mud, then bracing the tank against the weight of the water. Now the job was done. He was satisfied, content.

He didn't look content. He almost never did. He looked angry, which, for the moment at least, he wasn't.

He was here for the night. He might have made it back down before sundown, but Ruckus, the mare, was worn out from the hot climb. Better a rest, a night in the high country cool.

He'd made camp between the spring and the corral, arranging his bedding and gear around an old fire pit. He started toward it. Then he stopped.

High above, just beyond the snow line, reflected sunlight flashed. Fats watched for a short while as the brightness flared, flickered, slowly dimmed, and disappeared.

He knew what it had to be. He knew too that it was none of his business, not anymore. But he was here. He had nothing he had to do. He thought he could get up there and back before nightfall.

He went to his camp and got an apple and walked over to the horse and fed her from his hand as he quietly told her what he was about to do and why. Removing the hobbles, he led her to the spring, where she drank, and then into the corral.

He went back to his gear and took out and strapped on a gun belt and holstered his old Colt Trooper .38 Special. He had no need of the revolver, but he wouldn't leave it unattended, even though he was almost certainly the sole human being around for miles. The only tool he wanted was already buttoned into his shirt pocket.

He studied the mountain, fixing in his mind the route he would try to take. Then he started to climb. Soon he was sweating and sore, ankle, knee, hamstring. He angled up across rock-strewn slopes, around boulders and outcrops, over spreads of broken granite. He stopped three times to catch his breath and plan out passages. After two hours, he had reached the snow.

He could see it now, the airplane, fifty yards above him. Snow slopped over most of the identifying red letters and numbers on its side, but that didn't matter. The V-tail and back-pack engine offered identification enough.

The Cirrus Vision SF50, newly purchased by a Dallas air taxi service, had gone down in a storm two years before. The small jet's emergency locator transmitter had ceased sending over the Turquoise Range, thirty miles from Blue Lake, Nevada, but the National Transportation Safety Board calculated that the aircraft might have crashed anywhere in a largely trackless two hundred square miles of canyon and gulch, thick stands of timber and snow-shrouded peaks. Search planes fitted with the latest technology had failed to find it. Fats could see why.

Most of the aircraft was still buried, but after two mild winters and exceptionally hot summers, enough snow had melted to expose both the distinctive tail and, wedged beneath an overhang of rock, the nose and the cockpit window and the open clamshell door.

More interesting to Fats was the track in the snow, now sun-softened and smoothed, that zigzagged up to the wreckage. Someone had been here, he guessed a month or so ago. He also could guess who. And why.

He rested for a few minutes, enjoying the cool that rose from the snow, the soothe of a breeze. He turned and looked out through the heat haze to the darkness of another range fifty miles away. What he could see of the desert was brown and empty.

He turned his attention to the path again. Then he stepped into the snow, cracking the thin crust and sinking a few inches into the soft wet sag of a slow melting. He waded up the switchback trail to the plane.

Pulling out his phone from his shirt pocket, he carefully photographed the crash site, the snow and the rock, the distinctive V-tail of the plane and the red lettering and the engine piggy-backed onto the fuselage. Then he moved up to the door, which had sprung open, it appeared, in the crash.

The dead men were still strapped into their seats. Almost two years in the snow and the dry mountain air had made them mummies of a sort, skin dark and papery. The pilot's head was twisted to expose black blood and broken bone: jagged rock had torn away the side window and shattered the man's skull above his eye. The passenger showed no wounds. His dry and slightly shrunken eyes were wide open and his mouth was agape, as if death had amazed him.

The bodies seemed not to have been disturbed. The passenger's clawlike hands gripped an expensive leather attaché case. There was nothing in the cockpit that shouldn't have been there: operating documentation, charts, flight plan, a paper coffee cup. The cabin was empty.

Fats checked his phone for a signal, but he was high up a Nevada mountain, well beyond the range of the nearest cell tower. He buttoned his phone back into his shirt pocket. Then, noting the angle of the sun, he started down through the snow, taking care to tramp out all sign of the original trail. When he reached bare rock, he stopped and looked up at the plane. Already it was nearly hidden again in shadows.

He looked down the mountainside. He took a deep breath. The climb up had been difficult. The climb down would be treacherous.

He reached his camp at last light. After seeing to the mare, he put away his pistol, started a small cookfire, and laid out his bedroll. When the fire had burned to coals, he heated and ate a panful of venison stew.

The day declined. He cleaned the pan at the spring and washed his face in the icy water. He doused the fire. He said good night to the horse. He took off his boots and his shirt and crawled into his sleeping bag.

Night settled onto the mountain. Fats lay on his back, aching all over and tired but not really sleepy. The wind slowed into stillness. Stars came out in clusters. Life of some sort stirred in the brush. Silence swelled.

He awoke to the scream of a lion. The eerie, awful sound, so like that of a stricken woman, seemed to hang in the night. The frightened mare snorted, thumped her hooves heavily. Fats got up and made his way to the corral in the darkness. He stroked the mare's nose, talked quietly to her, told her that she was in no danger, that the lion was a long way off, that the cry wasn't a threat, just a female in heat calling for a mate. Slowly the horse quieted.

Fats went back to his bed. He seemed to still hear the cry of the mountain lion. Then he heard nothing.

He was awake before dawn. As the gray chill brightened and warmed, he cooked coffee, then did his chores, replacing a couple of cracked corral poles. By mid-morning he was done. He saddled and packed Ruckus. Mounted, he gave the spring one last look. Then he nudged the horse toward the trail down to the desert.

August heat rose to meet their descent, became a not uncomfortable weight on his shoulders. Pinon and juniper thinned, opened to sage and spiny plants and tiny flowers that fought for water. Halfway down, Fats stopped, dismounted, wet a cloth, and rubbed the nostrils of the horse. He drank from his canteen, remounted, and rode on.

His pickup and horse trailer were parked at the trailhead. Dismounting, he took out his phone, found the signal strong, and without a message sent the photos of the downed plane to the Pinenut County Sheriff's Office. Then he turned his phone off again.

He loaded Ruckus in the trailer and drove in the heavy heat down the graveled road to Gull Valley and the paved county highway. After a couple of miles of dusty, shrub-strewn desert, he slowed at a dirt crossroad. On the valley side, the track was little more than ruts following what was left of Cherry Creek, a muddy trickle that slid from a culvert, past a field of alfalfa watered by a central pivot irrigation system, and out onto a small playa, where it spread and disappeared. On the other side was an arrowed sign: Cherry Creek Stables and Excursions.

Fats turned off into the narrow gap that wound through the desert hills, after half a mile reaching an enclave of a small pond, pasture, and ranch buildings. Except for a stint in the army, and a couple of years in Las Vegas acquiring an AA in criminal justice, he had lived here all his life. After over four decades, he knew every shape and shadow of the place.

Horses grazed in the creek-fed meadow. Ducks bobbed and nodded on the pond, which spilled over and dribbled water into the gulch. A big old barn, newer adjoining stables, and several smaller outbuildings all were painted a sun-faded red. Farm equipment and horse trailers sat shaded in one open shed, ATVs and Sno-Cats in another. Worn-out machinery and begrimed vehicles formed a neat square at the edge of the pasture. Nearby a Ram pickup was parked before a large white house, two-storied, screen-porched. At the far end of the ranch yard another, smaller white house stood alone.

The place looked prosperous. It wasn't, particularly, but all was tidy and well tended to, like the Rangle brothers themselves, Gull Valley gossips smirked, after Mary Tucker took them in hand.

Fats drove into the dirt yard and got out of the vehicle. Buddy, his nephew, looked out from the doorway of the barn, waved, and vanished. Fats's younger brother, Bill, stepped down from the house porch and, with a rolling limp, came over. He grinned. "Sheriff just called. Wants you to come in."

Fats moved to the back of the trailer, jerked the restraining bar, and swung open the door.

Bill Rangle's grin widened. "Mary's looking for you too. She expected you back yesterday."

"Told her I might not make it."

"She had to go by herself to see the bank."

"I'll talk to her tonight," Fats said. "First I need to deal with Dale Zahn."

"How 'bout I take care of your gal here?" Bill moved to the trailer door. "Buddy can put everything away while you get cleaned up."

Fats didn't move. "I found that missing plane. In the snow above Shoshone Springs." Fats showed his brother the photographs on his phone as he told him how he'd come to take them. He didn't tell him about the zigzag trail in the snow.

The two men stood for a moment, silent in the heat of the high sun. Both were not quite mid-sized, both thickset. Bill Rangle didn't have his older brother's bulk, but his shoulders were as wide, his chest as deep, his legs as stumpy. His features too were similar—pale blue eyes, snub nose, square jaw—but more finely formed. Beside him, Fats seemed a roughed-out model, not quite finished.

When Fats said no more, Bill asked, "There any reward?"

"Not that I know of," Fats said.

Bill backed the mare out of the trailer. Then he nodded toward the pasture, where a pinto gelding rolled in the grass. "Getting frisky, Splash."

The brothers silently watched. Then Fats said. "Tell me again about Strutter."

Bill stroked the mare's neck. "Come back from taking a family fishing and camping at Heart Lake. Said he'd left his .22 pistol at Shoshone Springs and was riding back up the next day to get it. A couple days later, he leaves us his horse to tend to, says he's off to Vegas to see a girl. Be gone a week, maybe longer. That was a month ago."

"And paid a week's board for Splash." Fats watched the pinto get up and begin to graze. Ruckus watched too, nickered, scraped at the dirt with an impatient hoof. "Where you suppose the money come from?"

Bill grinned. "Ill-got, knowing Strutter."

"And why take off all of a sudden?"

"Probably because he had the money." Bill grinned again. "True lust, seemed like. He'd been going on about this gal for a while. Liked her. Said she was a sexy little thing."

"He tell you anything else about her—name, where she worked, anything like that?"

"Salome. That's what she calls herself," Bill said. "Didn't say what she did. Moniker like that, a guy could guess, though. He talked like he knew her from before."

Fats took off his hat and ran thick fingers through his thinning hair. "When I see Dale Zahn, I'll make a missing person report."

"Seems like the thing to do," Bill said.

Fats gave the mare an affectionate pat. "Rub her down good. Lion spooked her last night. And she had a hard go in this heat."

Fats walked over to the small isolated white house, a bunkhouse remodeled into two rooms, with a kitchen and bath. The linoleum floor was cracked and torn. The furnishings were few, unmatched, old.

He slid the holstered Colt into a bedside table drawer. Then he showered and changed clothes. When he came out again into the sun, the horse trailer was in a shed and his saddle and tack and camp gear were gone from the pickup bed. At the barn door Buddy waved again.

Soon Fats was on the paved road headed for town.

Not that long ago, there hadn't been much in this end of Gull Valley. Stunted sage, dusty tracks to nowhere in particular, worthless land without water. He'd felt at home in it. Now the desert was cluttered. Somehow zoning laws had been changed, parcels of real estate transferred, commercial buildings put up. Roads sliced across the buckled earth to new homes sitting on forty-acre lots. Deep wells and drought had lowered the water table, and much of the vegetation, scant to begin with, had shriveled away. What had been dry and empty was now dead.

When he reached the state highway, where a new Shell truck stop commanded a corner, Fats turned toward Blue Lake. Passing the airport recently risen on empty acres owned, no one knew quite how, by a county commissioner, he finally gave thought to what he was going to tell the sheriff. The truth—or some of it, anyway. And some not. Everybody lies.

He thought too about Mary. His sister-in-law had wanted him along when she talked to the bank. He guessed she knew he wasn't going to like what the loan officer would have to say.

As the highway eased up a low hill, the dark mass of the Turquoise Range came into view, as did the tan foothills that bordered Blue Lake and the vast pale playa on which in wet years enough water spread to explain the town's name. A billboard blared the welcome of a dead cowboy movie star who had once owned a ranch in Gull Valley. Weather-worn homes slumped in the sageland, some with small horse sheds and corrals, some with yards littered with dead machines. The highway slid past them and the Blue Lake Indian Colony, down what locals called The Rise and into town.

In the late-afternoon heat, the wide, sun-beaten Blue Lake streets were mostly still. Fats turned at Cottonwood Creek Park and idled up to an empty space before the old stone of the Pinenut County Courthouse. The newer concrete block building beside it housed the county jail and the sheriff's office.

He was reaching for the office door when somebody pushed it open from the other side. The woman who came out was small and well set up, wearing work clothes—boots and broad-brimmed hat, jeans, long-sleeved shirt. She also wore, in a holster clipped onto her belt, a 9mm Beretta.

The sight of him jolted her out of an intense inner occupation. "Oh, Norman."

Fats touched the brim of his hat. "Donna."

Strain crimped a corner of her smile. She seemed angry, unhappy and trying to hide it. "I ran into Mary at the bank. She said if I saw you to tell you to turn on your gol dang phone."

"I forget," he lied.

Her smile this time came brittle, as if about to crack. "Busy summer? Horseback riders, campers, fishing parties, all that?"

"Busy enough," Fats said.

For a moment neither spoke. She patted the pistol on her hip. Then her face changed as she nodded at the office door. "You don't miss it?"

"Nope."

"Because he could use your help, Dale." Her voice roughened as she spoke her husband's name.

Fats met her gaze. "I'm happy doing what I'm doing."

She bit her lower lip. She did that, he knew, when she was uncertain, unsettled. "Are you, Norman? Happy?"

"I'm fine," he said brusquely.

"It's so hard to tell with you, the way you're always glowering." She tried her smile once more. "I always expect you to start to growl."

"Yeah," he said, in fact feeling an old anger, cold, gathering in his throat. "Need to talk to the sheriff, though."

"Yes, of course. I didn't. . . ." Abruptly, again patting her pistol, she moved aside. "It's good to see you, Norman."

"You too," he lied again, reaching again for the door.

Inside, the workspace was cooled by a humming central air system. Fats didn't know either of the two young male deputies who eyed his entrance, but he nodded to Caroline Sam, a Paiute woman he'd served with for some years. She was tough, trustworthy. They got along.

She smiled. "Finding that plane. You'll be on TV, Fats."

"Not a chance," he said. He knocked on the frosted-glass of the door to the sheriff's private office but didn't wait for an invitation to enter.

Dale Zahn leaned back in his chair. For a moment he was silent. Then he said, "Fats. Have a seat."

As Fats sat, the sheriff turned to a computer terminal, punched keys, and brought up one of the photographs of the crashed airplane, "I thought we should talk before I send these to NTSB. This is Mount Adams?"

Fats nodded. "Above Shoshone Spring."

The sheriff sorted through the photos. "It seems straightforward enough. The plane flew into the side of the mountain and buried itself in the snow. Maybe it was the storm. Maybe mechanical failure. Or pilot error. The Feds can sort it out." He paused, then looked at Fats. "Anything else I should know?"

"No," Fats lied.

The wall behind Dale Zahn was hung with framed certificates, his diplomas from the University of Nevada, Reno, and the University of Nevada, Las Vegas, law school, as well as several awards and commendation letters for service with the Las Vegas Metropolitan Police Department. On one side wall was a door leading to interview rooms, cells, and a back exit. On the other was a row of group photos of former Pinenut County sheriffs and their deputies. In one of them Fats recognized his own unmistakable shape.

"The NTSB folks aren't going to be happy with you, Fats. You trampled all over their crash site. You know better than to stomp around like that."

Fats shrugged. "Wasn't a crime scene."

"It was clearly an accident, though. The same protocol is involved," the sheriff said.

When Fats said nothing, Dale Zahn rose, went to a small refrigerator, and withdrew two bottles of water.

The Pinenut County sheriff was rangy, handsome, with the easy smile of a man sure of himself in all situations. His wife joked that he'd been elected because he looked like what people thought a sheriff should look like. Fats, who had been two grades behind him in school, knew he was tough, shrewd, and ambitious. He was no more honest than he needed to be, no less corrupt than any other local Nevada politician. He accepted favors from and made deals with men who had business with the county. Women liked him, and he them. Few Pinenut County voters had yet discerned that he was a hustler.

He handed Fats a bottle. "How'd you find it?"

"Luck," Fats said. "When the sun's in the right place, for a couple of minutes it shines on the window. I seen the glare."

The sheriff swiveled his chair again to his computer terminal. He retrieved a file and paged through it. "The pilot was an experienced flyer who'd been with the air taxi service for several years. The passenger was a Deseret Construction VP. He'd been in Sacramento to deliver plans for a proposed land deal down by Death Valley. It was a day trip—no luggage, just an attaché case with business papers, which shows in the photos you took. Nothing of note in the official report or insurance claims." He leaned back in his chair and tapped his keyboard. The screen went blank. "Anything raise any flags?"

"No," Fats lied.

The sheriff took a sip of water. "Was it much of a climb?"

"Couple hours."

"That couldn't have been fun, in this heat. Why'd you do it?"

"I figured what it had to be. I thought it'd be best if we didn't have to wait to find out for sure. So families could be notified."

Maybe that was true. Partly.

"Well, you saved me a tussle with the mountain," the sheriff said, stirring in his chair as if ready to rise. "The Feds will take over now. We're done with it, you and me."

"There's this other thing," Fats said. "Strutter. We're a little worried about him." He told Dale Zahn what there was to tell.

The sheriff frowned. "He's gone a month and you're just now reporting him missing?"

"Didn't know he was," Fats said. "Vegas, a girl—that could lead to all sorts of things. And he knew we'd take care of the pinto till he got back. But you're right. I should of said something."

"Strutter Martin." The sheriff leaned back in his chair, posed as if in a ponder. "James. Runt. He hires out to ranchers to help with hay or cattle or water projects. Drives a beat-up old Ford 150, has a run-down single-wide out at Blackpool, lives on the edge of things."

"He's a relative," Fats said. "Shirttail. We share a great-grandfather."

"Had a file on him since he was a kid," the sheriff went on. "The odd burglary and theft, livestock rustling. Had him in here not long ago to talk about dope dealing. Never charged him. Does guide jobs for you and Bill. Draws unemployment."

"Might be nothing," Fats said. "Might be he got lucky."

"One way or another," the sheriff said, rising. "I've got a friend in Las Vegas Metro Missing Persons. I can ask her to look into it. And you can make an official report. That'll get us a warrant, and I'll have somebody look around Strutter's place in the morning."

"Don't need a warrant," Fats said. "I'm a relative. I know where he puts the key."

The sheriff frowned again. "Let's get the warrant, Fats. These days, we do things by the book."

Fats shrugged again. "Your call."

2

A half hour later, Fats was back out in the heat. County employees, workday done, were drifting out of the courthouse. Pickups and SUVs hissed and hummed as they passed over the hot soft pavement. The August afternoon sun hung heavy in the sky.

He'd filed a missing person report free of outright lies. He could tell that Caroline Sam sensed there was more to say, but she stayed silent, only observing, as he prepared to leave, that the situation was troubling. He agreed.

Fats turned on his phone and read the texts from his sister-in-law: she'd been to the bank, Bill had told her about the plane, she was headed home, she'd be making pizza and Fats was welcome to a slice. He texted her that he had a couple of things to do so he'd get his own dinner.

Then he climbed into his pickup and drove through town. Just past the diatomaceous earth–processing operation the locals called the Dirt Plant, he turned onto a highway that rolled over foothills strewn with sage and pinion. Slowly, a darkness ahead became an entryway, but before the highway vanished into Coldwater Canyon, Fats took a rough dirt track that twisted through bleak barren waste toward several grimy single-wides fronting a reed-rimmed pond.

Fed by a subterranean spring, the pool was roughly the size and shape of a baseball field, a dark blot in what was otherwise a desolation of sand and rock. Tall, dark green reeds cast shadows that blackened the water. Isolated, eerie, the place had seemed evil to the Shoshones. Settlers could make nothing of it and, after a try or two, let it be. Then, fifty years ago, Las Vegas developers put up an arc of cheap mobile homes and called the place Blackpool Estates. The enterprise, it turned out, was part of a scheme of corrupt moneymen to defraud a Blue Lake bank.

Most of the mobile homes were long abandoned, caved in or standing aslant, speckled with the bullet holes and splattered with the spray paint of vandals. Of the two yet inhabited, one was the home of an odd woman named Jenny Jones. The other belonged to Strutter.

Fats pulled up fifty yards away and sat, examining the dirt-encrusted trailer and the neat pipe corral and hay shed and horse shelter. Nothing moved but the sun. Eventually he got out of the pickup. The water in the pool smelled sharp, acrid. A few feet of wood frame and floor and rail, once a small pier, rotted at its edge.

He didn't need the key. The door jamb had been ripped apart. The door itself hung on a single hinge.

The rooms were hot and rank, strewn with soiled clothes, tools, dirty dishes, and magazines with photographs of women or horses. Drawers had been emptied, shelves cleared, pillows and bedding tossed.

Young roughs might have done the damage, but to Fats the mess suggested not a destruction but a search. In either case, it hadn't happened recently. The ruin was settled, dusty.

Fats moved slowly, carefully, looking. He found nothing to indicate who had gone through Strutter's place or what they had been looking for.

Stepping out into the sun, he saw a curtain shift in the other occupied unit. He walked over and knocked but got no response. He wasn't surprised. Jenny Jones, once a Blue Lake kindergarten teacher, had gone strange years ago, spoke to the Virgin Mary on a regular basis, and now was a ward of Pinenut County. He thought about questioning her, but decided not to. He probably wouldn't get anything sensible from her anyway.

Fats drove through twilight back to town, across the railroad tracks to a new steakhouse at the edge of the playa. He watched the emptiness out the window darken as he worked through a top sirloin. Diners came and went, a few familiar. Two men carried pistols. Fats nodded to them. No one spoke.

He finished his meal and went out into the night. He drove slowly across town, then turned onto an elm-lined street that ended at a copse of willows and a white, green-shuttered frame building. Once a home of some distinction, it was fronted by a small yard xeriscaped with colored gravels and yucca. A large parking lot was now occupied only by a new SUV, an old Chevy Blazer, and a flatbed stacked with hay bales. White-washed river rock edged a path to the front door, beside which a blue lamp dimly lit a small sign: Darla's.

He pulled in and parked. He started to get out, then didn't. He sat in the darkness, alone.

The heat of the evening seeped into the pickup's cab. Fats watched the house, the door. He didn't know why he was here, what he was doing. He grew angry, but at nothing he could name.

The front door of Darla's opened. A woman stood silhouetted in the light. A man stepped out into the night. The door closed.

Fats waited until the man drove off in the SUV. Then he started his pickup, flicked on the lights, and headed back to Main Street. A familiar urge had him coast past the Adaven, its window bright with neon beer signs, where there would be someone he could hit. But he drove on.

He stopped at Brunson's Liquors and bought a fifth of Jack Daniels. Then he headed home.

Later, he sat with Bill and Mary on the screened porch. The darkness slowly thickened. A rectangle of yellow light fell through the front door, glinted on the bourbon bottle and the bowl of ice sitting on a small table.

Fats tested his drink. "How'd it go with the bank?"

"They like the stable idea," Mary said. "They don't like the out-fitting."

Boarding horses was lucrative, the loan officer had allowed, and there was little local competition. The recent boom had brought people with money to Pinenut County, and the demand for stabling services was growing. Feed and vet bills were figured into the boarding fee, so the only real expense was labor, most of which could be done by the Rangle family: Bill, even crippled as he was, and Mary; Fats, if he was inclined; Bill and Mary's son Buddy, who had his father's feel for horses, and twins Steve and Sally.

Outfitting, on the other hand, was "problematical." It depended on forces no one could predict or control, from the local and national economies to the weather. In this part of Nevada there were no moose, few elk and bighorns—not much to attract the trophy hunter.

There were three other outfitters in and around Blue Lake. And the guiding and excursion business was a drain of resources: vehicles to keep running, tack and pack equipment to keep in shape, horses to feed and shoe and doctor, helpers to hire during hunting season.

"They called it a marginal enterprise," Mary said. "At best."

"I thought we were doing all right," Fats said.

"We're okay, now that the bank's paid off," Mary said, "but things are tight."

Light from the house shadowed her face. As a young woman, she'd been auburn haired and handsome, her appeal as much a matter of carriage and character and clear-eyed intelligence as lean body and pleasing features. Now her hair was iron-gray, her cheeks sun-scored, but she still gave men pause, even though she had no interest in them whatsoever.

She sipped from her glass, then went on. "They always have been," she said. "After your dad drank himself to death, when it was just Bill and you outfitting and selling a little alfalfa and running a few cows, you almost lost the place. Then after we gave up on cattle, it was only your deputy's salary got us through. Since you quit the sheriff, it's been the stable."

The stable was Mary's idea. They'd mortgaged the Cherry Creek place to build it. Now Mary wanted to borrow again.

"So," he said slowly, "what did they say we should do?"

"Split into two businesses," Mary said.

Fats understood. "Me do the outfitting, is that it? You and Bill run the stables?"

"That was their idea. If you thought you could make a go of it alone." Mary took another taste of bourbon. "Or we could give up outfitting altogether."

The night swelled with sound: the thump and nicker of horses, the whirr of insects, the faint sibilance of Cherry Creek. From the house came muted voices, Buddy on the telephone, a cop show on TV.

"If we just go on as we are," Mary said, "it costs us money. We still get a loan, we still can irrigate more pasture, add on to the stable, maybe not as much as we wanted, but. . .and the interest will be higher. And our risk is greater. A couple of off years could do us in."

She paused. "There's another thing. That Vegas consortium has bought up a lot of the water rights in Gull Valley. Nobody knows what they plan on doing, but anything big would take down the water table even more. Some wells are already going dry. If ours did, we'd have to drill deeper, which would cost us, and the electric bill for the pumps would be through the roof."

The Las Vegas group, Hydroneva by name, had made an offer for the Rangle brothers' water rights some months before. Bill and Mary and Fats hadn't sold. Many of their neighbors in Gull Valley had.

"If it gets so it's cheaper to buy feed than to grow it," Mary said, "we could still survive. But the outfitting would be a drain."

Fats hadn't known things were quite so bad. But growing more grass and building an extension to the stable were good ideas. All Mary's ideas were good.

A shrieking female wail, so like the cry of the lion the night before, sounded from the television. Fats shivered, sipped whiskey.

"We need to decide, Fats," Mary said. "You take over the outfitting alone, we quit it, or we keep on as we are. You're the one who'll be most affected, so it's your call. Bill and me will go along with whatever you want."

Fats looked at his brother. Bill hadn't spoken since they'd adjourned to the porch. Now he swirled the bit of ice left in his glass, but he still didn't speak.

"You two already talked about all this," Fats said.

"We knew pretty much what the bank would say. But I wanted you to hear it from them. So you'd know it wasn't. . .us."

So he wouldn't think that, to sustain her crippled husband, to settle or educate her three children, she was prepared to run off her brother-in-law. He didn't think that.

Mary looked at him. "We won't let this come between us, Fats. Like I said, we're good with whatever you want."

He knew already what he'd tell them. Bill and Mary and the three kids were the only human beings on the face of the earth he gave a damn about. He wouldn't place their livelihood in jeopardy. But he'd have to find something to do. He had no idea what that might be. "Give me a day or two."

Bill rose. "Time for this old buckaroo to hit the hay."

"I'll be there soon," Mary said.

Fats and Mary sat in silence on the dark porch. After a bit, he said, "Bill tell you about Strutter?"

She looked out into the night. "You think he's in trouble?"

"I don't know," he said. Then he added, "Probably."

"I ran into Donna," Mary said after a pause. "She's wound pretty tight. The ranch. Her marriage. Packing a pistol. For varmints, she said."

Fats said nothing, felt nothing.

The sheriff showed up near noon.

Fats was at the edge of the alfalfa field, having just finished realigning a sprinkler head on the rolling irrigation apparatus. He watched the county cruiser grow larger as it nosed toward him through the highway heat waves, then slow and pull in to a stop behind his pickup. He walked over.

The sheriff rolled down his window. "Can we talk?"

Fats got into the car. The air-conditioning was cold enough to sting his hot face, his damp neck.

"There's news," the sheriff said. "It isn't good."

He'd called his cop friend in Las Vegas and gave her what he had on Strutter. She got back to him quickly. Weeks before, Las Vegas Metro had impounded a pickup registered to James Martin of Blue Lake, Nevada, abandoned in the Trevi parking garage. Strutter had taken a room there, paying cash for a three-night stay. He'd never checked out. Hotel security said the bed hadn't been slept in. It appeared that he'd brought up his bag, taken a shower, changed clothes, and left, probably by cab. He'd never returned.

Fats stared out at the field and the desert and the haze-smeared horizon.

"They sent the usual notice. One of our nitwit new hires misfiled it. Other than that, they haven't done much. People disappear in Vegas all the time."

When Fats said nothing, the sheriff went on, "He had money. He paid over 600 bucks, cash, for a room. Where would he get it?"

"I don't know," Fats said. It wasn't quite a lie.

"Maybe he just lit out with his girlfriend."

Fats nodded. "Maybe."

"But if he was flashing cash, it would draw the attention of nasties."

The AC hummed. A puff of hot breeze stirred the alfalfa. Heat rose from the hood of the idling cruiser.

The sheriff fell silent. At last he said, "He's mixed up in something, Fats. Some kind of thieving, no doubt. Or more likely dope."

"Maybe," Fats said again.

"Caroline stopped by his trailer this morning. The place was trashed. But you know that, don't you?"

"Like I said, I'm a relative," Fats said. "I don't need a warrant."

"Did you learn anything?"

"Only that a month or so ago somebody was looking for something there."

"That was Caroline's read too. Jenny Jones might know who, but she's off her meds. I'll have Caroline give her another try. In any case, this doesn't look good for Strutter."

"No," Fats said.

"Drugs, you think, Fats? He messed with the big boys and they fixed him?"

"Could be." Fats rubbed his damp chest. "You got your cop lady friend on it now, don't you?"

"Ramona will do what she can," the sheriff said, "but she'd be the first to tell you they rarely find a missing person without help."

Fats said nothing.

The sheriff looked at Fats as if his silence spoke. Then he said quietly, "You ready to come back to work?"

"Not a chance."

Dale Zahn sat back in his seat. "You shouldn't take it personally, Fats. The Pinenut County constituency has changed—new people, new needs, new expectations. The election wasn't a referendum on your twenty years as a deputy. You just didn't know how to talk to them."

"And you did."

"That's right, I did," the sheriff said. "I talked my way into the job. I talked technology. I talked systems and Homeland Security programs and FBI courses and interagency cooperation. Which was what they wanted to hear. You talked domestic battery and runaway kids and meth labs and drunk cowboys driving pickups into the ditch. You offered them crime and guns and muscle, and I offered them security and computers and brains. So I won, you lost, and you quit in a huff."

Fats felt his anger thicken in his throat. "You made me out a thug."

"I didn't start that talk, Fats. Everybody knew you were apt to get physical sometimes." The sheriff shifted in his seat. "All that small-town tough stuff, that was the media, not me. And they were just reporting what was on record."

As if on their own, Fats's hands became fists. "Twice. Two incidents in twenty years. Not even a suspension either time."

"Two official excessive force complaints, along with the other not-quite-official stuff—dragging drunks out of cars, slamming suspects around, rough cuffing kids," the sheriff said. "People were half afraid of you. That's one of the reasons you were so good working actual crimes. Nobody was inclined to hold out on you."

Fats shook his head, as if silently denying what he knew to be true. With his thick body and big hands, he looked, and was, powerful. He could glare mean men into silence. People thought he was quick to violence. Around him they were wary.

Then the sheriff sighed. "It's two years, Fats. That's enough pouting time."

Fats looked out at the distant heat haze.

"The fact is, I need you," the sheriff said. "This job's 90 percent PR and politics. I need somebody to actually deal with the bad guys. And you need to get back at it."

"And you need to get fucked."

Dale Zahn grinned then. "I do, fairly often."

Fats nodded, his anger ebbing. "Word is you slept a couple nights at the jail lately. She'll throw your ass out in the street one of these days."

The sheriff grinned again, briefly. "A risk I'll take, Fats. Meanwhile, you should get back to what you're good at."

"I can't work for you, Dale," Fats said.

"Sure you can. Just swallow your pride, take the loss like a man, and get back to it." The sheriff shook his head. "Strutter had money, how much we don't know, but he got it here, doing something. In my county. I'd guess drugs, but who knows. There's something going on, and I want to find out what. Come back to work, check it out."

Again Fats stayed silent.

"There'll be a big fuss about that plane, Fats. I'll be happy to give you all the credit." The sheriff grinned. "Get you on TV."

Fats had had enough. He opened the cruiser door. For a moment, hot air pinned him to the seat. "I been on TV. I didn't much like it."

The day passed. Fats did his work. He thought about things.

He ate alone. Then he went to his desk and from a drawer lifted a file of glossy photographs of desert lakes and mountain meadows and families riding picturesque trails and men posed beside trophy kills. The photos were for a planned advertising campaign. Fats found the one he wanted, the only picture he had of his distant cousin Strutter Martin, all grin and cowlick, kneeling to hold up by the antlers a mule deer bigger than he was.

Fats looked at the photograph. Suddenly angry, he smashed a fist into his palm. Goddamn Strutter. What had he gotten himself into?

Then he packed a bag. On top of his clothes he lay his gun belt and holster and revolver.

Evening had settled into night. Mary and Bill sat again on the screened porch, studying the darkness. Fats stepped in to sit beside them. "I'll be gone a couple days," he said. "Las Vegas."

He'd already told them what the Vegas authorities knew. He hadn't told them that the sheriff had offered him his job back. He didn't want to complicate matters.

Bill spoke. "What do you think you can do down there?"

"Get away from the media fuss about the plane, mostly," Fats said.

He was half serious. On television he looked brutish, sounded dull-witted. Reporters tried to get him to say things he didn't want to say. They twisted the truth. They lied.

He went back to his house. He took the .38 out of his bag and locked it in a desk drawer. Then he went to bed.

3

Sprinklers sprayed the alfalfa with elegant arcs of water that glittered in the sunlight. Otherwise, the desert at this early hour was still and shadowed.

Fats Rangle turned his pickup onto the highway and met no one until he was nearly in Blue Lake. Driving through town, he passed the Dirt Plant and came to the road he had taken the day before. There the sheriff's cruiser was just pulling up at the stop sign. Fats gave Dale Zahn a nod. The sheriff nodded too. Both men drove on.

Soon Fats approached the cleft in the mountains that was Coldwater Canyon. Then he was in it. After a mile or so of twists and turns, the rock walls became hillsides that spread to hold green marsh and watery pasture and, eventually, alfalfa fields. A quarter mile on, a sign straddling a dirt road said that the place across Coldwater Creek was the Three Bar M.

Fats knew the ranch well. He'd once expected to spend his life working it. Generations of Manchesters had pieced it together. The name on the silver mailbox now was Zahn.

The green continued, pasture, fields, at intervals stacks of rectangular hay bales. Then the creek collected in a small pond, the hillsides lowered, and the canyon opened wider and disappeared into desert.

The sun rose in the empty sky. Heat gathered. Joshua trees appeared, bizarrely branched. Fats settled into solitude.

After a length of time, a gray stain on the horizon located Las Vegas.

Fats had spent two years in Las Vegas two decades ago. Even then, the seeps and springs that allowed life had been long overlaid with housing developments and strip malls. Sweltering summers and heavy use had already buckled and grooved the highways. Imported and pointless palm trees sagged in the sunlight. Now nothing was different, only more.

Fats found his way downtown. Traffic inched ahead. Fun seekers strolled and milled, music and barkers blared.

He parked in the lot of a small motel off Freemont Street. Beside it, a bank sign said the temperature was 109 degrees. In the motel office he learned he was in luck: the town was filling up for a big boxing match and some sort of water conference, but they had a couple of rooms left.

The office was cool, his room chilled. He dropped his bag and went back out into the heat. Memory and a city map he'd picked up led him to South Martin Luther King Junior Boulevard and the main offices of the Las Vegas Metropolitan Police Department. His luck held, providing a parking space near the entrance.

Inside, a cheerful, matronly officer directed him, and cool hallways took him, to the missing persons office, a room with a long counter attended by two uniformed officers. One, hearing what he had to say, disappeared through a door in the wall behind her. The other officer bent his head to a stack of papers.

After a few minutes, the door reopened. The uniformed woman who came through it was big and blonde, firm, fully female. She wore a smile and sergeant stripes. She stretched a hand across the counter. "Mr. Rangle? Ramona Clare."

Her grip was strong. She was inches taller than he was. Her hair was stylishly short, her eyes were pale blue, her features pleasant rather than pretty.

"Come on back," she said. "Dale called. He said you might be by."

He followed her into a small office. There was nothing in the room but what went with work.

Sergeant Clare showed him to a seat as she slipped behind the desk. "You're asking about James Martin, aka Strutter. You're the missing man's cousin?"

Fats nodded. "Sort of."

She turned to her computer. "We've got a file on him. Not much in it, I'm afraid. We know where his pickup is. We know he checked in at the Trevi. I can help you with those folks, if you want. Maybe you can help us with background stuff."

Fats told her what he could about Strutter's dead mother and long-gone father, his work history, such as it was, his probable petty thefts and dope dealing, his reason for coming to Las Vegas.

"Salome," she said, smiling. "If she's been picked up for anything, the name might pop up as an aka."

Fats showed her the photograph of Strutter and the mule deer buck. She quickly scanned the image and returned it. "Not much to him, is there?"

She hadn't mentioned the plane. Fats guessed that Dale Zahn hadn't told her about it. "I'd appreciate any help you can give me."

"Dale said to treat you right." Her smile became a grin. "I owe him. I worked for him for a while, gang unit. He got me out of a scrape or two. How's he doing, sheriffing in the sticks?"

"Seems to have a handle on things."

She sat back in her chair. "Well, Mr. Rangle, like I told Dale, I don't hold out much hope of finding your cousin. Not after this long. Chances are he's not even in town. If he is, he could be anywhere, shacked up or doped up. Or maybe he doesn't want to be found. Is there anybody he might be hiding from?"

"Not that I know of," Fats said. "His trailer was trashed a couple weeks ago. Might have been kids, though."

She leaned forward. Her shirt collar was open. The hollow at the base of her throat was dark. "Or he could be dead. People get killed all the time around here. Some we hear about only by accident."

"Well," Fats said, "maybe I won't find him, but I need to give it a go."

She looked at him. "Why?"

Fats looked at her. "I've got his horse."

Sergeant Clare offered to drive him to the impound lot. In an unmarked Ford Taurus, she made their way through the midday congestion. She wore silver shades against the glare of sunlight flashing erratically off glass and metal and plastic.

She talked about horses. She'd grown up in the Big Smoky Valley, where her dad was a farrier and small-time breeder of quarter horses. Ramona had ridden until she was sixteen, when her dad had gone bust and her parents split up and she moved with her mother to Las

Vegas. She'd had to sell her horse, Pete, a sorrel gelding. She still missed him, she said.

The impound lot sat amid streets lined with shaggy palm trees and shabby convenience stores and small frame homes that seemed abandoned. The enclosure abutted an open section of the extensive Clark County drainage system, designed to carry off the waters of flash floods. A pair of shiny tow trucks flanked the gate into a spread of vehicles dull with baked-on grime. In the window of a small shack a sign said "Office." Sergeant Clare parked before it.

Just inside the gate, Strutter's pickup gathered grunge. Soon Fats was sorting through the mess in the cab. He checked in the glove box, under the floor mats, behind the seats. He found the registration and insurance card, as well as a small hand ax and wire cutters, a quart of oil, fast food cartons and wrappers, a crumpled Camel filters pack, receipts for gas, and a nearly empty book of matches that he slipped into his shirt pocket.

Sergeant Clare watched him from the shade cast by the shack. He stepped over to her. "Had to look."

They went inside. She informed the lot man that Strutter's pickup was now evidence in an ongoing inquiry. Out in the heat, she told Fats, "That's so it doesn't pile up impound fees."

"Yeah," he said. "Probably already racked up more than it's worth."

They were pulling into the street when Sergeant Clare said, not quite casually, "You were a deputy, Dale told me. You. . .what? Quit?"

"Retired, technically. Can't draw benefits for years, though."

She adjusted her silver sunglasses. "I've thought about retiring. But I'd still have to find something to do. The only thing out there is security work, which doesn't interest me much."

Fats nodded. "My brother and his wife and I have a stabling and outfitting business."

"Lucky you," she said, her voice mildly envious, and something more.

Traffic on the Strip slowed near the Trevi Hotel and Casino. An entry drive circled a collection of columns and statuary and a spraying fountain. Signs directed those attending the water conference that began the next day. An access lane led to the underground parking garage, from which rose an elevator to the main casino floor and its cool antiseptic air, Muzak, and rows of shiny slot machines. Fats Rangle and Sergeant Ramona Clare waited with the concierge for a security man, who soon showed them to an upstairs room lined with CCTV screens.

In a few minutes, they were watching a tape of the registration desk camera tracking the approach of a small young man with a distinctive splay-footed, shoulder swinging stride.

"I see," Sergeant Clare said, "Strutter."

On the screen Strutter signed in. He paid for the room with cash he retrieved from a large leather wallet chained to his belt. Ramona Clare asked the security man to zoom in on the scene and run it again, and then again. The frames showed Strutter lifting bills from the wallet.

"Hundreds," she said. "He's got a lot of money there. Not too bright, is he?"

"Nope," Fats said.

They watched the small young man shoulder his way to an elevator. Sergeant Clare grinned. "Cock of the walk."

They went to another, smaller room filled with plastic bins neatly stacked and labeled. One of them held the clothes that Strutter had worn when he arrived as well as a clean plaid western-cut shirt, a pair of briefs, socks, a battered old toiletry bag, and a plastic pouch holding three condoms. No leather wallet. No chain.

Sergeant Clare, after a nod from Fats, thanked the security man. They made their way back to the reception area, then to her car. "Not much help," she said.

"We know he was here," Fats said. "He didn't have a lot of clothes, must not have planned a long stay. He had money. Ritzy place like this, I'd guess he wanted to impress somebody."

"Salome?" She laughed. "The names they come up with."

They headed back. As she drove, she probed, carefully. He found that he didn't mind.

In his terse, clipped fashion he told her how, after his army service, he'd come to Las Vegas to work security while he earned an AA in criminal justice at the community college. How, returned to Blue Lake, he raised alfalfa and did outfitting with his brother until he joined the sheriff's department. How Bill had broken his leg, pelvis, and hip when a horse fell and rolled on him, so the brothers, with Mary and the kids, went into the stabling business.

She told him she was divorced.

When she pulled into the Metro parking lot, she said, "I'll check on Miss Salome. And I'd like to know what you learn."

They traded cell numbers. Then he took the matchbook from his pocket. On the cover a stylized naked woman rode the arched back of a tailless cat within a semicircle of letters that spelled Manx Club. An address he didn't recognize. Phone number. "You know this place?"

"I wondered if you were going to share," she said, grinning.

The strip club, she told him, was downtown, not far from his motel. "It's part of Abel Lasky's complex—club, spa, and motel. Standard sleaze. Girls give lap dances in the club, more specialized services in the spa, and about anything men could want if they've got enough cash or credit for a motel room."

"I'll check it out."

"You'll want to be careful," she cautioned. "He won't like you nosing around. He's got goons, some have been up on charges—blackmail, assault, robbery. It's a real slow night at the Manx Club when somebody doesn't get bones broken."

"Twenty years ago there was more than one operator like that in town."

"They're still here," she said, "but Lasky's a little different. In Vegas, 'erotics,' as some call it, is a legitimate business. He wants to be seen as a regular businessman, get his picture in the paper with entrepreneurs and moguls and politicians. He supports local charities. He gives money to the UNLV athletic department. He plays golf with county commissioners while his bouncers are beating up horny tourists."

"If his place is so nasty, how does he stay in business?"

She shrugged. "How do any of these places? Connections. Corruption."

He put the matchbook back in his pocket. "Well, thanks for the help."

She took off her sunglasses. She grinned. "You can buy me lunch sometime. Or dinner."

He looked at her. "My pleasure."

"Dale said they call you Fats," she said. "Why is that?"

"I was a roly-poly kid."

She made a show of examining him. "Not much anymore. You aren't married, are you?"

"No," he said.

"Gay?"

"No," he said again.

"Good," she said. "Stay in touch."

He stepped out into the heat. He stood and watched until the Ford disappeared.

He got into his pickup and, as he waited for the cab to cool, he checked his phone for messages. He found two, both from Dale Zahn, who would have guessed, or asked Bill, where he was off to so early in the morning. Dale was passing on phone numbers. The NTSB wanted Fats to call, as did someone named Carroll Coyle, with a southern Nevada area code.

The first number rang the Seattle office of the federal agency. Fats arranged to meet one of their investigators in Blue Lake later in the week.

The second number reached Carroll Coyle's personal assistant who, in an ambivalently gendered voice, told him Mr. Coyle wished to speak with him, perhaps for a few minutes that evening at 9 at Reginald's Bar and Grill. Fats had no idea who Carroll Coyle might be, but he assumed that Dale Zahn had passed along his number for a reason. He agreed to the meeting, got the address, and hung up.

He drove back to his motel, parked, and set off on foot. The area around Fremont Street was crowded, carnivalesque. At one point it became a covered pedestrian mall, stuffed with performers and musicians and hustlers and hookers, tourists after sin and spectacle, and a few homeless men who camped in the nearby section of the drainage system. Downtown Las Vegas had once had about it a small-town aura that Fats had liked. Now it was just more plastic glitz.

Fats brushed off several solicitations, turned on a cross street, passed over the drainage tunnel, and soon found the Manx Club.

A tailless clawing cat outlined in red neon blinked over the entrance. Glass cases hanging on the walls held photographs of mostly naked women with stiff smiles and stiff breasts. Neon on an adjoining building advertised baths, steam, and massages. Across an alley the office of an old motel flashed a vacancy sign.

Inside the club, colored lights pulsed in the dimness. Music thumped and shrieked. The air-conditioning couldn't rid the big room of the smell of sex, sweat, stale beer and, faintly, disinfectant. On separate stages, three women worked rows of ogling men. At low tables or small sofas other women enticed or occupied other men. Large expressionless bouncers in black muscle T-shirts looked on.

Fats took a stool at the main bar, ordered a beer, left the change from $20, and told the bartender that he'd like to see the manager. He sipped his beer, checked out the bouncers. Most looked to be showing off gym muscles, but he couldn't tell which, if any, would know how to handle himself in a brawl. Habit had Fats shrug, loosening his shoulders.

An electric guitar screeched, catlike. A woman in hot pants and halter approached. She looked tired. When he politely declined her offer of company, she seemed almost relieved.

Different dancers took over but nothing changed. Fats had another beer, watched, and settled into a simmer of anger.

Finally, one of the big men, the left side of his face and entire left arm elaborately, colorfully tattooed, came up and jerked his head. Fats followed him through an archway and down a hall to a door that opened into a spacious office, expensively carpeted and furnished.

The room had the artificial, unused feel of a film set. Much as in Dale Zahn's office, one wall was adorned with plaques and letters celebrating civic and charitable efforts, another with framed photographs of men, mostly, grouped in casual poses. In each photo there appeared the eager smile of the man now sitting at the huge desk.

He was a tanned, trim, and taut fifty, his even features slightly snubbed, as if pressed against a pane of glass, hair dark and thinning, eyes dark and deeply set. He wore a summer-weight blue business suit. His cufflinks were gold, as were his wristwatch and the wedding band on his finger. "My manager is unavailable," he said. "Maybe I can help you. I'm Abel Lasky."

The words were not particularly threatening, but the voice was hollow, hard. Abel Lasky dressed for the boardroom but came from the streets. Fats remembered what Sergeant Clare had said about his aspirations. Everything about him would be put on, part of the role he tried to play, everything he said serving his own ends.

Another bouncer, his bald skull seamed and lumped, came in, placing himself behind Lasky. He folded his muscled arms, watching Fats with empty eyes.

Fats had gotten this far playing it straight. He decided to continue. He told Abel Lasky who he was and what he wanted, then handed him the photograph of Strutter with his kill. "This is the guy I'm looking for. He came to Vegas to see a girl named Salome. I thought she might work for you."

Something in what Fats said sharpened Lasky's gaze, raised a stiff false smile. "Strictly speaking, none of the dancers work for me. They're contract talent, from an agency. I don't always remember their names."

"Hard to forget a Salome," Fats said. "You'd remember Strutter too, if you'd seen him. The way he walks."

The big bald man behind Lasky hadn't moved, hadn't seemed even to breathe. Not like the big tattooed man behind Fats, whose breathing was deep, heavy, somehow menacing. Fats didn't like it. He took a step sideways and turned, bringing him into view. The goon grinned.

Lasky leaned back in his chair, raising the photo for the bouncer behind him to see. "Boo?"

"Yeah," the big man said.

This piece of business seemed to Fats to be staged. Abel Lasky knew very well who Strutter was.

Lasky looked again at the photograph. "He's your cousin, you say. But this doesn't feel like a family affair, Mr. . . . Ringo, was it?" He leaned forward, his smile widening, becoming even more artificial. "When I look at you, I don't see somebody's cousin. I see a peace officer."

"It's Rangle," Fats said, "and I'm not a cop."

"Oh, I always accommodate the law, when I can," Lasky said. "In fact, I'm seeing you now, without an appointment, because my security people say you carry yourself like a lawman."

"I'm not a cop," Fats said again. "I'm a retired Pinenut County deputy."

Lasky leaned back in his chair. "You seem pretty young to be retired."

When Fats didn't respond, Lasky nodded, let his gaze swing to take in the wall of photographs as if seeking approval. "This has nothing to do with me or my business?"

"Nothing," Fats lied.

Both men were silent. Lasky looked at the photograph of Strutter. In the pause, Fats took a longer look at the wall of photos, recognizing a couple of entertainers, a couple of politicians, and, in a clutch of men in tuxedos, a woman politician of repute.

Lasky said then, "Tell me again why you're looking for this Swagger fellow."

"Strutter. He's my cousin and he's missing," Fats said. "And he owes me for stabling his horse."

"How much?"

"Not a lot," Fats said, "yet."

"He's missing a month? This is an expensive town," Lasky said. "What would he be doing for money?"

"I don't know," Fats lied.

Lasky looked again at the photo. Then he nodded and returned it. "Well, you're right about one thing. It's hard to forget a dancer named Salome. In fact, she's one of our most popular artists."

Fats said nothing. Abel Lasky watched him. So did the bald man, who began slowly to massage one fist, then the other.

"As I said, I always try to accommodate the law," Lasky said, smiling his bogus smile. "Ex-law too. I guess there's no reason you shouldn't talk to Salome. If she wants to, that is. Come back tonight, any time after 9. She'll be dancing."

Fats nodded. "Thanks."

Lasky leaned forward over his desk. "If this Swagger shows up in the meantime, we'll get in touch with you. Where are you staying?"

"I don't know yet," Fats lied again. "But I'll get back to you."

"Yeah," Lasky said. "You do that."

Outside, the late-afternoon sun beat down. Fats walked back to Fremont Street, where he slipped into a chilled café and, hungry, gave his attention to a chicken fried steak. Then he made his way to his motel. He took a nap, awakening near 9:00. He showered and donned a fresh shirt. After checking his city map, he went out into the gathering darkness to his pickup.

The evening hadn't noticeably cooled. The Strip blazed with lights, colored or plain, steady or strobed, bright. Fountains spewed water; canals and pools shimmered. Tourists thronged. Fats felt alien, apart, and angry. Stupid fucking people.

Reginald's was a secluded two-story brick building a couple of blocks off East Flamingo Road. The parking lot was nearly full of pricey automobiles. Inside, the atrium was dim, with dark wainscoting and pale plaster. A tuxedo-clad host gave him a brittle smile that softened slightly when Fats asked for Carroll Coyle.

Fats followed directions to an upstairs bar serving a handful of murmuring men in expensive suits and women in glitter and gowns. In a booth sat a man speaking on a mobile phone. Beside him stood a pretty young man in a conservative pale blue suit who, smiling, beckoned Fats, then stepped back.

Fats went over, waited for the phone call to end, then said, "Mr. Coyle."

"Have a seat, Deputy." It was less an invitation than an order.

Carroll Coyle wore a beautifully cut gray three-piece suit, a gray silk tie and, like Abel Lasky, gold appointments. The elegance of his outfit worked to increase his ugliness. His skin was lumped and acne scarred, his features bony and misaligned. His teeth, when he smiled, were too bright and white and perfect.

The young man—Coyle's personal assistant, Fats assumed—hovered, smiling.

"You found the plane and the body of the Deseret Construction executive," Carroll Coyle said without preliminaries. "How did that come about?"

Fats was instantly angry. "How do you know that?"

"The plane story is all over the news," Coyle said. "An informant gave me your name. That isn't out yet."

Fats swallowed his anger. He told Carroll Coyle what had happened. He showed him the photographs on his phone. He waited while Coyle studied them.

Coyle studied them carefully before returning Fats's phone. "What's in the attaché case?"

"I didn't look."

Coyle raised a skeptical eyebrow. "Where's the briefcase?"

Fats emptied his voice. "I didn't find a briefcase."

"You sure about that?"

Fats, anger thickening again in his throat, looked at him but didn't speak.

Coyle took out a small gold case, removed a card, and placed it on the table. "Send those photos to this number."

Fats gave the card a glance but left it where it lay.

Coyle rubbed the heel of his hand roughly against his jaw. "What's your interest in this matter, Deputy?"

"Zip," Fats said curtly. "What's yours?"

For a moment, Coyle glared. Then his expression changed. "That's none of your business. But let me tell you anyhow."

He paused again, obviously for effect. Fats waited. The pretty young man had vanished.

"Deseret Construction is a multi-billion-dollar company that does business all over the West. Part of doing business is contributing to political campaigns. Like many large, powerful organizations, Deseret has a special fund that they disburse these monies from."

He paused as if giving Fats time to comprehend. Fats just looked at him.

"Deseret people have reason to believe that someone has embezzled from that fund and that the embezzled cash was on the plane that went down."

Fats felt his fingers clenching into a fist. "And you think I took it. The money."

"If it was there," Coyle said carefully.

"It wasn't," Fats said. "At least, I didn't see it. It also wasn't mentioned in the initial report or the insurance claims, the sheriff says."

"Well, yes." Coyle cleared his throat, obviously arranging a response. "Because possibly it wasn't on the plane. Possibly the information the Deseret security people had was incorrect. In any case, the corporation isn't eager to let the world know they have an embezzler in their operation."

"You haven't said how much money we're talking about," Fats said.

"And you haven't asked," Coyle said. "Maybe you already know."

Fats flexed his fingers. "And you haven't said how this is any of your concern."

Coyle again rubbed at his chin. "Deseret has its home office in Dallas. They have, over the years, contributed to the campaigns of political candidates I managed or advised. They asked me to keep them abreast of the search for the plane. That, Deputy, is my interest."

Fats didn't know if any of that was true. But he didn't ask. Instead he said, "Ex-deputy. I'm retired."

"You find a missing plane," Coyle snapped. "Then you come to Vegas. Why is that?"

"I found the plane by accident," Fats said. "I didn't want to get caught up in all the hoopla around it, so I reported it to the sheriff and then lit out."

Coyle smirked. "And you were okay missing your moment of fame, interviews, TV?"

"All that's a pain in the butt. Television cameras don't like me. Neither do reporters. And they lie," Fats said.

"I can imagine what they make of your snarling dog act."

Fats ignored that. "Anyway, I drove down here to look for my cousin. He came to Vegas to see a girl. That was a month ago. We haven't seen or heard from him since."

The bar was filling up. Voices swelled. Then the sound changed as a woman entered. She was small and slim and fair, not quite beautiful, but in person more attractive than she was in the photograph on Abel Lasky's wall. She seemed to Fats pleasantly imperturbable and completely contained as men, eager for her attention, at once gathered around her and parted to let her pass.

Coyle's assistant came up and said softly. "Judge Barlow isn't quite ready to leave."

"Of course," Coyle said.

But even as he spoke, she stepped over. "I don't mean to interrupt, Carroll. The speaker of the assembly wants a word about tomorrow's schedule."

Coyle slid from the booth. "No problem, Your Honor. But you might want to make the acquaintance of this gentleman. This is

Deputy Rangle, the man who found the plane that went down with the Deseret vice president."

Fats rose awkwardly. The judged smiled as she extended a hand. "I'm Vi Barlow. How do you do, Deputy?" Her hand was small and warm and firm.

"Ex-deputy," Fats said.

"The crash was up near Blue Lake, where Dale Zahn is sheriff? Dale and I were in law school together. How are he and Donna getting along up there?"

"Fine," Fats said.

He felt drawn to her, her quiet calm, her self-sufficiency. He would have said more but couldn't think of anything. Somehow, with Vi Barlow, there was nothing more to say.

The judge smiled again. "Give them my regards, would you?"

"Yes, ma'am, I'll do that," Fats said, watching with Carroll Coyle as she smiled and then moved to part a path through the attending men.

Carroll Coyle motioned Fats back into the booth. "What are you drinking?"

Fats had thought they were finished. But he sat. "J D rocks."

Coyle lifted a hand. The young man nodded and moved to the bar.

Carroll Coyle watched Vi Barlow leave and the crowd dwindle.

"We had a little fund-raising affair for the judge this evening. The people in this bar ten minutes ago were worth a billion dollars, easily. One of these days she'll be governor, at least. Maybe she'll go all the way." When Fats didn't respond, Coyle frowned. "You know who she is, don't you?"

He did. Violet McEwan Barlow was a former district court judge who before election to the bench had served as an ADA, then as legal advisor to the Clark County Commission. While on the bench, she had presided over several water law cases, establishing a regional reputation. She was said by all involved to be honest, impartial, independent, and informed. Widowed a few years ago, she now attended various gatherings with appropriate escorts, but whatever private life she had she kept private. Born and bred in Pioche, a graduate of UNLV and its law school, she was spoken of favorably in political circles. Environmental organizations, real estate firms, and construction companies all promised, should she run for higher office, their support and money.

"She'll be speaking at the conference tomorrow," Coyle said. "Maybe you should go to hear her. You've got water troubles yourself, I understand."

Coyle's assistant returned with their drinks. Fats sipped bourbon. "I do?"

"You pump water for your alfalfa in Gull Valley, you and your brother. The word is, somebody's after every drop—surface, ground water, all of it."

"Somebody?"

"Somebody. Them. It doesn't really matter who they are because they're all the same."

"We were approached by an outfit called Hydroneva."

"They would be a somebody." Coyle smiled coldly. "They or some other somebody will be coming at you again. You may find you could use a friend."

Fats understood that he was supposed to be impressed that Carroll Coyle knew the Rangle brothers' business. He was, although it made him angry. He was also supposed to be enticed by Coyle's offer of assistance.

Fats drained his drink. "What do you want from me?"

"Your consideration. Back in Pinenut County, if and when things come up, I hope you'll consider my interests."

"I don't know what your interests are."

Coyle too drained his drink. "Sure you do, Deputy."

"Ex," Fats said.

Coyle made as if to rise, then didn't. "How's your search going? For your cousin? It must be hard for a cow county ex-deputy to get information down here, Vegas being what it is. You need some local help?"

Fats didn't want to tell him about Sergeant Ramona Clare. "Wouldn't hurt."

Coyle picked up his phone. "There's a PI, Doc Wills by name. Ex-cop like you. He knows the town. I'll let him know to expect you in a half hour or so."

"I don't have money for an investigator."

Coyle shook his head. "He owes me. He can give you a day or two."

Fats checked his watch. It was nearly 11. "He'll be there this time of night?"

"Probably." Coyle slid out of the booth as the pretty young man appeared. "And don't forget the water conference tomorrow. You might learn something."

Fats rose too. He picked up the card that Coyle had put on the table. "I'd like to hear what Judge Barlow has to say."

"Two hundred and fifty thousand," Coyle said then. "A quarter of a million. That's what was or wasn't on the plane. Peanuts to those here tonight, but for a lot of people in Vegas it's enough to kill for."

4

The night had cooled to warm. The city lights cast an eerie aura, dulled the black, dimmed the stars. Somewhere in the darkness a cat yowled.

Once back on East Flamingo Road, Fats slipped his pickup into a stream of traffic nearly as heavy as it had been at midday. The Strip, when he got to it, seemed alive: lights and water and people, pulsing. Music blared into mere noise.

The address Coyle's assistant had given him turned out to be a Dolly's squeezed into a small mall near the Mandalay Bay. The mini-casino door opened to a roomful of men and women clustered at a brief bar or seated at tables or in booths, all hunched over video poker machines. Fingers jabbed. Plastic keys clicked. Some gamers snacked as they played, some drank. No one spoke, except to the machines.

One of the men stopped playing. He sat at the back, a coffee cup and a cell phone on the table. He was dressed like a tourist, straw fedora and dark glasses and a blue shirt printed with lavender palm trees. His face was thin and fish-belly pale, his bare arms all bone and knotty veins, his hands lumpy. He looked old or ailing or both.

Fats approached. "You'd be Doc Wills."

"And you'd be looking for somebody." The words came with a wheeze.

"Carroll Coyle said you might be able to help."

Wills nodded Fats to a seat. Then he punched up a poker hand, started to play as he said, "Talk."

Fats told him what he'd been telling people since he got to Las Vegas. He also told him about his visit to the Manx Club and his plan to return there to talk to a dancer named Salome.

Wills breathed loudly, harshly. He shifted in his seat, stretching smooth a section of shirttail that didn't quite hide a hip holster. As he listened, he dealt and drew to poker hands, always betting the maximum.

Finally, he asked the Vegas question. "Money?"

"Some," Fats said. "Maybe just enough to attract attention."

"Don't take much in this town." The PI paused, struggled for breath.

Fats was getting a sense of Doc Wills. He was sixty or a bit more, and in bad shape, but still hard, tough, an ex-street cop who'd never left the street.

Wills went on. "Druggies, derelicts, busted tourists, whores, lots of folks will do you for a buck or two. The thugs at the Manx Club don't even need that. There's one, name of Boo, who pounds people for the fun of it."

"I met him, sort of."

Again the ailing man gasped after air. When he could speak, he said angrily, "Forty years of Pall Malls. Quitting didn't help. Now the medicos want to hook me up to a tank of oxygen. The day that comes is the day I fucking check out."

Fats didn't doubt it.

Wills dealt another hand. Ace high. Drew four cards and paired it. "You'll want to be real careful, you go back there asking questions. You maybe can handle yourself, but Boo usually has help, just in case he needs it."

"I'm not looking to trouble anybody," Fats said, aware that that might not be true.

"You don't appear to be packing."

"I'm not looking to shoot anybody either."

"Need backup?"

"No thanks," Fats said. "Anything else you can you do for me?"

"Sniff around. Nothing happens in this town that somebody don't know about." Once more Wills sucked after air. Then he took a card from his shirt pocket. "I've got an office upstairs."

The card established the bona fides of M. D. "Doc" Wills, retired Las Vegas Metro sergeant, licensed private investigator. Fax and cell number.

Fats gave Doc Wills his number.

Wills dealt himself two pair, kings and sevens, tossed the sevens, drew a third king. "How's Coyle fit into this?"

"Good question," Fats said. "Who is he?"

"Hot-shot political consultant. Advises candidates for local and state offices. Knows where the bodies are buried and who buried them." Wills wheezed, scraped at his throat. "This is on his tab. Got to be a payoff for him somewhere."

"Seems like it, don't it?"

Wills removed his dark glasses. His brown eyes were red rimmed, red veined, the skin beneath them pouched and smudged. His stare was stony. He put the glasses back on.

He punched a finger at the video poker machine, again bet the maximum, and dealt himself two jacks, four hearts, tossed the off jack and drew for the flush and hit a rag.

Fats, as he stood, asked, "Ever come out a winner?"

"Always," Wills wheezed. "I own the place."

The Strip was all color and clamor, the night gaudy, the crowds itchy with expectation. Fats drove slowly, growing angry again. Assholes.

Back at his motel, he checked his messages. Dale Zahn was driving down the next morning. He had business to do, and he thought he'd drop in to hear Judge Barlow. He had new info too about Strutter, and he wanted to get together. Fats didn't respond. Ramona Clare said she'd share what she'd picked up if he'd buy her breakfast at 7:30 at Huffman's, a cop café a couple of blocks from the Central Station. Fats texted that he'd try to make it.

What he was about to do would cost him money. He used the ATM at the nearby bank. The printed receipt showed enough left in his account to pay for—maybe—enough gas to get home.

The streets were quieter now: engine murmurs and distant uneasy voices. His footsteps sounded softly as Fats passed over the drainage system. Soon, in the balmy darkness, he saw the lights of the Manx Club.

Inside, music throbbed and wailed, men drank and dampened, women hustled and danced, black T-shirted bouncers showed their muscles. Fats got a beer. As he had that afternoon, he left his change. Bills and coins disappeared beneath the bartender's practiced hand.

"Salome," Fats said.

The bartender looked past him, slowly swiveled his head. Fats followed his gaze.

She was dancing on the largest of the three stages. She was small and dark and young, with big eyes in a pretty, fine-featured face and a thin-lipped, disdainful smile. Her hair was boyishly short, her body but for her breasts boyishly slender. From the foliage tattooed on her left shoulder, tendrils twisted down to cradle a breast, unnaturally large, firm, bullet shaped.

She wasn't an especially talented dancer, but she was good at what she did, toying with the leering, grinning men who rimmed the stage, now enticing, provoking, now ignoring them. The men claimed her attention with money, placing on the lip of the stage bills that she bent for and slipped beneath the cord of her G-string.

She slithered around a chromium pole. Then she looked at Fats Rangle.

He was startled when her eyes met his. They were a distance apart; he might have been mistaken, but even as she turned, she kept her eyes fixed on him. She seemed to know him.

He tried to place her. But in twenty years as deputy, he'd dealt with so many women: coke and meth whores, pros doing a stint at Darla's, low-life girlfriends of the criminally stupid, and runaway teenagers, and abused and abandoned and angry wives. She might have been almost any, or several, of these. But he didn't remember or recognize her.

But whoever she was, she had recognized him. Her sneer said so.

He got another beer and took it to a small empty table near the arch leading to the back. He sat, sipped, watched. He could understand her appeal to Strutter. She was his age, his size, and pretty, cartoonishly sexual with her tight tidy bottom, shapely limbs, and exaggerated breasts. And she was alone, dancing, it would have seemed to Strutter, only for him.

Eventually a new set of dancers took to the stages. Salome stepped down and patted her forehead with a towel she then draped around her neck and over her breasts. She made her way through waving $5 and $10 and $20 bills toward the folded $100 now stiffly sticking up from Fats Rangle's fingers.

"Can we talk about Strutter?"

She pinched the bill. He tightened his grasp of it. She looked at him. She was flushed, damp, her makeup crumbly. Strands of dark hair were pasted to her temples. Her big dark eyes went hard. "Talk? Is that all you can manage, Fats? Yeah, we can talk."

She slid the bill from his now unresisting fingers. She tucked it into her G-string and stepped past him. "I'll be back."

He finished his beer. He located the several bouncers, big and still and solemn. The one called Boo wasn't among them. The dancers performed almost desperately. The patrons seemed dissatisfied. Some left. Some got louder. The bouncers stirred. Fats could almost feel their anticipation.

Salome returned, changed into a skimpy red bikini and fresh makeup. "One hundred gets you a session in a VIP room. Or—" She offered him a smile, small, mocking, "—a big spender from Blue Lake might want the motel. That'd be more."

Fats looked at her. He saw no sign of drugs, nothing in her big eyes but anger. "Let's try the VIP room, shall we?"

He followed her through the arch, down the hallway, to a door that opened into a room with a minibar, a large couch, a DVD player and television screen, a patch of bare floor, and a chromium pole. The walls were posted with photographs of naked women. Fats couldn't locate the CCTV cameras or microphones, but he knew they were there.

The young woman who called herself Salome placed herself before him, close. She'd combed the sweat from her hair, doused herself in a sharply floral scent. Among the leaves inked on her shoulder were small, delicate flowers. She sneered her smile as she dragged a red-nailed finger slowly over his crotch. "What's your pleasure, Deputy? I can—"

"Where's Strutter?"

She spat her reply. "How the fuck should I know?"

"He came to Vegas to see you."

She stiffened her back and shoulders, presenting her outsized breasts. "To see these, more like it. All kinds of dildoes come to see these. Even deputy sheriffs from Blue Lake."

Fats gave her a longer look. "Do I know you?"

Derision deepened her scowl. "No, Fats, you don't know me at all."

"Maybe not," he said. "But right now, I want to know about Strutter. He left Blue Lake a month ago, said he was coming here to see you."

She took several sexual steps to the couch, sat, and patted with an inviting hand. "He did. He had cash this time, so we went to the motel and he got his money's worth. Then he left. He said he was going out to score some weed and he'd be back. That was the last I saw of him." The words came clipped, rehearsed.

"How come? What's your best guess?"

"Who cares?" She shrugged. "There's all kind of action in Las Vegas, if you've got money. Maybe he found something he liked better."

"Or something found him."

"What? You think somebody did him?" She scoffed contemptuously.

"He had some money," Fats said. "And he wasn't real careful. And this is Vegas. He—how much did he have when he got here?"

"Dumb dildo, I told him—" For a moment she seemed to soften. But only for a moment. "He had a little over 9 grand. He made me count it, like I wouldn't believe it was real otherwise. He wanted to hire a limo, see shows, have room service at the Trevi. And he wanted. . ." She trailed off into silence.

Fats asked, "He say where he got it?"

"No," she said. "He—was it yours, the money?"

"No," Fats said.

"That's what you're really looking for, isn't it—the money? He stole it, didn't he, either from you or somebody you're working for? That's why you're here?"

"I'm here because he's missing and he's my cousin and I have his horse."

She rose from the couch. "Dumb dildo."

"Maybe so," Fats said, "but he liked you. Talked about you."

She adjusted the bottom of her bikini. She shook her head slowly, said quietly. "He had this stupid idea that I'd take off with him, we'd make it to Mexico, buy a little ranch and raise horses, live nice and simple."

Mexico, horses, the simple life with a fantasy woman—that would appeal to Strutter.

"Can't buy much of a ranch with $9,000."

"The thing is...he said he had more. Lots." She gave him a heavy-lidded look. "He must have. Why else are you here?"

"He didn't say how much he had?" But Fats thought he already knew.

"He was dumb," she said, "but he wasn't that dumb."

"He had it stashed somewhere?"

"Said he'd hid it right in plain sight, whatever that meant." She allowed herself a smile, small, hard. "All I know for sure is that he didn't have it on him."

Fats fell silent. He wasn't going to get any more out her, not now, not here. "You turned him down, the Mexico deal?"

Her sneer returned. Her preposterous breasts jutted. "Do I look like somebody who'd run off with a dildo like Strutter Martin?"

Heat clung to streets and sidewalks. Neon colored the faces of the tourists milling before the entrances to bars and casinos. Sounds merged into an anonymous urban hum.

Fats Rangle walked through the Las Vegas night, thinking about money. Strutter had come to town with $10,000 in his pocket. He could only have gotten it from one place. And he fantasized about buying a horse ranch in Mexico, which would cost much more. Maybe as much as Carroll Coyle said had been embezzled from the Deseret Corporation.

Fats walked on. As he retraced his steps over the underground drainage channel, he sensed that he was being followed.

The tail wasn't very good. Turning a corner, Fats glimpsed his shadowy shape. Then, among the determined fun seekers and weary drunks, he caught his image reflected in shop glass. It was the tattooed bouncer, a block back, and then, in the shine of a liquor store window, nearer, coming fast.

Fats understood too late and had only half turned when the thug shoved him into a dark, narrow alleyway and the fist of the bald bouncer called Boo. The blow caught Fats high on his forehead. Streaks of color swirled in the dim light as he stumbled deeper into the alley. Boo hit him again, just above his eye. Fats reeled into the darkness, instinct keeping him on his feet. If he went down, he knew, he was finished.

The tattooed bouncer came up, fist raised, and Fats, dizzy, sick, threw his own fist into the man's chest, driving him back into the wall. The mugger gave out an animal cry, enraged. Boo too was angry now, his face dark and ugly.

Fats knew he was about to be hurt. But he could do some damage of his own. A kind of angry elation cleared his head. It had been a long time since he'd hit anyone.

"Losing your punch, Boo?" The voice was calm, hard. Wheezy.

The alley entrance silhouetted a small man wearing a fedora. Doc Wills stepped into the dimness. "Two sucker shots and you can't put him down."

The bouncers stood silent, chests heaving. In the darkness down the alley something scurried. Out on the street, tires hissed on the warm asphalt.

Wills moved closer. Light from the street glanced off the pistol in his hand. "You maybe didn't know he was a friend of mine."

"This ain't nothing to do with you," Boo said. He was still breathing heavily.

"It is if I say it is." The PI coughed a short hard hoarse cough.

The tattooed bouncer rocked up eagerly onto his toes. He flexed, fisted his hands. "He's old, Boo. Sick. He ain't nothing."

"Shut the fuck up," Boo said, and slowly sidled toward the mouth of the alley.

Doc Wills stepped back, waved the weapon. His smile was unpleasant. "Give Abel Lasky my regards."

Fats leaned back against the alley wall. He watched the two heavies become shadows and then disappear. A knot of ache had formed on his forehead. He touched the pain above his eye, drew back fingertips stained with blood.

"It's nothing, a nick," Doc Wills said. "A band-aid will fix it."

"Yeah," Fats said. "Thanks. How'd you come to be here?"

"I thought Lasky might want to give you a Vegas hello." Wills coughed deeply, painfully. "I didn't figure you for such a yokel."

Fats nodded. "Walked right into it, didn't I?"

"Kept to your feet, though. That's something, I guess." The ex-cop no longer wore his dark glasses. In the ambient light of the alley his eyes seemed dark holes in bare bone. He holstered the pistol. "I figure you for a guy who'll take three punches to give one. Looked like you were ready to have some fun."

"Maybe next time," Fats said.

"Next time, if you want to ask questions in Vegas, you better pay fucking attention to what's going on around you."

"I'll do that," Fats said.

From the depth of the alley came a harsh squeal, then the scrape of claw on concrete.

"All kinds of killers out tonight," Doc Wills said.

Back on the street, they parted. Fats made his way to his motel. He was still awash in adrenaline. He wouldn't sleep much.

The sign at the bank said the temperature at nearly 2:00 was eighty-nine degrees.

Huffman's was crowded with cops, most men, both uniformed and in plainclothes. Ignoring the news show flashing silent images on television screens, they joked and argued and attacked their breakfasts. They were loud, nearly boisterous, eager to be out on the street. Fats watched them with envy.

He'd gotten to the café early, slipped into a two-person booth, sipped coffee and read the room and watched the door. When Ramona Clare came in, he was not the only one to admire the way she filled her neatly pressed uniform. He rose, squared his shoulders.

She saw him, removed her silver sunglasses, and grinned. Joining him in the booth, she studied the treated gauze he'd taped over the small gash on his eyebrow and examined the purple-yellow lump high on his forehead. Her mouth pursed wryly. "Welcome to Las Vegas."

"I misjudged Lasky."

She laughed. "You wouldn't be the first."

She'd just done ninety minutes in the gym, she said. Her color was high, her blue eyes bright. She shone with health.

They ordered. As they waited for their food, Fats tersely told her about the fun in the alley, about getting help from a local PI he'd contacted. He took out Doc Wills's card. "Know him?"

"I do," Sergeant Clare said. Her voice had gone flat.

Fats caught the change of tone. "The bouncer, Boo, he seemed afraid of him."

"He should be, if he's got any sense," she said.

"I don't get it," Fats said. "Wills is on his last legs, seems like."

"Doc Wills did over thirty years on the street," she said cautiously. "He put away a lot of perps, closed a lot of cases, but he didn't much care how he did it. People got hurt. Or they disappeared. Nobody messed with him. They still don't."

"Disappeared?"

The waitress arrived with Ramona Clare's melon cubes and Fats's scrambled eggs and bacon. When she'd gone, Sergeant Clare said, "Doc Wills killed three men, bad guys, all in the line of duty: righteous shoots. But some said there were others, maybe for money. Word was he had his own little cemetery staked out in the desert."

Fats crunched bacon. "He's a killer?"

She shook her head. "Who knows? On the street, that kind of rep can be an asset. Maybe it's just talk."

"How did he manage to end up owning a Dolly's?"

She looked at him. "The Vegas way."

Fats watched Ramona Clare fix her fork in a cantaloupe cube. Her hand looked smooth, strong, female. His own hand felt huge, heavy.

They ate silently. Fats had the feeling that Ramona Clare was studying him. He didn't mind.

She took out a small notebook. "About Miss Salome. Or Miss Edna." She grinned. "Doesn't have the same ring, does it?" She flipped pages, found what she'd copied from the records.

Edna Louise Kachuba, born in Reno twenty-seven years ago to Elena and Gus Kachuba. Mother OD'd. Father disappeared. Foster care. Teenage trouble, fighting, truancy, shoplifting. Sent to live with an uncle and aunt, Alec and Masie Duggar, in Blue Lake. Ran off. Appeared on Las Vegas streets. Questioned about burglaries thought to be the work of a teenage gang. Suspected of involvement in early-morning muggings on the Strip. Arrested twice for solicitation. Last known address an apartment complex on Paradise Road.

Fats listened attentively, wrote down the address. Then he said, "I talked to her last night at the Manx Club. Strutter had been there. He had over 9 grand on him, didn't say where he'd got it." He paused for a moment, then added only, "He told her he'd be back, but she hasn't seen him since. Or so she says."

Sergeant Clare stuffed her notebook into a pocket. "You didn't need any of this then."

"It all helps," Fats said, "especially the address. I want to talk to her again, away from the club."

"You don't believe her?"

"Everybody lies. And she knows more than she said." He finished his coffee.

"Besides which, she's the only lead you've got," she said. "The money. Where does a guy like Strutter get that kind of money?"

"I don't know," Fats lied. "Maybe he stole something—cars, cattle, jewelry. Haven't heard of any major thievery around Blue Lake, but I'm out of the loop these days. I'll check when I get back."

Sergeant Clare pursed her lips, frowned. "A pip-squeak cowboy in Abel Lasky's club with $9,000. Nothing good can come out of that. I—oh, look."

She was staring at one of the television screens. On it, Dale Zahn stood outside the Pinenut County Courthouse, smiling his sheriff's smile as he spoke silently. Then came a drone shot as the camera swooped over Shoshone Springs and up the rock and snow to the crashed airplane.

"I saw this at the gym," Ramona Clare said. "That's the plane that went down with the Deseret Construction executive."

NTSB officers in dark caps and jackets busied themselves about the wreck. Their steps had chewed up the snow. A small white tent covered the plane's clamshell door.

"They said. . ." Ramona Clare paused, gave Fats a long look. "They said the plane was discovered by a local guide. That wouldn't have been you, by any chance?"

"Dumb luck," Fats said. "I was mucking out a spring. Saw the sun glance off the windshield. Reported it to Dale. Then I took off."

"Or else that would be you being interviewed up there." Dale Zahn had reappeared on the screen, smiling, handsome, at ease. "On TV he comes across. . ." She couldn't find the words she wanted.

"He looks honest and competent, so people think he is."

"Is that why he beat you in the election?" When Fats didn't immediately respond, she grinned. "You can find almost anything on the internet these days. Even stuff about Norman Rangle and the campaign for sheriff of Pinenut County, Nevada."

"He looks good on TV," Fats said. "I don't. I look. . .ugly. Mean."

"Are you?"

"I'm a kitty cat."

"Do you ever smile?"

"Sometimes," he said. "I try, anyway."

On the television, Dale Zahn was replaced by a pair of pretty newsreaders.

"He's in town, Dale," Fats said. "At the water conference. Wants to meet me there."

"Oh, is he?" Her surprised expression was not quite convincing. "Tell him I said hello."

The café was emptying. Fats paid for their meal, and soon he and Ramona Clare were out in the heat. They crossed the parking lot to her car.

"What's your plan?" she asked.

Fats told her. Try to talk to Salome. Edna. Talk to Dale Zahn. Then, unless he learned something to help his search, which he doubted would happen, back to Blue Lake. "I've got to meet with the NTSB people."

Ramona Clare grinned. "If you end up staying the night, give me a call. I owe you a breakfast."

It didn't mean anything. She was just being polite, friendly. Probably.

Fats had just started his pickup when his phone shivered. Doc Wills wheezed, "There's talk. Some fuss outside the Manx Club a while back. Maybe your guy, maybe not."

Fats said, "Any way to find out for sure?"

"Coyle told me to give you a couple days," the PI said. "I'll keep at it."

Fats thanked him and clicked off, then pulled his pickup into the street. Traffic was heavy and halting. Engine exhaust smeared the hot air, which rose in wavering columns. Fats drove carefully, trying not to get angry.

He found his way to Paradise Road. Boxy apartment buildings and block warehouses huddled in the heat. A midsized casino hotel. Weedy desert lots glittery with broken glass. A few shops and offices occupying what had been modest homes new when the road was a busy state highway.

Paradise Arms was a relatively recent construction already in decline, four floors of pink painted concrete. Dusty yuccas flanked the entrance. In the rectangular pool, a man and woman played. Around it, a few mostly bare females broiled. The young woman who called herself Salome was not one of them.

Fats parked and took the hot, jerky elevator to the fourth floor, found her door, knocked, waited, knocked again.

The door eased open a chain length. In the narrow gap, he could see a cheekbone, freshly bruised, still puffy and red. Her voice was hard. "Go away."

"We need to talk, Edna," he said.

"Go away," she repeated, starting to close the door.

Fats put his hand out and pushed. The door was hollow, the chain cheap. "I don't want to have to bust in."

After a moment, she undid the chain. Fats stepped inside and shut the door behind him.

She tightened the belt of her thigh-length black silk kimono. "You're asking for more of what you got last night, Deputy."

"Looks like you got some too."

In the sunlight that streamed into the room from a balcony, the swelling on her cheek was more pronounced, spreading toward her temple, and the hues more vivid. She'd been slapped, Fats thought, and hard.

"I got you to thank for it. And I'll get it again, when whoever Abel Lasky has watching me tells him you were here."

Fats frowned. "Why would he want to have you watched?"

"Because he thinks Strutter's just waiting for a chance to come get me and light out with the money to Mexico. Or that I might try to skip out and go get it."

"Did Strutter tell you where the money is?"

"God, you're like the rest, aren't you?"

"I know Strutter," Fats said. "He wouldn't be able to keep from bragging, especially to you. Maybe he wouldn't tell you where he'd stashed it, but he'd tease, give hints."

For a moment she sat silently, eyes unfocused. "All he said was that it was in plain sight, where nobody but him could see it."

"In plain sight where? At his trailer, at Blackpool?"

"He said once he could see it from his kitchen," she said. "But it wasn't like he went on about it. He mostly talked about his horse and that ranch in Mexico he was planning to buy."

"And he didn't tell you where he got the money?"

"No. But he had to have stolen it," she said. "Most likely from drug dealers. Who else would have that kind of cash?"

Fats thought about it. Probably she was lying. But maybe she wasn't.

"Look," he said. "I'm sorry I got you a slap. I'm sorry if my being here is going to get you another one. I'm just trying to find Strutter."

"Well, you see him here anywhere?" she snapped.

The small studio was sparsely furnished, with a kitchenette, breakfast bar, and bathroom. Neat, well kept, a few female frills. Nowhere to hide.

"What got you the smack?"

She glared, as if it had been his hand that marked her. "I didn't work you hard enough about the money."

"Tell me again about what happened with Strutter," Fats said. "The truth this time."

"Or what, Fats? You'll wallop me too? You look like you're about to."

Fats studied her: her short dark hair, her big dark eyes. He still couldn't place her. "I'm just trying to find this little guy who left his horse with me."

"Yeah," she said. "Okay. If it'll get you out of here."

She sat on the sofa, tucking her legs beneath her, tugging silk tightly over her knees, brushing at the swell of her breasts. She gave him a story that might not have been a lie.

Strutter had shown up with a wallet full of cash. Nine thousand plus. Trying to impress her, he said he had a lot more, started blabbing about the Mexican horse ranch he had enough cash to buy, so she knew he had more money somewhere—if he wasn't lying, which was possible with a dildo like him.

Abel Lasky smelled money. He wanted it, and he wanted to know where it came from. He wanted to know how much more Strutter had and where it was. Salome was supposed to find out, but didn't. Strutter told her finally that he had it stashed away, then he left, going after some grass. She never saw him again.

Fats knew all this, more or less.

When Fats showed up, she said, Lasky assumed he was after the money, probably drug money, and that Fats was working for the dealers that Strutter had ripped off. Again Salome was supposed to find out how much there was and where it might be and where Strutter had got to. She hadn't. Abel Lasky thought she hadn't tried hard enough. She got popped.

"You think he's dead?"

The question silenced her. Her big eyes sought something out the French doors, in the sunlight, in the empty blue sky.

Then she said, "Abel Lasky doesn't think so. Otherwise, he wouldn't be looking for him. Strutter's run off, or he's hiding. But who from? And why hasn't he gotten in touch with you or...me?"

Those were the right, the obvious questions.

She looked up at Fats. Then she spoke in a voice he hadn't heard yet. "I mean, I hope he's not dead. I hope he's down in Mexico, riding a horse."

So somewhere under the tattoos and makeup there was a soft spot in Edna Kachuba.

"You knew him back in Blue Lake," Fats said.

"They'd messed him up too, the welfare people."

Fats looked at her. The bruise seemed even uglier. "Can you cover that with makeup?"

"Yeah," she said, "But I probably won't. They like it, the dildos. It turns them on."

Fats looked at her even more closely. But he couldn't place her. She was just one of Abel Lasky's dancers. "In Blue Lake, did I give you a hard time?"

She smiled then, again defiant. "I like that you don't remember. Maybe you will someday."

5

In the parking lot, a black Escalade idled. Sun glare distorted the driver's face, but Fats assumed he was one of Abel Lasky's goons. Fats let pass the urge to brace him: nothing he could do would keep the young woman who called herself Salome from getting another slap.

The pickup's air-conditioning fought the heat and lost. Traffic was heavy, slow. A black Escalade appeared and reappeared in his rearview mirror. Maybe he was being followed. But there were a lot of black Cadillac SUVs in Las Vegas.

Parking at the casino was a problem. Then the elevator was full, hot bodies pressing against other hot bodies. Fats, more and more irritated, was near to saying the hell with it when the car stopped on his floor.

Stepping out, he was greeted by an amplified female voice. He followed it to the open doors of the grand ballroom, where men and women filled rows of straight-backed chairs, listening. Fats slipped in, found a piece of wall to lean against, and he too listened.

Small, slender, wearing a simple peach-colored cotton dress and pearls, Vi Barlow looked delicate, even fragile. But she spoke with quiet force, calmly, her phrases measured, her tone assured. She spoke of crises, current and to come.

Water from the Colorado River, the primary provider for Las Vegas, was over-allocated, the flow recently reduced, the levels in reservoirs perilously low. Short-term shortages—droughts—had long been a problem, but now climate change threatened the entire American Southwest with aridification. Ranchers, farmers, and miners needed water, for which they had to compete with politically powerful cities. Rights to rivers and streams were all already owned, many, courts had held, by Native American tribes. Aquifers were being depleted faster than they could be replenished. Pipelines were expensive and environmentally harmful. Conglomerates were buying up water pumped or promised, to what end no one could say. Conservation efforts had been offset by population expansion. So far, desalination projects had not been encouraging. Interior Department policies were uncertain at best, and Bureau of Reclamation projects ineffectual.

Judge Barlow gave grim news but she seemed untroubled by it. Fats was impressed. He found himself prepared to accept whatever she would say.

She paused, sipped from a waterglass. Then she smiled. "Let me simplify. If other sources of water are not developed, all economic efforts in the Southwest deserts must be scaled back and urban growth must end."

These, she said, were immediate issues. But they were specific, local aspects of much larger problems, problems of global overpopulation and resource exhaustion, of air and sea pollution, and of irresponsible human husbandry of planet Earth.

Her audience stirred. She had laid out the situation so clearly that it could not be mistaken or muddied. But she did not presume either to pooh-pooh the problems or to offer solutions. Instead, insofar as desert issues were concerned, she appealed now to the interests and energies of her audience, observing that those men and women in attendance—tribal representatives, miners, ranchers, scientists and academics, bureaucrats, politicians—were the ones tasked with working out the future. She did not doubt, she concluded, that they would do so satisfactorily.

Applause came enthusiastically. People rose but seemed unwilling to leave. Many milled and shuffled about Judge Barlow, as if seeking her acknowledgment, her approval. Dale Zahn was not one of these. Fats watched as the sheriff of Pinenut County rose from his seat and, spying him, came over, drawing glances from around the room as he moved. With his white shirt and string tie, he wore a dust-colored summer-weight suit, carefully creased, the jacket cut to accommodate a shoulder holster. His black boots were glossy, his belt silver buckled. He held his white Stetson in his hand. He looked like a costumed actor on his way to a film shoot. Like Abel Lasky, Fats thought, Dale Zahn was playing a role.

He grinned at the gauze above Fats's eye. "You found some fun, did you?"

"Some," Fats agreed.

The sheriff gestured toward Judge Barlow. "What do you think?"

"Seems like the real thing."

"A lot of people in Las Vegas are betting a lot of money that she is."

For a silent moment, the two men watched her: calm, controlled, smiling. Noticing them, she turned and spoke to the man hovering at her elbow, Carroll Coyle. He listened, then made his way through the press of people and approached. He was again beautifully dressed, again appointed in gold.

"Deputy. I understand you found amusement after we parted last night." He extended his hand, but not to Fats. He smiled his too-bright smile. "Sheriff Zahn, nice to see you again."

Dale Zahn took the proffered hand, flashed his politician's smile. "Been a while, Mr. Coyle."

"I imagine we'll be meeting more often," Coyle said, "once Judge Barlow starts to campaign."

Fats didn't know what that meant.

"The plane Deputy Rangle here found—you've been involved in its recovery."

"At the edges," the sheriff allowed. "The Feds are running the show."

"I've told Mr. Rangle of my interest in the matter," Coyle said. "I'd like to talk to you about it this evening. Judge Barlow is barbecuing for friends and supporters. She'd be pleased if you could attend." He nodded then at Fats. "You too, Deputy."

"Ex," Fats said. "Thank the judge for the invitation, but I'm heading back to Gull Valley."

"Too bad," Coyle said without real regret. "But I know she wants to talk to you, Sheriff. Political stuff. And, as I say, I've a couple things I'd like to go over with you."

"I'll be there," the sheriff said.

Coyle again extended his hand. Dale Zahn again took it. Fats had the sense that some sort of show had just ended.

As the sheriff watched Coyle make his way back to Judge Barlow, he said to Fats, "Jenny Jones's memory improved a bit once she took her meds, Caroline says. Strutter's place was trashed by a big man and a small woman. Big black ride, probably an SUV."

"I met a big man last night, a couple of them," Fats said, touching the bandage over his eye. "The dancer that Strutter came sniffing after, she's small. And a black Escalade may be on my tail."

Fats was guessing. But Lasky would have sent someone to Strutter's place to look for him and the money, and Salome had lived in Blue Lake, would know her way around.

Dale Zahn looked at him. "And?"

Fats hesitated. But it was time. Better that he told the sheriff about the money before Carroll Coyle did. "You suppose there's a nice quiet bar in this place?"

Crowds of tourists and badged conference-goers clogged the hallways. Fats had to check his impulse to shove his way through them. There were too many people, it was too hot out, Las Vegas was too ugly, he'd had too much of it all.

His anger ebbed as he and Dale Zahn finally sat over frosted beer glasses in a corner of a lounge on the main floor. The air here was cooled nearly to cold. From hidden speakers came a faint accordion playing a tune vaguely Italian.

Calming, Fats sipped his beer. Then he told the sheriff about the track in the snow and what it meant. "Had to be Strutter got to the plane before me. Nobody else was up there."

The sheriff eased back in his seat. The pistol in his shoulder holster made a small lump in the smooth fabric of his jacket. "You deliberately scuffed out all sign of him."

"Let's say I didn't try not to," Fats lied. "I was beat and it was the easiest way up and I didn't much give a shit."

"And?"

"And Strutter hadn't said nothing about finding the plane. He didn't want anybody to know."

"Because he stole something from it."

"That'd be my guess," Fats said.

"And you covered it up." The sheriff watched him, unperturbed.

"It just wasn't none of my business anymore."

"Being an ex-deputy, you mean," Dale Zahn said drily. "And you wanted to protect the runt. So you tracked up a crash site and then made a false report."

"Arrest me," Fats deadpanned.

"You lied to me." The sheriff seemed almost amused.

"Everybody lies," Fats said.

The sheriff took a long swallow of beer. "What else?"

Fats told him all of it then. He told him about money, the ten thousand dollars Strutter had come to Vegas with, and the $250,000 that was missing, maybe, from the crashed plane. He recounted what the pole dancer Salome, née Edna Kachuba, had said, described Abel Lasky's interest, summarized his conversation with Carroll Coyle.

When Fats had finished, the two men sat silently. Voices came in murmurous waves from the casino. Strings replaced the accordion.

"Strutter?" The sheriff said finally, "You think he's dead?"

"That or on the run, maybe from Lasky, maybe from Carroll Coyle."

"Abel Lasky—I had dealings with him, back in the day. If there's big money to be had . . . but why Coyle?"

"I don't know," Fats said. "The money—he acts almost like it's his."

"He wouldn't kill for it, would he? Two hundred and fifty thousand is a chunk of cash, but . . . I didn't read him that way."

Fats thought about it. "There's another guy you probably know from your cop days down here. Name's Doc Wills. A private badge now."

"I know Doc," Dale Zahn said. "Nasty mother-humper when he wants to be."

"Coyle loaned him to me to help find Strutter," Fats said. "My guess is that he's really keeping tabs on me. The muscle I ran into last night are afraid of him. Your Sergeant Clare gave me an idea why."

Dale Zahn nodded. "He'd chill Strutter for 10 grand, no question. For nothing, if he had a mind to."

Fats drained his beer. "Lasky thinks I'm working for drug dealers and Coyle thinks I stole the money from the plane. Both of them know I'm looking Strutter. They're hoping I'll find him."

"Imagine that." The sheriff showed his grin. "As far as Coyle knows, you were the first to get to the plane and whatever was in it. If thieving went on, who else could have done it?"

Fats shrugged. "They can think what they like. Don't make it so."

"Two hundred and fifty thousand dollars," the sheriff said again. "You buy the story about embezzlement?"

"Not really," Fats said.

"Coyle talked about politics? So this cash would most likely be gray money?"

Fats nodded. Dirty tricks money. Money moved through so many accounts that it finally becomes untraceable.

"That's why it didn't show up on any of the official reports. If there was cash on the plane," Dale Zahn surmised, "Strutter got it. He's not all that bright, but he knew better than to bring a quarter of a million dollars with him to Vegas. He took out 10 grand to party with. The rest's back in Pinenut County, stashed somewhere."

Fats nodded. "Probably."

"Any idea where?"

"Not a clue," Fats said, lying.

The two men sat, silent once more. Around them the casino did its business. Money moved.

Then the sheriff said, "What we're saying is Strutter stole a quarter of a million dollars that there's no record of. That wasn't there. That didn't exist."

"I'm guessing," Fats admitted, "but yeah."

"The thing of it is," the sheriff said, "if a fellow was to find it, he wouldn't need to report it, would he? There wouldn't be anything officially to report. But you probably already figured that out."

Fats said nothing.

"Don't give me that look," the sheriff said carefully, watching the ex-deputy. "You're not incorruptible. It's no secret, Fats, favors and deals and payoffs. You're just like the rest of us."

Fats said nothing.

After another long silence, the sheriff suddenly grinned. He slid from the booth. "You sure you don't want to try Judge Barlow's barbeque? Mingle with money?"

Fats stood. "I'm gone."

He was in the Trevi parking garage when his phone hummed and shivered. Doc Wills wheezed into his ear. He had a bit more on the commotion outside the Manx Club the night Strutter disappeared. Somebody got hurt. Nobody knew much about it.

"What's your guess?" Fats asked.

"Probably your boy," Wills said. "It was quick and quiet. Lasky don't usually do harm that close to his club, though. It might have been just an old-fashioned mugging. Then again, somebody hauled off the body. If there was a body."

"But Lasky's looking for him, for Strutter."

"Which means he didn't do him," Wills said, "assuming he got done."

"That the best we'll get?"

"Yeah," Wills said. "I'll keep an ear out, but I don't expect there'll be much more."

"Yeah," Fats echoed. "Anyway, I'm heading home. Thanks for the help."

There were several black SUVs in the parking garage, but none followed him out.

The drive back to his motel was less frustrating. Fats was going to pick up his bag and check out and be on his way. Already he was beginning to relax.

In the motel parking lot, a green Bentley convertible idled. From it slipped the pretty young man who the night before had attended Carroll Coyle. "Mr. Rangle," he said, "I'm so glad I caught you." His voice was low and throaty, his smile soft, his air affable. He wore seersucker. He seemed not to sweat.

Fats climbed out into the heat and accepted an elegantly embossed card: Mr. Terry Blume. "I have a message from Judge Barlow," he said. "She hopes that you might find a way to attend her barbeque this evening. She'd like to talk to you about a horse."

Fats was puzzled. "What horse?"

"I don't know. I was to give you the message. And this." He withdrew from his pocket a folded sheet of Violet Barlow's personal stationery, on which a small neat hand had written directions. "Is there an answer?"

Fats didn't really think about it. "Yeah. Sure. I'll be there."

"Wonderful."

Fats took a step, then stopped. "How did you know I was here, at this motel?"

Terry Blume smiled. "This is Las Vegas, Mr. Rangle."

After the Bentley was gone, Fats reconnoitered. No goons. No Doc Wills, as far as he could tell. All he learned was that the temperature was 111. He went up to his room, entering cautiously, but he found no one and no sign that anyone had been there.

His plans now changed, he took a nap. He slept deeply for several hours and awoke groggy, regretting having said he'd attend Judge Barlow's party. All he wanted was to get away, back to the desert.

He showered and dressed, then went to the motel office and checked out. The nap would hold him, he'd eat barbeque and talk to Vi Barlow about a horse, leave as soon as possible, and drive back to Gull Valley in the dark and relative cool.

Joining the thinning rush hour traffic, Fats pointed his pickup toward Mt. Charleston and the declining sun. Las Vegas, beyond the fuss and flash of the Strip, was much like every other city in the desert. The usual franchises with their loud signs, the familiar residential tracts with their artificial arcs and angles, the empty parcels of scrub sage and dust, all seemingly without pattern or purpose. Fats, driving through the sameness, gradually ceased to see it.

Following Vi Barlow's directions, he took a cross street to a lane that eased up a brushy knoll to a spread of recently constructed houses: Shadow Springs Estates, according to the sign. Here Fats turned onto a graveled road that dropped into a gully littered with debris left by the most recent flash flood. Then the road rose again, bringing into view various ranch buildings and enclosures. These were fronted by a large hacienda, old but in good repair: red tile roof and thick whitewashed adobe walls, arched windows and entryways, and a courtyard decorated with yucca and sage and shaded by cottonwoods and elms.

Fats parked in the dust of an improvised lot at the end of a row of vehicles, SUVs and midsized sedans and pickups, mostly, but also a few glitzier machines, noticeably a white stretch limousine with Texas plates. Mariachi music and heat met him as he made his way to the crowded main courtyard, in the center of which bubbled a low-flowing fountain. A white-hatted cook basted a spitted quarter of beef. Plates of food covered a long table. A red-jacketed Latino served a small bar.

The gathering had a neighborly, backyard feel to it, some men in coats and ties but as many in shorts or chinos and shirtsleeves, women in summery dresses or sleeveless tops and designer jeans. Money people, many of them, but also some old friends of Vi Barlow, Fats guessed, and supporters attesting to their loyalty.

Carroll Coyle, in an off-white suit, greeted and glad-handed. When he spied Fats, he slid through the crowd. "Deputy. Her Honor will be pleased you could make it. She'd like to speak with you."

"About a horse," Fats said.

"So I'm told." His smile flickered falsely. "Get yourself a plate and glass. She'll be with you as soon as she takes care of a few obligations."

At the moment the judge stood in the shade of an immense elm, the center of a semicircle of three men in green-tinted Ray-Bans. Two were burly, wore their jeans and poplin jackets like uniforms, and stood so that between them they commanded all approaches to the third man. At ease in shorts and a Dallas Cowboys jersey, he was smaller than the other two but, judging by the angle of his sunglasses and the set of his shoulders, their superior. Vi Barlow was speaking. The smaller man listened carefully. The big men watched.

Fats followed Coyle's suggestion. At the buffet table he made himself a meal, and at the bar he got a Coke. Then, as the evening shadows lengthened, he ate, standing up, observing. Men and women moved about the courtyard, into and back out of the house, swirling around either Vi Barlow or the man in the Cowboys jersey and dark glasses. People ate and drank and talked. All seemed to know why they were here. In this, as in most things anymore, Fats was not one of them. He felt restive, itchy, ready to disappear.

He was finishing his meal when he was motioned over by Carroll Coyle. As he moved through the crowd, he could feel in his chest the scrutiny of the two big men. Fats took them for muscle: expensive and worth it.

"Mr. Mohr," Coyle said to the other, smaller man, "this is Deputy

Rangle, the fellow who found the plane and the body of your vice president. Deputy, this is David Mohr, CEO of Deseret Construction."

Mohr was fifty, maybe, and fit. His sunglasses hid his eyes. He held out his hand. "Deputy. I wanted to thank you personally for your effort. Not knowing Carl Portman's fate was a burden for everyone, his family foremost, but for those of us who worked with him as well. He was valued and respected. I understand we might never have known what happened to him if it hadn't been for you."

Fats took the offered hand, met the firm grip. "Dumb luck."

"I don't believe in luck, Deputy," Mohr said. "I believe in resourcefulness. That seems to be a quality you possess."

Fats couldn't get a read on David Mohr. The voice was soft, the mouth hard. His jaw seemed permanently set, his lips barely to move as he spoke. His Ray-Bans, pointless now in the deepening twilight, somehow suggested distance, as if he occupied an alien space.

"Well, Deputy—"

"Ex-deputy," Fats interrupted. "I'm retired."

"From law enforcement, yes, so I understand," Mohr said, "but in any case, we are in your debt. You and your brother have a business in Gull Valley. We have interests there. We might want to make use of your services somewhere down the line."

"We're available," Fats said soberly.

"Or you might weary of retirement. I'm sure we could find something interesting for an ex-deputy to do. Give Carroll here a call."

For a moment, Fats stood still, uncertain, even as the CEO of Deseret Construction nodded and turned away. Coyle too left him.

The day was disappearing, the crowd quieting. Festive lamps lit the courtyard. Vi Barlow was nowhere in sight. Fats again grew restless, and now faintly angry. He was about to say the hell with it when Terry Blume, still in unwrinkled seersucker, appeared. "Mr. Rangle, the judge will be down at the stables in five minutes. I'll show you the way, if you'd like."

Fats followed him. Passing the open archway into a large living room, he saw Dale Zahn standing before a massive fireplace, scowling at the clawlike hand that Carroll Coyle rested on his forearm. At the same moment, Fats recognized the big blonde grinning at him.

Terry Blume led him around the house, then pointed across a wide and shadowed lot. The stable was, like the other structures, old and weathered, looked little used. It might, from its size, once have sheltered a dozen animals. Now Fats was watched by only one.

The gray gelding shuffled in the stable corral, snorted, moved up to lean his dappled neck over the top rail. He nickered, inviting attention. Fats stroked the horse's nose and talked to him, quietly telling him what he saw and thought. Old: mid-twenties, at least. Some good blood, maybe Arab, well-configured but thin and listless. A faint rasp in his breathing. Tired, maybe ailing.

"What is it, boy? You catch something?"

"A mild viral infection. But it's more what he's lost."

He hadn't heard her come up. Now Vi Barlow, small and waiflike beside his bulk, smiled wanly. "His companions, one by one, have died off. The last one went a few weeks ago. Omar's never been alone before."

"That'll put a horse off his feed," Fats said.

"We hear that horses are social animals, that they need the company of their kind, but we sometimes forget that they feel deeply—affection, loss, loneliness." She smiled. "He seems to like you. What were you talking to him about?"

"Just getting acquainted, Judge."

She patted the horse's neck. "You and I could do the same, Ex-Deputy. I understand they call you Fats. I'd like to, if you'll allow it. And I'm just Vi."

In boots and jeans and plain white blouse, she wouldn't have been out of place on Blue Lake sidewalks. For all her considerable achievements she was, Fats thought, still a girl from Pioche. As he had when they first met, he found her presence somehow heartening. She seemed, even when speaking, quiet, still even when moving.

"Shadow Springs Ranch has been in the Barlow family for generations," she said, stroking the horse. "But it hasn't ever been really profitable. Not enough water, poor range—you know the problems, I'm sure. My husband had started selling parcels before he died, and since then I've gotten rid of the rest. The only thing of value left is the ranch house. I've lived here since my marriage, but it's time to move on."

Fats followed that. "You're selling?"

"Not exactly. I'm deeding it to Clark County. The commissioners don't know what they'll use it for, but they're excited to get it."

"Pretty big gift," Fats said.

"Oh, I'll receive. . .considerations," she said. "But the point is, I need to find a place for Omar. I've decided that I'd like to board the old guy with you and your brother in Gull Valley."

Fats was surprised. "We'd be happy to take him."

"I know there are good stables around here, but. . .the politics are complicated," she said. "I've thought this through, and settling Omar with you is the best thing for him and for me."

As night fell, Vi Barlow and Fats Rangle stroked and rubbed and patted the old horse whose future they were determining. She had taken the trouble to research Cherry Creek Stables, and knew most of what she needed to, so her questions were few and sensible. His answers were simple, direct. He quoted her a price, tentative until confirmed by Mary. He told her, briefly, about his family. She told him that Omar was finishing an antibiotic cycle but would be ready to move soon. Fats said that he could bring down their best trailer and carry the old horse to Gull Valley.

The matter was quickly settled. She and he smiled as they formally shook hands. Proper papers and signatures would come later, but they were, at least to Fats, unnecessary. He would never need more than Vi Barlow's handshake.

He said good-bye to the horse, as did she, and the two of them started back through the shadows. Soft lamplight created a yellowish aura around the courtyard and glowed in the house windows. A Mexican guitar thrummed. The edge was off the heat, the evening turned almost pleasant.

"Finding that plane," Vi Barlow said. "How did that happen?"

Walking beside her, her blonde hair catching the light, her white blouse arranging the darkness, Fats felt oddly protective of her. He told her about the flash of sunlight.

"It's a wonder that no one else saw it."

"The real wonder is that I did. The sun moves."

She understood. "There would be only a brief period, minutes at most, when it would strike the plane just right. But might somebody else have seen it too?"

"Nobody else gets up that way much," he said. "If anybody was to spot it, it'd have to be one of us."

"Us?"

"Me," Fats said. "My brother. Buddy, my nephew. And a distant cousin who helps out from time to time."

"Oh, yes, that would be the young man you're down here looking for," she said. "Carroll told me. Have you had any success?"

"Nope."

They reached the corner of the house. Voices murmured. Vi Barlow stopped, placed her hand lightly on his arm. "Good luck finding your cousin."

"I'm heading back to Blue Lake. I'll have to leave it to the Vegas police, at least for now," he said. "But thanks. And thanks for the hospitality."

"You're welcome, Fats," she said. Then she added: "Young men sometimes get lost in Las Vegas. Let's hope your cousin isn't one of them."

Ramona Clare stood alone at the courtyard entrance. She grinned again as he crossed over to her. She was waiting, it turned out, for him. "I've been dumped. Dale is tangled up doing politics. Or so I'm supposed to say."

Like Vi Barlow, she was outfitted in boots and jeans and a simple white blouse. In them she was all heft and health, looked ready to wrestle steers. Her color was high. Her grin was playful, and something else. She was a bit tipsy.

Fats nodded. "I don't guess you'd have much trouble hitching a ride."

Her grin spread. "I already had a couple of offers. But Dale said you'd take me home. And I wanted to say hello."

"Hello," Fats said.

"Hello," she said, laughing.

Fats hadn't played this game for a long time. He wasn't sure, in fact, that they were playing it now. But the signs were there, had been since they met.

"I'm on my way out of town," he said, "but if you're ready to go, I can drop you off."

"I've seen enough," she said. "Nice old place. When E. E. Barlow was alive, money and politics came here to breed, or so they say. Still do, from what I saw tonight." She laughed again. "I don't imagine you were talking about campaign contributions with the judge?"

He led her to his pickup, telling her briefly about Vi Barlow's horse.

In the parking area, empty spaces marked the departure of several vehicles, including the white limo. Fats held the pickup door open for her, a gesture that charged Ramona Clare's grin. He climbed in, started the engine, flicked on the lights. As he pulled out of the dusty lot, he asked, "What should I know about David Mohr?"

"Speaking of politics and money," she said.

"Are we?"

"He's had Deseret Construction buying property all over the state. Buying politicians too, some say, or at least influence. What he's up to is anybody's guess," she said. "He's supposed to be smart. Tough. Not so much corrupt himself as a corrupter. Why?"

"He offered me a job," Fats said. "Sort of."

"Doing what?"

"Didn't get that far," Fats said.

Console lights turned her skin and hair a faint rose. She smiled at nothing in particular. Then she caught his look. "What's on your mind, Ex-Deputy?"

"You," he said. "And Dale."

"I wondered if you'd be interested enough to ask," she said. "When he's in town, Dale brings me to these things sometimes, because Donna knows there's nothing between us anymore. There never was much, a couple of bumps in the night when I was between husbands. Now I give him an excuse not to notice the women coming on to him. Most of the time."

"But not always," Fats said.

Her grin faded. "What happens between a husband and wife is their business. Dale and Donna, they seem to have worked things out since they left Las Vegas. This town can be hell on marriages."

Fats drove toward the distant glow of the Strip. Ramona Clare talked. If failure in marriage were a crime, she said, she'd get life without parole. She was a three-time loser. In this town, in her line of work, there were too many temptations to betrayal. She'd been both cheated on and cheater. She had nothing good to say about her husbands and lovers, but nothing bad either. If she blamed anyone, it was herself. She'd had impossible hopes, made inappropriate plans, chosen foolishly, ended up with shouting or silence. Now she took men as they came, which was, these days, less and less frequently. She'd leave Las Vegas, she said, but she had nowhere to go.

Fats said nothing. He wasn't prepared for her intimacies. They might have constituted an invitation. Or not. He wondered how much she'd had to drink.

"You and Dale," she said, "You ran against each other for sheriff. He beat you pretty bad, it sounded like. But you're...friends?"

"No," Fats said. "We've just known each other all our lives."

"And Donna?"

After only a slight hesitation, he said, "Her too."

They settled into silence. He drove carefully, following her instructions to a curve of homes, every third one the same, at the edge of Summerlin. Her house was dark. Streetlamps shone on a new SUV parked before her garage. A sprinkler system misted a small patch of lawn.

She grinned. "You want to come in?"

"I need to get going," he said.

She looked at him. "Don't be an asshole, Fats."

He looked at her. "Yeah. Okay."

They stepped out into the heat of the night. She worked her key in the front door and went inside. Fats followed her into her house, into her bedroom, into her bed. Both made noises, but neither spoke until they finished.

As they lay in the dimness, she said, "I needed that. It seemed like you did too."

"Been a while," he admitted.

"What," she wondered playfully, "does an ex-deputy in Blue Lake, Nevada, do for love?"

"Nothing," Fats said. "Or go to the pros."

"Ah," she chuckled throatily, "a real romantic."

"At least I don't have three exes."

She rose up on an elbow to look down at him. "You really are an asshole, aren't you?"

He didn't know why he'd said that. He had regretted the words almost instantly.

Light from the street diminished the darkness. Shadows softened her face. She seemed now older, more worn, more real.

He raised his thick hand and stroked her throat, much as he had that of Vi Barlow's old horse.

"It's just simpler, with whores. They don't want anything but money." He removed his hand. "I never slept with a woman who didn't want something from me."

When he was a deputy, he was often approached by women in want—other men's wives and girlfriends, divorcees, welfare mothers, druggies, cop groupies. With them he often had been an asshole. But now he didn't say that.

She looked at him. "Well, I don't want anything, Fats."

"What is this, then?"

"I don't know," she said. "Another bump in the night? You're off to your family and business in Blue Lake. Maybe we'll never see one another again."

He didn't know what to say to that.

"It's easy to leave a lover in Las Vegas, Fats. What happened happened. It's done. Now there's only now."

He didn't know what to say to that, either.

She touched his flaccid penis. "You're short and fat and ugly, but I like you." As she spoke, she removed her hand, rolled away, and slid out of bed. Then she said, "I like the way you don't mind that I'm taller than you are." For a moment she stood before him, large and female, naked and shadowed. Then she moved, went into the bathroom.

Fats lay quiet, damp. He listened to the sound of water running in the bathroom. He felt as he usually did after sex—empty, almost angry.

He got up, found his clothes where they'd been flung, and began to dress. Ramona, now in a short terrycloth robe, slipped back into the room. She sat on the edge of the bed and watched him. Buckling his belt, he said, "I'll be back in a week or so, fetching Judge Barlow's horse. I'd like to take you out to dinner."

She smiled. She rose from the bed. "I'd like to be taken."

He followed her through the house—kitchen, living room, French doors leading to a small patio and smaller lawn. It all seemed strangely unlived in.

At the door, Fats sensed that he should say something. He hadn't felt this obligation before, leaving a woman. Now he couldn't manage words. He opened the door and went out into the night.

Fats found his way to West Flamingo Drive and a 7/11, where he gassed up, bought coffee and bottled water, and relieved himself. Peeing, he caught the smell of sex and the softer scent of Ramona Clare.

The lights of Las Vegas glowed, seemed almost to throb. Interstate traffic, when he rose up the ramp into it, was hurried but finally beginning to thin. He drove carefully until he was free of the pull and pulse of the city. On the state highway, vehicles were few, business and residential lights fell away, and darkness dominated the moonless, shadowless night. Fats turned off the AC and cracked open his window, letting the warm desert air wash over him, and he began to feel clean.

The scent of Ramona Clare had stayed with him. Now the idea of her rose in his mind. He didn't understand her interest in him. As she said, he was short, fat, and ugly. She said she didn't want anything from him. But everyone lies.

6

Sunlight streamed into the kitchen where Fats sat with Bill and Mary. The kids were at their chores. The coffee pot was nearly empty, Fats had pulled in while Mary was fixing flapjacks and eggs. She'd set him a plate. As they ate, he'd told them about the deal he'd made with Vi Barlow to stable her old gelding, Omar. Mary, pleased, promised to do the paperwork that afternoon. Now, in the morning stillness, she and her husband waited for Fats to say what he had to say.

A barn cat padded up to the screened back door, a blob of gray fur dangling from its mouth. The cat carefully placed the dying mouse on the mat, then began to wash. The mouse twitched once and was still.

Fats told them everything about Strutter and the plane and the money. Mary had questions. When he'd finished, they sat silently as the heat grew weightier. The cat, curled, was asleep.

"Lots of this you don't know for sure," Mary said at last.

"Sure enough," Fats said.

"About Strutter being dead."

Fats took a deep breath, let it ease from his lungs, then told them what he'd concluded during his drive through the darkness.

"He wouldn't go off without his horse. Or at least making arrangements."

"That doesn't mean—"

"Yeah, it does," Bill interrupted. "Only thing he gave a rat's patoot about, that pinto."

"Maybe he's dead, maybe not," Mary insisted. "But in a way it doesn't matter. He'll show up or he won't. But the money—if he really stole it, if he hid it around here somewhere, those guys who banged you up, they'll come looking for it."

"They've been here once already," Fats said. "Trashed Strutter's trailer, looking."

On the porch the cat awoke, stretched, showed its claws.

"Think I ought to get me a carry?" Bill asked, not smiling.

Fats hesitated. The question made the matter ominous. "Wouldn't hurt. Mostly, though, just keep an eye out."

"And maybe a loaded twelve-gauge near to hand." Bill made as if to move.

"While we're talking," Fats said. Driving through the darkness, he had decided to tell them he'd give up outfitting. Now he did.

Bill looked at the cat, which watched him without concern. Mary looked at her brother-in-law. "You sure, Fats?"

"It's the only thing that makes sense."

"Sell most of the machines and gear and stock?" Mary said.

Fats nodded. "I can handle that."

"And then. . . help out with the horses?"

"Till I find something else to do."

"We've contracted for a photographer's week in the mountains that Buddy's handling, and a few deer hunters this fall. But if we don't take any more, we can be shuck of it by the first of the year." Mary paused, then in a different voice said, "This something else you'll find to do—what would it be?"

"I don't know for sure," Fats said, "but everybody and his dog is offering me a job these days."

They weren't surprised that Dale Zahn would want him as a deputy. Even with all the changes in Blue Lake recently, Fats had a better sense of local crime and criminals than Dale would ever develop. Caroline Sam kept the office running smoothly. The three of them would make a good team.

They *were* surprised by what David Mohr had said. What sort of service they could be to Deseret Corporation wasn't immediately clear, but if Fats wanted to go on their payroll, his wages would make them not only solvent but secure.

"All this just because you found their dead vice president?" Mary asked.

"All I know is what he said." Fats shifted in his seat. "Besides, it felt sort of like a test. Like he was trying to figure me out."

They sat for a while in silence. Then Bill rose. "You're getting real popular there, Fats. We've had newspeople calling for you. Missed your chance to get on TV."

Fats scowled, grunted. He rose too. "Good."

Mary wrinkled her nose. She looked at Fats. She smiled wryly. "Made a friend in Vegas, did you?"

He frowned. "Huh?"

Mary shook her head, still smiling. "Go take a shower, Fats."

The meeting with the NTSB official was mostly a matter of form, but boxes had to be checked, blanks filled, reports confirmed, so he and the agent went well past noon. She seemed to already know the answers to her questions, which were obvious or obligatory. Fats's responses were terse and to the point. Neither brought up the zigzag trail.

Although investigators couldn't be certain, she told him, they thought that mechanical failure had brought down the plane. The bodies of the pilot and passenger had been removed. Plans were to helicopter out the plane in pieces.

They'd talked in a small conference room in the courthouse. When the agent left, Fats busied himself with some county records. Searching through files, paper or electronic, was not a task he was especially good at, and to get any real information he'd need to go to Carson City, but he was able to determine that officers and owners of Hydroneva had worked hard to hide their identity behind lawyers and brokers, subsidiaries and holding companies.

What this meant, Fats couldn't say. But it didn't much matter. He wasn't sure why he was looking anyway. He gave it up.

Outside, as if pressed down by the heat, Blue Lake barely stirred. For a moment, Fats stood on the courthouse steps, uncertain. He had nowhere he needed to go, nothing he needed to do, but he was restless. He wanted something to happen.

He got in his pickup and again drove toward the mountains and Coldwater Canyon, again taking the dirt road to Blackpool Estates. A hot breeze slid through the dark green reeds around the water. The curtains in Jenny's window did not wave.

Fats parked where he had before, but this time, ignoring Strutter's single-wide, he went into the corral. The ground was clean, raked, Splash's droppings collected into a mound that Fats probed carefully with a fork. He searched the space shaded by a corrugated metal lean-to, moved and replaced three hay bales, and checked around the water trough. In a small shed, he found tools and tack, camping gear, old horse blankets and pack satchels, and garbage bags, one half full of litter Strutter had hauled down the mountain on his last guiding trip. What he didn't find was a briefcase and a quarter of a million dollars.

The sound of an approaching engine brought him out into the sun. The white and green pickup raised a thin rooster tail of dust. The driver's door bore the brand of the Three Bar M.

Donna Zahn pulled to a stop and slid out of the cab. Squinting into the sunlight, she tugged at her hat brim, seeking to shade, maybe to hide, her eyes. She patted the handgun holstered on her hip, as if for reassurance. "I thought that was you, Norman," she said. "Any clues?"

Dale Zahn would have told his wife that Strutter was missing and that Fats was looking for him. Not, certainly, about the zigzag trail. Not, probably, about the money.

"No," Fats said. "I just had a hunch. Nothing in it, turns out."

"It doesn't look good for Strutter, Dale says." Everything about her seemed stiff—voice, feeble smile, shoulders—as if she were trying to hold herself together.

"No," Fats said again.

She bit her lower lip. "I understand that. . .in Las Vegas, you went to a party at Vi Barlow's. You and Dale and Ramona Clare."

Fats knew then why she was there. Anger thickened in his throat, chest.

"Sergeant Clare helped me trace Strutter's movements," he said roughly. Then he gave her what she'd come for. "Dale brought her to the party, I took her home. The last time I saw him, he was politicking."

His tone turned her away from him. She looked at the distant haze, the sun-blasted land, the dark reedy pool. She spoke as if to the emptiness. "I'm sorry, Norman. You're right to be disgusted with us, both of us. Dale has you help his adultery and I try to get you to help me catch him in a lie. We're using you. That's not right."

Fats didn't reply. But his anger, like the dust raised by her arrival, slowly dissipated. He looked at her and felt nothing at all.

She took his silence as an accusation. Again she scraped her teeth across her lower lip. "I've told you, Norman, I'm sorry for what we—for what I—did with you. To you."

As she stood stiff and unhappy in the heat, he saw how the summer sun and winter wind had dried her up, brought out the bone beneath her features, cut and seamed the skin around her mouth, rippled her throat. She looked runneled, eroded, worn away. The desert had done it, and her desolation.

Once the set of her shoulders would have moved him. No longer.

"I have to go," he said.

"I want to check on Jenny," Donna said. "She—Dale and the county have tried to get her into town, to the elder care facility, but she won't go."

"This's home for her," Fats said.

"I don't see how it—I mean, it's spooky, this place, everything dead-looking, even the reeds, the water. . ." Something new came into her voice then, silencing her.

Fats said nothing. In the window of the single-wide, a curtain moved.

Fats left Donna Zahn alone in the dust and heat. He drove back to town, where impulse turned him onto a cross street and soon into an older neighborhood without curbs or sidewalks, small homes that were, despite additions and minor modifications, all alike, some well kept, most not. He pulled up before a gray clapboard, green-shuttered house. A small sprinkler wetted a patch of lawn bordered by rose bushes. A paunchy old man in overalls and gardening gloves and a broad-brimmed straw hat stopped snipping dead blossoms to watch him.

Fats got out and walked over. "Mr. Duggar."

Alec Duggar was a widower, a railroader on disability with diabetes. Fats had known who he was since boyhood. He couldn't recall them ever having spoken.

"Deputy."

"No more," Fats said. "But I'd like to ask a couple of questions. About Edna Kachuba. Your niece."

It was a long moment until Alec Duggar said, "What kind of questions?"

Fats told him about his search for Strutter and the missing young man's connection to the exotic dancer who called herself Salome.

"Salome," Duggar said thoughtfully. "Scripture tells some ugly stories. You suppose that's what she wants for the guys that gawk at her dancing? Their heads on a plate?"

Fats nodded. "Could be."

"She all right?"

"You don't do what she does and not pick up a few bruises," Fats said. He was going to say more, then didn't.

"A couple months," Alec Duggar said. "That's all she was here before she run off. Upset Masie, she was still troubled by it when she died. Thought we hadn't done enough for the girl. But she was beyond doing anything for by the time we got her. Pissed off at the world. Had a right to be, I guess."

Fats said. "She said she knew me, but I can't place her. She in some kind of trouble while she was here?"

"Not really. Got rounded up one night with a bunch of kids smoking dope down in Cottonwood Creek Park, but nothing came of it. You was one of the officers on it."

Fats remembered, vaguely, the night. He didn't remember Edna Kachuba.

Alec Duggar looked at the clipper in his gloved hand, as if he couldn't fathom its purpose. Then he looked up at Fats. "But she had better reason to remember you, Deputy. We was in the Wagon Wheel, watching, when you beat hell out of that tough that time."

Fats said nothing.

"Thought you was trying to kill him."

Fats sighed, said, "He was wrecking the Adaven Bar. I went there to arrest him, and he caught me coming in and knocked me though the door into the street. Then he came out after me."

"I didn't see the first punch," Alec Duggar. "But all the rest was you, pounding on him."

"He got in his licks. But he was resisting arrest."

"You was having fun."

"There was an investigation," Fats said carefully. "I was exonerated."

"Sure you was. Cops, deputies, always are, ain't they? That's the way it works."

Fats, despite himself, didn't disagree.

Duggar said, "Anyways, she seen it, Edna. Wasn't long after that she lit out."

"Did she ever come back?"

Another pause. "Matter of fact, yeah."

A month earlier, Edna had appeared at the door with a muscle-bound bald man. They had arrived in a big black Cadillac SUV. She wanted to know about Strutter. They'd already been to his trailer at Blackpool. They asked about his friends, where he liked to hang out, where he might have left his horse.

"Wasn't much I could tell them," Alec Duggar said. "Strutter, he's just a guy around town."

"You tell them he hired on for us, or that we probably had his pinto?"

"I might of, if it'd just been her. I mean, she's tough and all, but I never thought she was actually mean. But the ape she was with, he was trouble you and your brother didn't need. Besides. . ." He paused again. In the heat and silence the sprinkler swished softly. Then he said, "I got the sense she didn't really want to find him. Strutter. Or that maybe she already knew where he was and didn't want the crud she was with to know."

"Thanks for keeping them off us."

"Didn't do it for you, Deputy. But your brother and his family, they're good people."

"Still," Fats said.

As he got back in his pickup, his phone shivered. It was Mary. He had a visitor.

The green Bentley convertible was parked in the shade of the house. In the pasture, Terry Blume and Buddy moved among the horses.

Bill came out of the barn and, as Fats parked, rolled his way across the yard, a holstered pistol on his hip.

"He brought a good-faith check from Vi Barlow. Said the vet said we could come get the old guy in a week or so." After a short silence, Bill added, "Knows horses. Wouldn't have guessed, a fellow like that."

"Probably a lot about him a guy wouldn't guess," Fats said.

"He wants to talk to you. Asked if he could look around while he waited."

"Well, let him look," Fats said.

A half hour later, Terry Blume sat on the porch with the Rangle brothers. Despite the heat, he looked comfortable, his white shirt still crisp, his pearl bush hat unstained. "Judge Barlow is interested in property in Gull Valley," he told Fats. "Carroll Coyle thought maybe I could see what's available. He hoped he could hire you to show me around tomorrow, scout the territory for her."

"I can give you a tour," Fats said. "No charge. What sort of property we talking about?"

"As I understand it," Blume said in his soft-spoken manner, "she might buy but would prefer to build. She's looking for a getaway, a place to escape to but not so distant that she couldn't get to Las Vegas or Carson City fairly quickly if she had to. Now that you've got a decent airport out here, Blue Lake and Gull Valley would do nicely."

Mary stepped onto the porch, waving the young man back into his seat as he started to rise. "Sit. Sit. Here."

She handed him a manila envelope. "If the judge will look these over and sign them, Fats can bring our copies back with the horse."

"I'll see that she gets them, Mrs. Rangle," he said.

As Mary disappeared into the house, her husband said, "You treat horses like somebody who grew up with them."

"I spent summers at my grandfather's place outside Wallace, Idaho. He raised Appaloosas."

"Big money in the breed, I hear," Bill said.

The two men talked horses. Listening, Fats decided that Terry Blume wasn't chatting but investigating. Bill felt the same, it turned out. After an hour, having promised to come out for breakfast, Terry Blume left for the room he'd taken at the Desert Vista Motel. As the Bentley disappeared into the gap in the brown hills, Bill grinned. "Think we passed inspection?"

At noon the next day, Fats and Terry Blume were sitting in pickup shade, lunching on the sandwiches and fruit and cookies Mary had packed for them. Fifty yards off were the ruins of a small homestead: warped and weathered wood, rusted wire, dugouts of various sorts and sizes. Small pools of water stood nearly still in a willow-bordered stream bed. Only the pasture, tinted a pale green here and there, and the old pole chutes and corral showed signs of recent use.

"Carsten place, people call this," Fats said. "Ain't been a Carsten out here since before World War I."

"Folks have to call it something, I suppose," Terry grinned.

"Crick hardly ran at all this year," Fats said.

Terry Blume looked out through the heat shimmer at the distant desert, the dun foothills, the mountain darkness. He took up an expensive-looking camera, aimed, pressed a button. "This would be a nice place if the water flow was dependable."

"You could say that about a lot of places out here," Fats said.

They had spent the morning looking over properties that Fats knew were, or could be, for sale. In most of these locations, water seeped or trickled or flowed, but not amply enough to sustain an enterprise of any consequence. Here a few head of cattle allowed the owner to take advantage of tax laws, there a patch of alfalfa earned extra income, but except for a big garlic farm owned by Beatrice Foods, all serious efforts at agriculture had long since been abandoned. Two major mining operations now left their smooth, swelling slag piles, while older, smaller efforts were being reclaimed by the desert.

"You know anything about an outfit called Hydroneva?"

Terry Blume shook his head.

"They're buying up water rights all through the valley. Nobody knows what they've got planned."

"A development of some sort, you think?"

Fats shrugged. "There's talk of it. Ritzy places served by an air shuttle. Or big farming—enough water and anything'll grow."

"Or speculation? Guessing the price of water's got to go up?"

Fats shrugged. "Could be. There's a lot of betting on the come out here."

"These wells people are drilling—how does their cost compare to the sort of setup you've got?"

Fats told him. Throughout the morning, Terry Blume had asked the kind of questions that a prospective buyer or builder might. But Fats knew the young man was checking out not just Gull Valley but as well, and especially, Cherry Creek Stables and Excursions. And himself. Fats didn't mind, for it made it easier for him to ask questions of his own.

"Your boss, Coyle, what does he actually do for people like Judge Barlow?"

"Primarily he counsels them on political matters."

"What would be political about building a home out here?"

Terry Blume uncapped the plastic bottle of water he'd taken up. He drank, grinned. "Everything is political in Nevada."

"Even moving an old horse to Cherry Creek Stables?"

"Even that," he said. "Imagine the fuss if the judge put Omar with you and then it was discovered that you and your brother were involved in nefarious activities."

"Which you're here to sniff out," Fats said. "Why don't you just ask us?"

"Mr. Coyle already knows pretty much all there is to know about you." Terry Blume's smile was at once innocent and ironic. "But he doesn't think you've told him all you know about that airplane."

"But Judge Barlow has no connection to that plane," Fats said. "Coyle really sent you out here to snoop for David Mohr and Deseret Corporation."

The young man pushed up the brim of his bush hat, as if to see more clearly. His expression opened. "I'm here to get a sense of you. There are stories, stories in which you might be seen as the villain. A lot of people around Blue Lake are afraid of you. You're quick to anger, they say, and you like to knock people around. The important question, though, is whether you tell the truth."

Fats almost smiled. "Everybody lies."

"Yes," he said, "but usually there's a reason. Mr. Coyle thinks that a quarter of a million dollars might be reason enough for you to make up a tale."

"And you'll decide if that's so, then hustle back to Vegas and tell Coyle what you think, and he'll tell David Mohr, who sort of offered me a job."

Again Terry Blume hesitated. He looked out at the desert. Then he said quietly, slowly, "I'm attached to Carroll Coyle, Mr. Rangle, but he'll tire of me soon enough. I've already tired of him. I do what he tells me as best I can, and I won't betray him, but my deeper interest is Vi Barlow. She's the real thing. She'll go far. If I'm conscientious and careful, I might be able to go with her."

Fats got to his feet. "Sounds like a plan."

They spent the rest of the day checking out a half dozen possibilities. Otherwise, they just raised dust. Fats drove and was content. Terry Blume was equally satisfied to drive and look and say little.

They were at the far end of the valley, edging along the foothills of the Turquoise Range, when Fats said, "Speaking of water."

Cresting a sage-littered knoll, he eased the pickup to a stop. Before them the land was patched dun and green, desert and meadow, sage flat and field and pasture. Ponds collected water from sough and spring. The small flows that were Eagle Creek and Molly Creek fed irrigation ditches. On a rise, several outbuildings and a large old barn served the ranch house, got up to look rustic.

"Water makes it a different world, doesn't it?"

"Just like in Las Vegas," Fats said.

Terry Blume laughed. "Might this place be for sale?"

"Don't know," Fats said, then told him what he did know. This was the old Rocking W, once owned by a movie and television cowboy. His son had had big plans for the place, some kind of western museum or monument to his father, but nothing came of them. He leased out the fields and pasture but never came to the ranch himself. Word was that ineptness, booze, and a divorce had left him in bad financial shape. "He's sort of goofy about this place, they say. He might just sell," Fats said, "but the deal would be pricey, probably a lot more than the judge could come up with."

"Then again," Terry Blume said, "who knows what kind of financing she might be able to arrange?"

He took several photos. Then Fats drove on. Not too far up the road they came to an abandoned house, paint peeled in places to bare wood, windows broken, shingles lost, and an old alfalfa field being reclaimed by the desert.

"Zahn place," Fats said.

"Zahn as in Dale Zahn?"

"His folks. Managed to hang on till Dale got a scholarship and a couple part-time jobs and was off to the university. Never looked back."

"Some people in Las Vegas think he's got something: brains, résumé, all that Clint Eastwood charm." Terry Blume kept his eye on the ruined house. "But there's other talk too. Character issues."

Fats didn't know what that might mean. He didn't much care. He drove on.

Long shadows sharpened the glare of the sun by the time Fats took the Cherry Creek turnoff. Coming out of the shaded narrow passage into brightness, for a moment he saw before the house only shimmer and blur. Then, slowly, a smudged shape became a large black SUV. Two dark figures flanking the vehicle might almost have been shadows themselves. Fats felt his abdominal muscles tighten.

Bill stood on the steps of the porch, at his hip a pistol snug in its holster, in his hands a pump shotgun, the barrel of which he slowly swung from Boo, Abel Lasky's bald goon, to his tattooed accomplice, both hatless, in black T-shirts and dark glasses.

As Fats slowed the pickup to a stop, Buddy came out of the barn and started for the house, but with a raised hand Bill sent his son back. Fats turned off the engine, nodding to Terry Blume: "No need for you to get involved in this."

"I don't imagine you'll require my help," Terry Blume said, popping open the door. "But I'm here."

Dust slowly settled. Fats stepped out into the still heat. He let his gaze, like the barrel of Bill's shotgun, shift from one big man to the other, even as he spoke to his brother. "What've we got here, Billy?"

"Trespassers," Bill said.

"Fuck that," Boo spat, red-faced. "We want the girl."

Fats gave him a long look. "What girl?"

"You fucking know what girl." The tattooed one leaned forward, quivering, like a dog straining against a chain. "Either you give her to us or we take her, your choice."

"What makes you think she'd be here?"

"You talked to her," Boo snapped, "then you left town, and nobody's seen her since. It figures she'd come out here with you."

"You're guessing." Fats spat in the dust. "She gave you the slip and you don't know where the hell she got to."

"I told them there's no girl here," Bill said calmly, still waving his shotgun. "Told them to get their hind ends off our property. They didn't. That mean I can shoot them?"

"Not legally, not unless one of them comes at you." Fats's smile was small, hard. "But I can arrest them."

"So why don't you have the gimp—"

"Easy, Mitch," Boo said. "It's all bluff. He ain't a deputy anymore, he can't arrest shit."

"Citizen's arrest, it's called." Fats took off his hat and set it carefully on the hood of his pickup. He squared his shoulders, settled his weight over his hips, bent his knees, rocked slightly onto the balls of his feet. His hands felt heavy. "Maybe you'd like to resist."

Boo's pate was pinking under the glaring sun. Sweat stippled his forehead. He was uncomfortable, uncertain. "You're looking for an excuse for this asshole to shoot me, ain't you?"

Fats shifted, loosening his shoulder muscles. "Would you shoot this piece of crap, Bill?"

"Sure would," Bill grinned. "I ain't shot a piece of crap in, oh, days."

"Fucking gimp ain't about to shoot nobody." Mitch, the tattooed hulk, moved.

The shotgun boomed. The side mirror on the SUV disintegrated. Terry Blume laughed.

The report seemed to hang in the still air, like the dust. Bill jacked another shell into the chamber, grinned. "Dang. Missed. But ain't that double-ought nasty."

"How 'bout it, then?" Fats said to Boo, again rocking, ready.

The sun blazed. The silence deepened. Boo looked from brother to brother. "I guess not. Not this time."

"Figures," Fats said, sneering. "Fucking bully is all you are."

"Well, I ain't." Mitch managed a small smile. He nodded toward the barn, in the door of which Buddy stood with a rifle. "A few too many guns right now, but your day'll come."

Fats put his hat back on. "Go on. Get out of here."

"That goes for you too, sweet meat," Mitch sneered.

Terry Blume smiled.

The two big men eased back, slipped into the SUV. Soon they were raising dust. Fats and his brother watched them vanish into the gulley.

Terry Blume removed, reset his hat. "That was fun. You haven't seen the last of those two, though."

Bill nodded. His expression sobered. He looked toward the barn, where Buddy still stood holding the rifle. "Glad Mary and the twins weren't here. But we'll all have to be careful from now on, till this thing is over. Whatever the hell this thing is."

"I didn't mean for so many people to get involved," Fats said. He turned to Terry Blume. "They'll be looking to hassle you, too, you give them half a chance."

"We don't travel in the same circles," the young man said, smiling, "but I'll stay alert."

Fats looked around him: horses, pasture, pond, buildings—all as it should be. Home. "I'll call the sheriff. And somebody should give Alec Duggar a head's-up, let him know these thugs are around."

"Me?" Bill asked.

"He don't much care for me," Fats said. "He'll take it better if it comes from you."

"And I should be on my way," Terry Blume said. He thanked Bill for his hospitality. He told Fats that he'd report to Carroll Coyle, show him the photos, let him pass them on to Judge Barlow. "Soothes the soul, doesn't it, driving around the desert?"

"For some of us, anyhow," Fats said.

Terry Blume stepped over to the Bentley convertible. Then he stopped, turned. "I'm out of the loop on all this. These goons, they have something to do with Judge Barlow?"

"Not that I know of," Fats said. "But I'm pretty much out of the loop myself."

Fats watched the convertible until it disappeared. Then he sat on the porch while Bill was inside, phoning. Returned, Bill sat too.

"Duggar says the muscles already been to his place, looking for the girl. Says they made threats. Now, he says, he's packin'."

Fats scowled. "That's all we need, more guns."

"Hell," Bill said, settling a hand on the butt of his pistol, "this is Nevada. Half the people in the state carry something these days."

When Mary and the twins came back from town, Fats let Bill and Buddy tell them what had happened. He went to his house, grabbed a beer, and took out his phone. He gave Dale Zahn a brief account of the incident. The sheriff said he'd have deputies keep an eye out for the thugs and on Alec Duggar's house. He said too that he'd call Sergeant Clare and ask if she could get any additional information on the dancer Salome. He told Fats to check with her the next day.

Then Fats told him that he was thinking about giving up the excursion business. Dale said he'd be looking for work. Fats said it'd be a while, first of the year maybe before he'd cleared away everything and met all obligations. Dale said they could talk about that the next time Fats was in town.

After hanging up, Fats took out his old Colt. He cleaned and oiled it. He handled it, felt its heft. Then he put the pistol back in its holster and the holster and gun belt back in the drawer.

He had another beer as he fixed and ate a ham and cheese omelet.

Boo and Mitch had come from Las Vegas searching for Salome. They hadn't mentioned Strutter. Fats wondered why.

The question stayed with him the rest of the evening, which he spent in the pack shed, looking over frames and straps, buckles and bags and panniers. Sorting, he got a sense of what might go to auction, what should be tossed, what kept. Most of the gear was old, still serviceable but nothing anyone would want to pay good money for. Had he chosen to go on with the business, he would have had to replace the wear and rot. One more reason to get out.

Darkness had fallen by the time he finished. A breath of breeze took the edge off the heat. In the moonless night, stars spectacularly spangled the black sky. The yard light lit a yellowish circle. In his brother's house, windows shaped lamp light. Fats stood for a moment in the night. Then he walked to his house, threw open the windows of his bedroom, took a cool shower, and stretched out on the bed, naked.

He awoke with a start. He lay listening but heard only the faint shush of the creek. He got up and, in the dark, made his way to the front door, eased it open. All the shadows were familiar.

Suddenly Fats was angry. He wanted to hit someone. But there was no one there to hit. He had a sudden sinking feeling that there never again would be.

Ramona Clare phoned the next afternoon. She had no news about the missing dancer. "Like I said the other day, this happens all the time. People disappear. All we can assume is that if Abel Lasky is looking for her, she probably isn't dead."

"Maybe," Fats said.

"The important question, though," she said, "is why he's looking for her in the first place."

"He thinks she can lead him to Strutter."

"As far as that goes, Fats, you haven't troubled to tell me why you and Dale Zahn and half of Vegas are looking for this guy."

"I've got his horse."

"That accounts for your interest, maybe," she said, "but not Dale's. And the only thing that interests Lasky is money. Other than what Strutter had in his big wallet, I don't see any money anywhere in this." Before Fats could respond, she added: "And even that money, you ever find out where he got it?"

"Dale thinks from drug dealers, most likely. So does Lasky."

"But you don't?"

"Probably something like that."

After a moment, she said, "You don't lie very well, Fats."

"Not enough practice," he said, lying.

"No," she said, her voice changing, thickening. "I think it's just because you're tired."

"You think so?"

"I do. I mean, climbing mountains, chasing after missing buckaroos and exotic dancers—that has to poop a guy out. You need a vacation."

They were now in a different kind of conversation.

"I also think you need to rescue Strutter's pickup. I can take a few days—what if I was to drive it up there for you?"

"It's been impounded."

"Well, yes," she said slowly, "but there are ways around that."

"What ways?"

"Just...ways." Her voice changed again. "I could bring it up there and ride back with you when you come down to get Judge Barlow's horse. In between, we could...ride. Camp."

Fats stayed silent.

After a long moment, Ramona Clare said, "Unless you have something better to do, Fats. Or someone."

"No," he said. "It's just that I may need to stick pretty close to home for a while."

"That would work too," she said. When again he didn't speak, she added. "I could be there this time tomorrow."

"Yeah," Fats said. "Let me call you back. An hour or so."

"Do that," she said.

He called Dale Zahn. Abel Lasky's goons had left town that morning, taking the road to Las Vegas. Then Fats talked to his brother, who just grinned. He called Vi Barlow's office and left a message that he'd be down to get Omar in a week.

He called Ramona Clare. "We could go to Heart Lake. Day up, a couple days there, day back. A day to Vegas."

"How do I get to your place?"

He told her. Then it was her turn to go silent. Finally she asked, "Do you have any actual enthusiasm for this adventure, Fats?"

"A whole bunch," he said.

She laughed.

7

Late the next afternoon, Fats rose from his kitchen table, where he'd been working on a supply list, at the sound of an approaching unmuffled engine. From the door he watched as Strutter's pickup parked beside his own and, after a moment, Ramona Clare climbed from the cab into the settling dust. She doffed a straw Stetson, ran a hand through her hair, removed her silver sunglasses, grinned. "Whose bright idea was this, anyhow?"

"Yours," Fats said.

"Hardly worth the effort. This critter's on its last legs. The AC's just a wheeze," she said. "I'm wilted."

"Don't look it," Fats said.

She looked hale, able, at ease. Her Stetson was old, her blouse and jeans were washed into softness, her boots were glossy. Her grin was full of fun, and something else. "I need a shower and a cold beer."

"We got both," Fats said.

From the pickup she retrieved a good-sized bag. "Lead me to 'em."

Inside, she gave only a glance to the few rickety furnishings, the cracked linoleum, the bare walls. She dropped her bag on the bed as if establishing possession. After a quick look in the bathroom, she flicked shooing fingers at him. "I may be a while."

While she showered, Fats parked the grimy pickup beside Strutter's horse trailer. Then he went back to his kitchen table and completed his list: foodstuffs, paper goods, treats for the horses, first-aid items, beer, .38 ammunition. Most of what he'd pack up the mountain was already stacked neatly just inside the barn door. The three-horse gooseneck trailer sat in place by the corral gate. Loading up in the morning would be quick.

"You said something about a beer?"

He rose and got her an IPA from the refrigerator. "You mind

drinking this on the way to town? There's a few things we need yet.
And we could have dinner."

"As long as your pickup's air-conditioning works." She pulled gently
at a button on her blouse. "A person could melt in here. You ever
thought to get a unit for this place? Maybe at least for the bedroom?"

"I never much mind the heat," he said. "But I'll crank up the cold
in my rig."

Outside, before she got in the pickup, Ramona looked about:
stables and barn, corrals and pasture, creek and pond, and riding
trails that climbed toward the mountains and out to the desert.
"Nice place, Fats."

"We like it."

"Judge Barlow's old horse will too."

On the drive into town, Ramona drank her beer and told him how
she got Strutter's vehicle out of impound. Favors and falsehoods,
she said, nothing actually criminal, no lie that couldn't be made to
seem a simple mistake, if anyone ever inquired, which they wouldn't.

"Sounds like not much has changed down there."

"In my experience, Fats," she said, "nothing does. It's just different
people doing the same old thing."

They drove through the heat. The AC fan whirred. Every now and
then they looked at one another.

As they approached the state highway, she said, "Pretty dry out
here."

The desert was everywhere some shade of brown. Nothing green
grew. Roads and roofs were thick with dust.

"Hasn't rained for six months, and not much then," Fats said.

"There's a hurricane churning down Baja way," she said. "They
think it'll stall out and break up over Vegas. Maybe get remnants
up this far."

"Won't help the drought, though," Fats said. "Flash floods and
dried mud is about all we ever end up with."

Blue Lake was quiet, the streets still, almost empty, although the
Safeway parking lot was clumped with vehicles. Inside, the store
was comfortably cool. As Fats and Ramona passed up and down
aisles, other shoppers noted the novelty—the stubby ex-deputy sheriff
wheeling a cart with an unknown big blonde in silver specs. Some

stared. An old man outfitted in gun belt and holstered Glock nodded to Fats, a woman whose son he'd once run in for drug possession glared, another woman smiled, but no one spoke until, as they were assessing steaks laid out in the butcher's case, behind them a voice purred, "Ramona, is that you?"

Donna Zahn's smile was fixed firmly to her face. She nervously nudged her empty shopping cart forward, back. "This is a surprise. What brings you to Blue Lake?" Her voice was thin, fluty. She turned to Fats, twisting her smile. "Or should I say who?"

"Hello, Donna," Ramona said, removing her sunglasses. "How are you?"

"Fine. Fine," Donna said. She bit her lower lip. "It's been a long time, hasn't it? I . . . I understand you've been helping Dale look for Strutter Martin. Any sign of him?" She was trying to make conversation, but she was clearly on edge, teetering. She patted her holstered Beretta. "I hope he's all right," she went on. "But . . . it doesn't look good, does it?"

"No," Fats said.

Donna bit her lip again, abruptly changed the subject. "You just missed Dale. He's in Carson City for a couple of days. He said, Norman . . . he told me you're going back to work for him?"

"Nothing's set yet."

Donna looked around the store, as if for help. Then she nodded at the cart they'd nearly filled. "Planning an outing?"

Ramona Clare put a hand casually on Fats's forearm. "We're camping up at . . . what is it, Fats? Heart Lake?"

Before he could respond, Donna Zahn spoke, her sudden smile faked and forced. "I think this is great, Norman."

He stayed silent.

"The two of you, I mean."

It was edgy and artificial, almost a question. Neither Fats nor Ramona answered.

Color rose up Donna's throat. "Anyway, I hope you have a good time."

"We plan to," Ramona said.

"Yes, well . . ." Donna worried her lip. "Is there anything you'd like me to tell Dale?"

Ramona smiled. "Not at thing."

After a feeble half wave, Donna wheeled her cart away.

Ramona grinned, "Norman, is it?"

"Yeah," he said.

She waited. When he said no more, she put on her sunglasses. "I've got questions, Fats."

"Later, okay?"

"She's . . . straining."

"Yeah," he said again.

They finished their Safeway shopping, stopped at the Seed and Feed for feed cake for the horses, at Barry's Guns and Ammo for a box of .38 shells. Fats found a parking place outside the Wagon Wheel café. They went in and ordered dinner.

Fats didn't know the waitress. She didn't know him. Once she'd taken their orders, he said, "Wasn't so long ago, I'd've been able to ID every person in the place. Not now."

Ramona looked around. The café was nearly full. "There are four people here carrying pistols, Fats. What are they afraid of?"

"Hillary Clinton."

She looked at him. Then she grinned. "I believe that's the first time I've heard you make a joke, Fats."

He kept a straight face. "Who's joking?"

They talked horses. Fats planned to ride Ruckus, and he thought Ramona could get up on Splash, who needed the work. He told her what she should know about Strutter's gelding—he might be a little frisky at first but a tight rein would settle him down. Fats thought he'd pack Daisy, a small, sure-footed buckskin mare.

Ramona asked about his family. He told her they'd see Bill and Mary that evening, maybe the kids.

She lifted an eyebrow. "What did you tell them about me? What do they think is happening?"

Fats forked a bite of his chicken fried steak. "Just that we're going to the mountains for a couple of days."

Again she studied him.

"They thought it was a good idea," he added.

"And you? What do you think, Fats?"

He chewed, swallowed. Then he said, "Tell you the truth, I'm trying not to think."

She nodded. "Good. Let it happen, whatever it is."

They ate in silence. Over coffee she said, "You're thinking about going back to the sheriff's office?"

He hesitated. "It's an option." He told her then, in a few words, why he would be giving up outfitting.

She listened carefully. Then she said, "I'm sorry, Fats. I can tell you'll miss it. But things change, don't they?"

"Didn't you tell me an hour ago that things never change?"

She grinned. "I lied."

They finished their meal. Before leaving town, Fats stopped at Brunson's Liquors and bought a fifth of Jack Daniels.

"Take it easy with that stuff tonight, Fats," Ramona said, grinning. "I want you sober."

"As a judge."

They drove back in the gathering darkness. After unloading, they walked over to the big house. Bill and Mary were on the porch. Fats made introductions, gave Mary a handful of credit card receipts, and passed his brother the bottle of bourbon. Mary went after ice and glasses. Soon the four were settled with drinks and each other.

Mary conducted a friendly inquiry. Ramona responded, repeating what she'd told Fats about growing up in the Big Smoky Valley, about having to sell Pete, her sorrel gelding. "I haven't ridden since," she said. "I imagine this time tomorrow I'll be a little sore."

"Splash rides easy," Bill said. "And the goin' will be slow."

They talked about her job. She'd become a police officer because she thought the work would be interesting. Sometimes it was. She preferred working with men, which she had for several years. She had thoughts about going for a detective position, but finally she'd switched to missing persons, where a woman could make rank without getting on her knees.

At that remark, Mary snorted. Bill laughed.

They talked about Donna Zahn. She was a woman with big worries, Mary said. They talked about Strutter. Ramona repeated what she'd told Fats in her office: he could be hiding out, or gone, or dead. They

talked about Edna Kachuba, who could be anywhere. They talked
about Abel Lasky and his goons, Boo and Mitch.

"They won't be back, them two," Bill scoffed.

"Don't be so sure," Fats said. "I still ain't happy about leaving
you here alone, specially since I'm the one got you into this mess."

"We can take care of ourselves, Fats," Mary said. "You go on.
You can use a little. . .R and R."

That seemed somehow to end the conversation. When Bill handed
him the bourbon bottle, still more than half full, Fats stood, as did
Ramona. They said good night. Walking back through the pale yard
light, Ramona touched his elbow. "R and R? That what it's called
these days?"

"Fits good enough," Fats said.

Heat hung heavy inside the house. Ramona made for the bedroom.
Fats stood in the doorway, watching her sort through her bag.

She turned to him, grinning. "This isn't the biggest bed in the
world. Things are likely to get. . .slippery."

"If the heat bothers you. . ." He couldn't quite finish.

"If the heat bothers me what, Fats?" Her mouth shaped itself into
a mischievous, almost childish pucker.

"It won't cool down till near sunrise," Fats said.

Ramona smiled away her pout. She placed herself before him, lay
her forearms on his shoulders, leaned her face toward him. "What's
a little sweat between friends?"

Two hours after sunup they were at the trailhead, the trailer and
pickup parked, Daisy packing a carefully arranged load, Ruckus
and Splash saddled and eager to go. Fats watched Ramona with
Strutter's horse, murmuring, stroking, patting before she got up on
him, reined him out of a little crow-hop, and nudged him forward.

He talked to Ruckus, telling her what was in store. Then, letting
Ramona take the lead, Fats gave a pull on Daisy's rope, and they
started up the mountain.

The rising sun had already wiped away the pre-dawn cool but,
climbing, they stayed ahead of the serious heat. Neither spoke until
mid-morning, when they stopped to give the animals a blow.

Ramona's grin was different now, filling her face. "I'd forgotten what it was like, Fats—the sounds in the quiet, the smells of sage and pines and horses, all the little signs of life, everything just...*here*."

He checked Daisy's pack, offering her commendations and encouragement. Tugging at a strap, he asked Ramona, "How you doin'?"

She bowed her back. "I'm a little stiff, but nothing serious. I'll be ready for a nap when we get to the lake." Her grin changed. "I didn't get a lot of sleep last night."

Soon after they remounted, the trail steepened, asking for all of their attention. The horses labored, went frothy at mouth and chest. When they reached the level ground that was Shoshone Springs, they nooned. Fats saw to the horses. Ramona made a meal of cold ham and biscuits, bananas and cookies and coffee. Fed, they lolled about the small fire.

"I could camp right here," she said with a sigh.

"We're only a couple hours from the lake," he said, "and the goin's easy enough."

She looked around. "This is where you saw the plane, isn't it? Where exactly was it?"

He pointed up the mountain. "At the snowline. It's still there. Sun's in the wrong place to spot it, though."

"You climbed up there? Up to the snow?" She craned her neck, removed her sunglasses. "Whatever possessed you?"

"Seemed like the thing to do."

"I don't see why."

"It was there. So was I."

"That's hardly a reason."

"Maybe I was just curious."

She tossed the dregs of her coffee into the fire, frowning. "There are things you aren't telling me, Fats."

He looked at her, her eyes, her mouth, the hollow at the base of her throat.

She went on calmly, quietly. "I don't know why you think you need to keep secrets from me, but if you don't trust me, there's not much I can do about it."

Fats watched her put back on her sunglasses. Then he said, "I knew what it had to be, but I guess I wanted to get to it before the sheriff did."

She shook her head. "That's it? Some kind of pissing contest between you and Dale?"

"Seems pretty silly when you say it, but yeah."

"And what about the other stuff, Fats? The stuff about Strutter and money? There has to be more than what he had on him. Too many people are looking too hard for him."

The fire crackled. A puff of breeze swayed the flames.

"All right," he said. "But let's wait to talk till we're set up at the lake."

The trail from the spring was less difficult, roughly following the tree line, now weaving among boulders and granite ledges, now moving through stands of pine and juniper. They reached the lake at mid-afternoon.

The campground was deserted. Fats chose a site near a narrow feeder creek, and after they unburdened and wiped down the horses, fed them apples, and set them, hobbled, to graze, he helped Ramona pitch camp. Once the tent was up and the packs unloaded, Ramona started a small fire and arranged stores and equipment while Fats took an ax to chop more firewood. When he returned, they sat on stones and drank coffee.

The alpine afternoon was warm but, after the heat down on the flat, comfortable. A light breeze stirred the surface of the water, freshened the faintly pine-scented air. Around them, gray granite rose into snow.

"Do we have it all to ourselves, Fats?"

"Probably," he said. "It's five miles or so around the lake, there's a couple of other camping spots, but anybody up here ain't interested in us."

Ramona grinned. "So I can skinny-dip without worrying about oglers."

"I imagine I'd ogle some," Fats said. "But not for long. The water's real cold."

Ramona laughed. "You don't strike me as an ogler, Fats."

"Not my first choice," he said, then sipped coffee.

After a bit, Ramona suggested a walk to smooth away some of the saddle kinks.

Fats got to his feet. "If you don't mind a little hike, there's a nice view spot not too far."

Before they set off, he took up and cinched on his revolver.

Ramona raised an eyebrow. "You think you need that?"

"Don't like leaving it, is all," Fats said. "I don't know why I even brought it along. Nothing up here I'd want to use it on."

"Like all those guys in the café yesterday, packing pistols to no point."

"Oh, they're making a point," he said. "Ain't their fault if nobody gets it."

Fats set off on a path that edged the lake for some distance, then turned up into a narrow, boulder-strewn gully. The incline was steady but not steep. They took it slowly, breathing deeply of the thin mountain air, until the way widened and leveled out into a small granite shelf.

"Look," Fats said.

The sky was blue and empty. The far horizon was a gray smudge. The desert was a pattern of earth tones, swirls and flushes.

Ramona took it in, her chest swelling rhythmically. "It looks almost liquid, doesn't it, rivers of rock and dirt?"

Fats nodded, he too catching his breath. "All of it was underwater a long time ago, they say. A view like this, you can see how that might be."

They looked at the desert. Then they turned and looked at the lake, roughly heart-shaped, sun-sheened still water surrounded by stone and conifers and patches of marsh. The sigh of a light breeze didn't disturb the silence.

"This is worth the hike, Fats," Ramona said.

Eventually they started back down. Shadows were long by the time they reached camp. They corralled the horses and served them feed cake, and Ramona gave them a quick brushing while Fats put away his pistol and started supper—Dutch oven biscuits, bacon and beans, fried potatoes. They ate as darkness gathered. By the time they had cleaned up, night had fallen.

They sat at the fire, sipping bourbon and water from their coffee cups. Darkness enclosed, contained them. The moonless night sky came aglitter.

"In Las Vegas," Ramona said, her head tilted skyward, "you can't see this. What do they call it—urban glow? The city lights washing out the stars? They're still there, just not visible."

The fire crackled, the little rivulet hissed.

Then her mouth set in a playful pucker. "Now about this Norman business..."

"A high school thing," Fats said slowly. "We went together. It was her way of...well, I don't quite know what it meant, really."

"Teenage girls," Ramona nodded. She let her pause linger. "You haven't been in high school for a long time."

"Yeah," he said, "I don't know what it's supposed to mean now either."

"She's reminding you that the two of you had something special. Maybe that you still do, in a way?"

"No." He held up his cup, looked at it, but he didn't drink. "We don't."

"She's...changed. I hadn't seen her for a while," Ramona said. "She looks old."

"The desert does that," Fats said. "Dries people out. Women especially. And like Mary said, she frets: two girls in college, the ranch, Dale's carrying on."

The fire popped, seemed to sigh. "Did you sleep with her, Fats?"

"A couple of times. Kids, hardly knew what we were doing." His voice had thickened, gone gruff. "I guess that had something to do with the Norman business too."

Firelight flickered over her face. "There's a story here, isn't there?"

"Not much of one," Fats said. "One you probably heard a hundred times."

"Make it a hundred and one, Fats."

He downed his drink. He took up the bourbon bottle and poured. For while he sat silent. So did Ramona. At last he spoke. "After high school, she went off to UNR. I went into the army. We were sort of engaged. Unofficial. At least I thought so. Then she dumped me."

"Why?" Ramona asked. "What happened?"

His voice changed. "Dale Zahn happened. Knocked her up."

"How? I mean, had they had something going all the time in Blue Lake, or—"

He stood abruptly. "I've said all I have to say."

"You're angry," she said.

"Maybe so."

"Sit down, Fats." She waited, and when he finally took his seat, she said calmly, "You're angry about a lot of things, aren't you?"

"Maybe so," he said again.

"Your reputation—I asked people, Fats. They say as a deputy you were...*physical,* dragging people out of cars, slamming them around, goading perps into fisticuffs. That was anger, wasn't it."

"Drunks, reckless drivers," he said. "And toughs looking for trouble. And guys beating on women, kids. Stupid fuckers. I never gave anyone anything they didn't have coming."

"I hear that a lot in Vegas, too," she said. "And nobody accuses you of being mean, not exactly. Not cruel. Just...quick on the draw, maybe. Just angry."

"Yeah," he said. "Maybe. Probably. Yeah."

The fire pulsed, seemed alive.

"These people you talked to," he ventured, "that'd be Dale Zahn, wouldn't it?"

"I asked him about you, yes," she said. "He said you were a good deputy, that you saw things, made the right connections. He said you scare some people, you look so powerful, dangerous, always scowling, and you use their fear. He said he'd have you back in a minute."

Fats finished his drink, started to speak, stopped.

"It's not necessarily a bad thing, anger," she said. "Most cops I know are pissed off most of the time. It's the only thing that lets them deal with all the nastiness and stupidity they run into. It's that or drink or drugs or money. Or sex."

He raised his cup. "Here's to anger."

She touched his wrist. "I prefer sex."

The next morning they rose and breakfasted late, then lazed about camp. When the sun was high enough to warm the shallows of the lake, Ramona bathed. Fats watched, which she didn't seem to mind.

As she toweled herself dry, he said, "All your working out, you take good care of yourself."

"I have to," she said, grinning. "The bod's all I have to bargain with."

"No, that ain't right," he said.

Her grin changed, became a smile of a sort he hadn't seen before.

Later they went riding. The mountain was traced with trails, he told her, used by deer and in the summers by campers like those he escorted into the high country. They rode up to an abandoned fire lookout, then down to an aborted digging, then to a seep tracked up by thirsting deer and a good-sized bobcat. They made a long circle back toward the lake. The water was within sight when suddenly Ruckus stuck her front hooves into the earth, stuttered, snorted, while Splash shook his head and did a dance against Ramona's tight rein.

Making soothing sounds, she patted the horse's neck. "What is it?"

"Look," Fats said, pointing up the trail. A lion had dragged its kill under the lean of a long-downed pine tree. The deer's hoof, leg, and haunch still showed. "It's fairly fresh. Last couple of days, I'd guess."

"He's close by, watching?"

"Could be. Or could be miles off. They're solitary critters, range over a big territory. But he, or she, is no threat to us."

"Splash doesn't think so," she said. "He wants out of here."

"That can happen." Fats touched Ruckus with his heels, and they started down the trail.

The horses were still jittery when they got back to the campground. Fats and Ramona fed them apples and rubbed them down, he talking to them all the while, but they kept them in the corral. Then, while Ramona began supper, Fats rigged his flyrod, tied on a BH Prince Nymph, and cast for trout, unsuccessfully. From time to time, patches of ragged, gray-bottomed cloud shadowed the lake. The evening grew cooler. Fats and Ramona ate broiled rib eye steaks and potatoes baked in coals. Their talk was quiet, their silences comfortable.

At one point, she asked about his old Colt. "There aren't many of them still around, except in collectors' cases. Does it have some significance to you?"

He wanted to say no but found he couldn't. He'd bought the pistol years ago, at auction, in a sale of the effects of a small Gull Valley rancher who'd gone bust. The weapon had been outdated even then, the model long discontinued. The auctioneer couldn't get a bid on it. Fats, for no reason he could have given anyone, raised his hand.

"Peace officers haven't carried these Colts since the sixties," he said. "About all they're good for anymore is keeping down the varmint population. I just. . . ."

"What?" Ramona laughed. "Thought it deserved a good home?"

"Something like that," Fats said, and he wasn't joking, quite.

He cleaned up while she gave the horses feed cake. They drank coffee as the darkness gathered. Then, because he'd said he would, he told her about Strutter and money.

"Let me see if I've got this straight," she said when he'd finished. "You think Strutter found the plane before you did. You think he stole a briefcase full of money, $250,000, that somebody might have but probably hadn't embezzled from Deseret Construction, that you think is probably political money. You think he took $10,000 to Las Vegas to pay for some fun with Salome, née Edna Kachuba, and stashed the rest, probably in this part of the country. That's what you think."

"Yes."

"I'm struck by how little actual evidence you have, Fats," she said. "All you've got is an old trail in the snow and a horny little guy's bragging."

He shrugged his square shoulders. "Yeah, I know."

She stared into the fire, musing. "So Strutter, he hooks up with Salome, flashes his wallet, talks big money, and disappears."

"Yes."

"Then a month later you find the plane, come down to Vegas, and hear the story about the embezzled money from Carroll Coyle, who says he represents Deseret Construction and who lends you Doc Wills to help look for Strutter, but who is probably also keeping tabs on you. And you get jumped by a couple of thugs who work for Abel Lasky, who is looking for Strutter and the big money—drug money, he thinks—that he told Salome about."

"Yes."

"Then the CEO of Deseret Construction offers you a job, an offer which may or may not be innocent, legitimate. And Judge Barlow decides to board her horse with you, which also may be on the up-and-up."

"Yes."

"Did I leave out anything?"

"Just Dale Zahn. He knows all of this. It's his idea that if someone ended up with the $250,000, he couldn't be accused of theft because officially the money doesn't exist. The idea seems to be that in this to-do, we're now partners."

"Which means that Dale is looking for Strutter, or the money, too." She sighed. "But it's all guesswork, isn't it?"

"Not all of it," Fats said. "Strutter had money we can't account for, he told Salome he had lots more, and he's disappeared. So has Salome, seems like."

She looked at him. "And then there's all these people making you unsolicited and suspicious offers—Carroll Coyle, Deseret, Vi Barlow, Dale. Anybody else?"

"Well," Fats said slowly, looking at her, "there's this woman who seems almost too good to be true."

A gust of wind brightened the coals. The darkness deepened.

Ramona got to her feet. "You really are an asshole, aren't you, Fats?"

Fats was up at dawn, fishing. Trout were taking Black Gnats, and after an hour he'd caught several, releasing all but the largest two, which he fried with eggs in bacon fat. The sounds and aroma announced breakfast.

Ramona left the tent and poured herself coffee and looked around. Her tone, when she spoke, was flat, empty, meant to maintain distance. "The weather's changed."

The day was not noticeably cooler, but a high, thin overcast grayed the sky, and scattered, wet-looking clouds scudded over the lake.

Fats nodded. "Must be that hurricane you mentioned."

"Must be," she said woodenly.

They ate. They cleaned up after their meal. They drank coffee.

Fats finally broke the silence. "Like I told you that night at your place, I never slept with a woman who didn't want something from me."

"If that's actually the case, it's about the saddest thing I've ever heard," Ramona said rigidly. "But it sounds like bullshit to me."

"You think so?"

"I think that's just what you tell yourself so you don't have to really get close to anybody."

Fats stared into his coffee cup. "I'm not much on barstool psychology."

Ramona looked at him steadily, silently, until he met her eyes. "Do you see what an insult it is, the idea that I'm fucking you because I'm after something?"

"That wasn't—"

"Do you see what that makes me? And what could you have that I'd want bad enough to whore for it? The only thing I ever wanted from you, Fats, is you." Her face was flushed, her voice rough with indignation. "I thought you were a man I might connect with, and I've been up front about it. I haven't been coy or cute. No games. There's nothing else going on here."

He nodded bleakly, as if in confirmation of his worst fear. "Look, I'm sorry. I don't blame you for being pissed."

She looked away, out over the lake, as if to dismiss him.

He struggled on. "I didn't mean anything, really. I don't even know why I said it. Maybe because I can't quite believe my luck."

They sat silently. In the corral Ruckus nickered, nosed against Splash's neck. Then Fats said, "It was all a lie."

Her gaze came back to him. "What was a lie?"

"The thing with Donna. Turned out, I wasn't really her boyfriend, not really. I . . . she was pretty, you know, and trim, a competitive barrel racer, and one day she'd own the Three Bar M. By the time she got to high school, half the studs in Pinenut County were lined up to take a run at her. She didn't want any part of them. She had plans of her own, school and rodeoing, maybe. She . . . she took up with me so nobody would mess with her."

He looked over at the corralled horses, as if he might be speaking to them. "Then she went up to UNR and got pregnant," he said. "I was in the army. She Dear Johned me. Said she didn't, you know, love me. Never had. I was just a *escort*. A blocker, like. Bodyguard."

"She actually told you that?"

"She's still proud of it. Telling me the truth, when she could have lied."

"Dale—what did he have to say?"

"Nothing," Fats said. "Why should he? It wasn't really about him."

Ramona frowned. "He stole your girl, Fats."

"Except she wasn't really my girl, was she?"

"Still. . ."

"For Donna, Dale had always been just this Gull Valley guy a couple years ahead of her in school. But at UNR, she saw him differently, through her sorority sisters' eyes, sort of—good-looking, smart, going places. She went after him," Fats said. "Dale did what most guys would do. He saw an opportunity, and he took it."

"What it comes down to, Fats, is she done you wrong." Ramona's mouth twisted into a sneer. "And she's to blame for your self-esteem issues and your trust issues and your anger issues."

"I don't know about all this 'issues' crap. And I never blamed anybody but myself." He tried to smile. He failed. "For being so fucking stupid."

"And now you're being stupid again."

"Yeah," he said. "Maybe so. Yeah."

She tried to smile. She succeeded. "Well, knock it off."

He saw that her anger had passed. He didn't know why. "We good?"

"We'll see," she said.

Under the cloudy sky, they no longer cast shadows. A cool breeze blew over the dark water. They decided to ride.

He took her to a high mountain meadow where someone, decades earlier, had built a rock and pole hut, for what purpose no one had ever be able to say. He showed her a grove of aspens, some of the leaves already yellowing, the white bark long ago carved by Basque sheepherders: initials, names, female shapes, crude genitalia. He led her to a small pond where, as the horses drank, a blue heron elegantly settled on the water.

Back at camp, they had a light late lunch. They talked. Ramona

remembered growing up in the Big Smoky Valley, the dusty summers and frosty winters and the solitude, even when with others.
Life in Las Vegas, after that, had always seemed oddly unreal. She
asked what he planned to do with Splash should Strutter not return
to claim him. She wondered if he could work for Dale Zahn, given
what she'd heard about their election campaigns.

"I was pissed, yeah," Fats said. "Still am, some. He made me out
a thug, him and the television people."

"All's fair in love and politics," she said, smiling. "Everybody lies
and nobody cares."

"What really got me was how many people in Pinenut County
went along with that."

"It's not hard to see why," she offered, "the way you scowl all the
time. You just look mean."

He shook his head. "But it wasn't only newcomers. People who'd
known me all my life, hardly any of them voted for me."

"Maybe they weren't voting *against* you so much as *for* Dale," she
said. "He's got a way with him, you know that, and he was a local
too. I imagine that not many men in Blue Lake, Nevada are going
to beat Dale Zahn in a popularity contest."

"Even so . . ."

"He's also ambitious," she said. "He's not likely to stay Pinenut
sheriff for long. If you take the deputy job and smile once in a while,
who knows what might happen?"

Fats looked at her. "Dale—he's got his eye on something?"

"Always."

It made sense. Dale Zahn's rise from a hardscrabble Gull Valley
alfalfa farm to the Three Bar M, from UNR pre-law to UNLV law
degree, from Las Vegas Metro to Pinenut County sheriff, all ele-
vations that seemed inevitable, effortless, actually had about them
careful calculation.

"Politics, you think?" Fats studied her. "Something to do with
Carroll Coyle? With Vi Barlow, maybe?"

"I don't know," Ramona mused. "When he quit the force, word
was it was for personal reasons. To save his marriage."

"You don't think so?"

Ramona shrugged. "Could be. You know the story, I'm sure."

He did. When Donna's dad died unexpectedly, she and her two daughters moved from Las Vegas to the Three Bar M. The separation strained the Zahns' marriage to the point that he decided it was more important to him than his career in law enforcement, or so he said, and he too came back to Blue Lake. He got on with the Pinenut County Sheriff's Office, worked with Fats and the other deputies. Then the sheriff announced that he wouldn't be running for reelection. Dale and Fats became candidates the same day.

"What other reason would he have for coming back home?"

"He was a good cop," Ramona said slowly, considering. "His record was impressive. And clean enough. But there was, well, talk. Maybe he was a bit too close to bad sorts—not tied to, necessarily, just. . .cozy. There were whispers about money, payoffs, nothing that could be proven, but maybe it was just time for him to take an early out. And maybe he knew that the Pinenut County sheriff would be retiring."

"The man who would know that ahead of time is Carroll Coyle."

"Yes."

"But at Vi Barlow's speech, they acted like they hadn't been in contact for a long time." Fats ran the back of his hand over his stubbly chin. "On the other hand, the judge and Dale go way back."

"I suppose she could have given him a head's-up. There's nothing wrong with that." Ramona grinned. "That's the way we do things in Nevada."

He grunted. "That's the way everybody does everything everywhere."

That night they enjoyed the darkness and the stars and one another. They slept well past sunrise and, once risen, they saw to the horses, had a big ham and egg breakfast, and then set about to strike camp. The day was gray again but warm, the ride to Shoshone Springs easy, the descent into the desert heat slow. They reached the trailhead in mid-afternoon.

They both checked their phones: she had a couple of work-related messages, which she quickly answered, he an assurance from Dale Zahn that Abel Lasky's enforcers were nowhere to be seen and were

most likely back in Las Vegas, as well as a reminder from Terry Blume
that Judge Barlow would expect him to pick up Omar in two days.
He texted acknowledgments.

They were back at the stables well before dusk, sweating in the
now humid heat. With Buddy's help they got the gear unloaded and
stowed, the trailer parked, and horses pastured. Mary stepped out
to offer them, after they'd rinsed off the camp soot and trail dust, a
spaghetti supper.

They shared a shower but managed, laughing, to make haste.

Faint rain from a drifting, ragged cloud dampened their walk to the
main house. The kids had eaten and scattered, so through the meal
Bill lubricated the conversation with Chianti. There'd been no sign
of the black Cadillac SUV, or of Edna Kachuba, neither here nor at
Alec Duggar's. A couple of Deseret Construction representatives had
stopped by looking for Fats, but it turned out all they wanted was
directions to the Carsten place. The only real news was the weather.
Temperatures had dropped a dozen degrees, and scattered showers,
most light and to little effect, had spread up from Las Vegas, where
heavier rain was causing serious flooding. Streets in new developments
were awash and mall storefronts not sandbagged were swamped. The
countywide drainage system had in places clogged up with debris,
some of which had made up the camps of the homeless who had
sheltered underground. Most of those had got out safely, but two
deaths had been recorded.

Mary asked about their camping, and Ramona told her about the
lion's kill. She admired Splash, hoping to be able to ride him again
sometime. She talked too about the desert stars, which she hadn't
seen since she was a teenager. Faintly flush, bright-eyed, she seemed,
at least to Fats, happy.

Ramona insisted on helping Mary with the pots and dishes. Fats
and Bill, out on the porch, could hear the two women talking.

"They get along," Fats said.

"Mary says she's pretty much what you need."

"Maybe so."

The women brought out coffee and sat. Mary answered Ramona's
general questions about the stabling business, then asked a question
of her own: why would Judge Barlow want to buy or build a place

in Gull Valley? Ramona couldn't guess. Fats, appealed to, said it was probably political. Bill said the Deseret Construction men who'd been by talked about the Carsten place as a building site. Mary wondered if maybe the Rocking W might be of interest to her—for someone with money to invest it had all sorts of possibilities.

She told Ramona then about their expansion plan. It was at bottom, she admitted, a plan to make use of water. Since the day Bill Rangle brought her to Cherry Creek, she had fretted at the sight of pond water spilling over into a ditch bound for nowhere. The waste affronted her desert-bred sensibility. For years she had tried to work out a way to use the overflow. Finally, with help from a hydrologist from the Department of Water Resources, she had.

Once the water dropped into the ditch beneath the pond, it was basically inaccessible. So, simply put, they proposed to take it before it got to the pond, to irrigate a piece of desert into pasture. It would cost money to chain and blade, establish a gradient that would allow flow, and either seed or sod, and fence off, and there would be labor costs, mucking and maintenance—they might have to hire help—but it would increase their pasturage, which in turn would accommodate the stable expansion they had in mind. All they required now was a loan from the bank. It should be approved in a few days.

Ramona listened, said appropriate things. Then, silent, they watched the night descend.

Fats's phone shivered. He took it out of his pocket, looked at it, put it to his ear, and said hello. He listened. Then he put the phone back in his pocket. He sat silently.

Ramona finally asked, "Who was it, Fats?"

"Doc Wills." He finished his coffee. "In Vegas, the drainage system flushed out a body."

After a silence, Mary asked quietly, "They're sure?"

"Seems like," Fats said. "Been dead a while, and the flood beat it up some, but there's the wallet on a chain, ID."

"They'll want somebody to confirm the identity," Ramona said.

"I will," Fats said. "If I can."

8

Ramona cracked her window and breathed deeply. "There's nothing like that smell, is there? Desert rain."

Before Fats could answer, his phone shivered. He took it out and listened, then said, "No problem. I'll see you tomorrow morning."

Ramona looked at him. She wasn't wearing her sunglasses. The faint lines around her eyes made her more human, attractive.

"Small change in plans," he said.

He'd intended to drive to Judge Barlow's hacienda and leave the horse trailer so he wouldn't have to tow it all over Las Vegas, but a mudslide had blocked her road. The county was clearing it, but it would take the crew the rest of the day.

"That was her?"

"Terry Blume."

They drove into a heavy shower. Rain roared on the pickup's cab, turned the windshield wipers' sweep into a frantic flailing. Gusts of wind dangerously swayed the trailer until they were past the downpour.

Soon small patches of blue appeared in the midday sky. Traffic congested, raising a vaporous scrim over the interstate. The shapes and signs of Las Vegas emerged from the mist.

Fats drove carefully, idled through a flooded intersection, avoided fast-running currents, following Ramona's directions to her house. While he parked and uncoupled the trailer, Ramona went inside. When he came in with their bags, she was just putting down her phone. She'd made an appointment with the medical examiner to meet at the morgue.

An hour later, with an assistant medical officer and a Metro homicide detective, they watched an orderly draw back a white sheet to expose ravaged human remains. The hair, what was left of it, was fair and stiff. The face was torn and lumped, hardly a face at all, battered flesh clinging to cracked bone. But despite the corruption and damage, Fats could discern blurred but familiar features.

Fats felt his fists opening and closing. He put one within the other to still them. "That's him," he said, his voice thick, rough. "Strutter." Ramona put a hand on his arm. "Easy, Fats."

The AMO's estimated date of death fit with Strutter's arrival in Vegas. Since then the body almost certainly had been in the drainage tunnel, the relative cool of which would have reduced the rate of putrefaction.

"Putrefaction," Fats repeated angrily, looking down at the flesh, the bone.

"Garbage collects down there," the detective said. "It stinks. The smell of a rotting corpse would just add to the stench."

The detective attended as a matter of policy and procedure: all deaths deemed suspicious were handled, at least until a different determination was made, by the homicide division. He told Ramona and Fats what the police knew. Strutter's body had been found when workers went to clear a tangle of debris that blocked the drainage system, but it hadn't been in the water long. The best guess was that it had been dragged to a secluded dry spot close to an entrance to an underground section, the nearest of which was a quarter mile upstream from the flood-caused clog.

"Dumped. Left to rot," Fats said, his throat constricting.

The detective gave him a long look. Ramona gripped his arm more tightly, as if in restraint.

The police theorized that Strutter had died in a mugging gone wrong. The cause of death, still unofficial and likely to remain so, was actually the medical examiner's best guess, given the condition of the vital organs and a particular predeath bruise. *Commotio cordis,* the AMO said, also known as lethal disruption, which occurs when a blow to the chest disorders the heart's rhythm and causes fibrillation and then cardiac arrest.

Fats told the detective about the money Strutter had brought to Vegas. The detective said that that, and the empty wallet still chained to his belt, made the mugging scenario more likely. Fats told him of his search for Strutter. He didn't mention the wrecked plane or the possibly missing briefcase filled with cash. The detective asked him to come in and give an official statement in next day or so. Sergeant Clare promised to send over the missing persons file. The detective gave Fats another long look, then said he thought they were through.

The storm seemed to be breaking up. Showers still darkened the horizon, but patches of blue, larger now, appeared more frequently. Streets steamed in the sun.

As Ramona drove home, she talked into Fats's silence. She talked about dinner. Fats had brought with him a change of presentable clothes, and as he was leaving that morning Mary had slipped him the business credit card. He'd told Ramona that he wanted to take her somewhere nice. She made a couple of suggestions.

He was having a hard time concentrating. He kept thinking about Strutter, dumped in a drainage tunnel, rotting. Corruption. Putrefaction.

At Ramona's, she found him a beer, then sat on a sofa and quickly scanned her mail. He waited, edgy, uncomfortable. The room was furnished cheaply, even anonymously, nothing in it speaking of her, less a home than a stopping place for transients.

His phone shivered. Doc Wills panted in his ear. "It was your guy, huh?"

"Yeah," Fats said, not surprised that the old ex-cop already knew what had just been established. Vegas was like that. Everybody knew everything but nobody knew anything. "Thanks for the heads-up."

"I've got another one for you. You're looking for a girl, one of Abel Lasky's bimbos. The day she went missing, she was spotted at a truck stop off I-15. Sergeant Clare can tell you what that probably means."

"I probably know," Fats said.

"There's one more thing," Wills wheezed. "The spot where they think your guy was stuffed into the drainage system, it's about two hundred yards from Lasky's place."

"The police think a mugging," Fats said.

"Could be."

"If so, why hide the body?" Rotting.

"Good question."

The line went dead. Fats stood still for a moment, Ramona Clare eying him closely. Then he told her what the gasping old PI had said.

"The truck stop," she considered. "Women, some pros but not all of them, they trade their favors for rides out of town. They hop from truck to truck, go all over the country." She shifted, so as to get a better view of him. "What it means is that she's probably not dead. She's on the run."

"Maybe," Fats said. "But there's all that money out there. If she knows anything at all, and I think she does, she'll be back after it."

"Back being. . .here, Vegas?"

"Gull Valley, Blue Lake. He would of left it where he could get to it quick."

"Not up on the mountain, then?" She nodded. "But you have no idea where, exactly?"

"Not a clue," he lied. He finished his beer. "I want to take a look at that drainage ditch."

"No, you don't," she said, shaking her head. "You're all snarl and growl, Fats. What you want is to hit somebody."

He didn't know what to say.

"You're angry, upset," she insisted. "You want to go down there and mess with Abel Lasky's head and get him to sic Boo on you so you can beat the crap out of him, or he can beat the crap out of you, it doesn't make much difference which."

He had nothing to say to that either.

"You're asking for trouble, Fats."

"Putrefaction," Fats said through gritted teeth. "They left him to rot."

"Fats. . ." Dismay sagged her features.

"I need to settle some things, settle them in my mind," he said. "I need some answers."

"That's not what you're likely to get," she said, almost angry herself.

He shrugged. "I don't think Abel Lasky will bother me, not if I've got things figured."

"Figured how?"

"I'll tell you later," he said. "If I'm right. In the meantime, you could call Dale Zahn and fill him in."

"I'd rather do that from the office," Sergeant Clare said. "Make it official."

"Whatever you think is best," he said. "But I won't be long, a couple hours at most. By then you might have decided where I'm going to take you to eat tonight."

She stood, still distressed. "You'll be lucky if you've got any teeth left to eat with."

The Manx Club's parking lot fit into the U shape formed by Abel Lasky's buildings. Fats found a space, and, as a light rain fell, he sat, getting his bearings. No CCTV that he could see. Automobiles of all sorts, including a late-model Mercedes, probably Lasky's, parked near the club's back door, beside a black Cadillac Escalade.

A bouncer in his black costume came out of the door, looked at him, and went back inside. Fats waited, but no one stepped out to challenge him.

The shower passed. He left his pickup and walked over to the street. Two blocks away, at the edge of an empty lot, he saw a low lumpy construction of concrete and wire fencing. He headed for it.

Water ran in the stretch of open drainage that led to the tunnel. The frothy flow, desert colored, slapped at the containing concrete. The wire fence that once would have prevented careless creatures and drunks from walking or falling into the channel twisted uselessly over the flood.

The scene told him nothing. Strutter's body had been hidden somewhere inside the tunnel, and the rising water had washed it a quarter mile downstream and into daylight, where it got caught in a junk jam. Probably the body had been lugged or dragged from the Manx Club parking lot, or near to it. A month ago. Any signs long gone.

It didn't matter. He knew all he needed to know. Besides, Ramona was right. He wasn't looking for evidence. He was looking for trouble.

He started back to his pickup, where trouble was waiting.

Fats Rangle was angry, but he wasn't about to be stupid. Approaching, he weighed the situation. Against the two black-clad bouncers he'd have only one chance.

Adrenaline tighten his abs, sent a shudder across his shoulders, altered his breathing. His hands became fists. He was almost happy.

"Look here, Boo," grinned Mitch, raising his tattooed arm in mock salute. "We got us a deputy. And not a shotgun in sight."

"Ex," Fats said. He smiled, moved close, and swung a fist as hard as he could.

The jolt of bone on bone ran up his arm to his shoulder, his spine. Fats instinctively crouched defensively as he wheeled, but no return blow came. Instead, Boo backed away, held up both hands, warding him off. "Whoa there," the big bald man urged. "No trouble. We ain't—Mr. Lasky, he wants to see you is all."

Fats didn't quite believe him. He too took a step back. His hand ached faintly but was still useful. He set himself. But Boo didn't move.

Mitch had gone down hard, his muscled torso blotting a puddle of rain water. Now, dripping, he struggled to get to his hands and knees. The corner of his mouth was bloody. His inked jaw jutted awkwardly. His eyes were full of pain.

Fats took another step back. "What about him?"

"He don't listen too good." Boo lowered his hands. "Mr. Lasky said no trouble, so there ain't gonna be none."

Mitch clambered to his feet, stumbled, leaned against the fender of Fats's pickup, his front soaked, his face pale even under the elaborate twists and snarls of his tattoo. He tried to speak but could only make a weak mewling moan. He swayed and would have fallen if Boo hadn't caught him. He was damaged, Fats saw, finished.

Boo was another matter. And there were more like him in the club. They could put the ruin on him. Maybe Lasky would hold them off, maybe not.

But he had questions, suspicions. And he was still angry. At the moment he didn't care much what happened to him.

"Okay," he said. "I'm right behind you."

Fats followed them, Boo supporting his stumbling partner, into the club, where music blared, lights throbbed, the air was chill and acrid on the tongue. They passed a couple of gawking bouncers who seemed about to make a move until Boo waved them off. Then they reached the hallway and the still silence of Abel Lasky's office.

Lasky wore tailored sports clothes, looked freshly steamed and barbered, might have just left the country club. He leaned back in his chair, glanced at Mitch, at the swelling and angle of his jaw, and then looked at Fats. "What'd you hit him with, Ringo?"

"Everything I had," Fats said, massaging his sore hand. "And it's Rangle."

"Mitch braced him," Boo said hastily. "I told him, but he did it anyway."

Lasky flicked dismissive fingers. "Get him out of here."

Through the opened door came a scream, perhaps music, perhaps something else. Then the door closed again on silence.

Lasky sat up in his chair, composed an amiable expression, and said evenly, "I didn't want a fuss, Deputy. I just wanted to apologize for my employees giving you a hard time."

"Ex-deputy," Fats said.

"Especially that...*encounter* at your place in the desert. That was a mistake, hassling you at your home."

Again, everything about Axel Lasky struck Fats as false, posed. Even, maybe especially, his apologies.

Lasky waved a hand loosely at the wall of photographs. "I've got important friends, as you can see. Turns out, so do you. And your important friends had a word with my important friends. So I apologize. Nobody will bother you. You can look for your pal Swagger in peace."

"His name is Strutter," Fats said angrily. "Even a fucking moron can remember that."

Lasky's small smile slipped, for a moment went brutish. "I try to get along, Ex-Deputy. Sometimes it just doesn't work out, though."

Fats registered the threat, angrily ignored it. He rubbed the soreness in his hand. "I just IDed Strutter's body. It'd been dumped in the drainage ditch up the street. It'd been left there to fucking rot. To putrefy."

Fats stopped. He was shaking. His voice was unfamiliar to him.

Uncertainty flickered in Lasky's dark gaze. It seemed real, like his flickering small smile. He hadn't known. Then he rose and came out from behind his desk, nodding at the small conference table. "Sit down, Ex-Deputy. Let me fix you a drink. I've got some very old bourbon here you'll like."

Fats, suddenly aware that his knees were quivering, sat.

At the wet bar, Lasky poured. He brought the drinks to the table, playing host. "Take a couple of deep breaths, flush out the adrenaline. Then tell me."

Fats drank the whiskey in a swallow. Then he said, "Strutter was here with Salome. He went out to score some dope, and somebody killed him. They took the money he had on him, and then they stuffed the body down the drainage ditch. The high water washed it out, what hadn't rotted away."

Lasky sipped his drink. Then he asked, "Do you know who this somebody was?"

"Not for sure," Fats said, "but I'd put money on the two assholes who just left."

Lasky performed a frown. "I wouldn't take that bet, Deputy. Ex-Deputy."

"I'm not saying you were involved." Fats went on. "You were looking for him. You didn't know he was dead. In fact, you didn't want him dead, at least not before he told you where you could find the big money he'd bragged to Salome about."

Lasky's mouth moved, as if he was about to say something. He thought better of it.

"I'd guess that's why they hid the body," Fats said, "so you wouldn't know they'd killed him. They didn't have the brains to move it later. They probably gave you a story about him running off."

"Lot of guessing there."

"In Gull Valley," Fats said, "they were supposed to be looking for Strutter, but Boo only ever asked about Salome."

"That doesn't mean much," Lasky said, but he held up his glass, examining his drink in another practiced pose.

Fats shifted direction. "Strutter had 9 grand in his wallet. You knew it. Where is it?"

"Good question," Lasky said. "So you're saying. . ."

"Whoever killed him took the money," Fats said.

Lasky nodded. "Makes sense."

"The killing doesn't, though," Fats said. "It probably wasn't planned. Might even have been accidental. But the rest of it, the covering up, was the deliberate work of somebody real stupid."

Lasky watched him. Then he said, "What now, Ex-Deputy? What do you want?"

"I want to find out who killed Strutter."

"Most likely we'll never know," Lasky said. "Bodies show up in Las Vegas all the time."

"No, you'll know," Fats said shortly. "Probably already do. I probably do too."

"Probably doesn't prove anything, though, does it?" Lasky frowned. "What about the other money, Ex-Deputy, the big money this Strutter said he had?"

Fats had several lies he might have told Abel Lasky. He decided to confuse him with the truth. "I don't know if there's more money or not. If there is, it belongs to some of your important friends up there." He waved a hand at the wall of photographs. "I sure as hell don't want to get into a face-off with them over it."

Lasky finished his drink. He rose, went to the bar, took the bottle back to the table, sat, poured into both glasses, and said, "It's not dope money, is it? It's money that was in that plane, that one with the Deseret vice president. But I hear you're the guy who found it."

Lasky had been talking to Carroll Coyle. That probably meant something. Fats had the sense that other conversations were going on, conversations about him that he was not privy to.

He didn't tell Lasky about Strutter and the tracks in the snow.

"What about the girl, Salome?"

"All I know is that she's lit out," Fats said. "Probably got tired of getting slapped around by your goons."

"Are you going to look for her?"

"No reason to," Fats lied. "I'm only here to pick up Judge Barlow's horse and haul him back to Gull Valley."

"Vi Barlow," Lasky said, rising. "You a friend of hers, are you, Ex-Deputy?"

Fats finished his drink and stood. "We're boarding her horse is all."

Lasky smiled again. "When you see her, give her my regards."

Fats nearly sneered. "Fat chance."

"You sucker-punched one of his thugs, so Abel Lasky invited you in for a drink while you accused him and the thugs of killing Strutter?" Ramona's lips twisted in mock amazement. "Is that what you're telling me?"

"Two drinks," Fats said. "And no, it was just the bouncers. I don't think Lasky even knew Strutter was dead."

She shook her head, laughing. "You should be down on the Strip rolling the bones, Fats, as much luck as you've got."

"What I've got," Fats said, "is important friends. At least, that's what Lasky says. Let's see if he's right."

He had returned to find Ramona on the phone, frustrated. She'd been trying to make dinner reservations at upscale restaurants, but the town, despite the storm, was filled with high rollers, and the expensive establishments were already booked. He could see that she was biting back her disappointment.

Now he took out his own phone, punched a few numbers. Ramona's eyes widened as she listened to him speak. Then he handed her the phone. "Terry Blume. He'll be a few minutes. He'll tell you what he's come up with. You choose. I'll be in the shower."

Some hours later, Ramona said, "This is almost perfect, Fats."

They had turned heads when they entered Reginald's dining room, the thickset deputy in western-cut clothes and the strapping blonde in heels and a green cocktail dress that bared her broad shoulders and deep decolletage. Ramona obviously enjoyed being looked at. Fats enjoyed her pleasure.

The room was crowded but quiet, their table centrally located but nevertheless secluded, the service faultless, the food delicious. They ate and drank, spoke little. There seemed nothing either especially wanted to say.

"Almost," he agreed now. His sister-in-law would go breathless when she got the credit card bill, but Fats didn't really care. Ramona's high color and wide smile were worth it.

They were idling over coffee when a murmur waved through the room. Vi Barlow, with a brief word here, a light touch there, made her way toward them. Fats rose.

"I wanted to offer my condolences, Fats," she said quietly. "I heard about your cousin. That must have been difficult, identifying his body after all this time."

"Thanks," he said.

Her smile came easily. "Sergeant Clare, it's nice to see you again. That green is perfect for you."

Ramona colored, pleased.

The judge turned back to Fats. "And I wanted to confirm that you'll come and get Omar tomorrow. The road's clear now, so there should be no problem."

"How's the old guy doing?" Fats asked.

"Better. He's up to a trip to Gull Valley, according to the vet," she said. "I'll try to be there to send him off, but if I can't make it, Jorge, the last of our stable hands, will help you."

Fats nodded. "I'll take good care of him."

"I wonder..." The judge had just met with a few political advisors and was waiting for Carroll Coyle to tie up some details, she told them. Fats took the hint, invited her to have coffee. With a smile, she joined them.

They chatted about horses for a bit. Ramona told her about Pete, the gelding she'd had to give up, and confessed that she'd like to buy Splash, Strutter's paint, if the legalities could be sorted out. The judge approved, jesting that a Nevada woman was often better off bonding with a horse than with a Nevada man. She talked in friendly fashion about learning to ride as a girl in Pioche, about the many mounts stabled at the hacienda when she first came to know E. E. Barlow, about Omar's present solitary state and loneliness.

"He won't have that problem at Cherry Creek," Ramona said. "He'll think he died and went to heaven."

Then somehow they were talking about Gull Valley and the properties Fats had shown Terry Blume. The judge was interested in the Carsten place. Its potential would be great if they could get the creek running all year round, which for some hydrological reason seemed possible. The Rocking W would of course be wonderful, but it was prohibitively expensive. For her, anyway. She happened to know, she said, that Deseret Construction was interested in the ranch, although she didn't know what they might have in mind.

They talked too about the plane Fats had found in the snow. Something—not suspicion, exactly, not mistrust—kept him from mentioning Strutter. He explained how he'd been lucky to spot it, which Ramona confirmed. He described the mummified bodies, so unlike the remains he'd identified that day. He told her about the attaché case in the skin-and-bones clutch of the dead passenger.

"Ordinary business papers, I understand," Vi Barlow said.

Fats agreed. "That's what they say."

A silence ensued. Then the judge broke it. "Not that the Deseret people weren't happy to get them back. But they were even happier that you'd found the bodies, so that the families could get closure."

"Glad I could help."

"They might even have given a reward, if anybody'd brought up the subject."

"They offered me a job," Fats said. "Sort of."

The judge smiled. "You don't strike me as a Deseret Construction sort of fellow, Fats."

"That'd be my read too," he said.

Carroll Coyle, as always beautifully suited, came in, came over, smiled his bright white smile. "May I join you, Ex-Deputy?"

"No, Carroll," Vi Barlow said abruptly, rising. "We've got things to do. Sergeant Clare, it was nice to see you again, and good luck with the horse. Fats, thanks for the coffee and the conversation. And if I don't meet you tomorrow, have a safe trip to Gull Valley."

Fats rose, stood standing until they were out of the room.

Ramona smiled. "It's easy to see what the fuss is all about, isn't it? She's...special." She sipped coffee. "I noticed, though, you didn't tell her that Strutter had gotten to the plane before you did."

"The fewer people who know about that the better, at least for now," he said.

Ramona made her mouth a moue. "That would be you and Bill and Mary and me and...who? Dale?"

Fats nodded. Ramona seemed to expect him to say more, but he didn't.

They finished their coffee. Fats called for the bill. The maître d' appeared and with a somber smile told him that their meal had been served with the compliments of the house.

Out in the warm, still slightly humid Las Vegas night, Ramona said, "The house, meaning Judge Barlow."

"Probably."

"In Las Vegas, you get comped only when they want something from you."

"She wants me to take good care of her horse."

"Is that all?"

"Probably not," he said.

Leaving the restaurant's parking lot, Fats drove as if from memory toward North Las Vegas, following side streets into an older, quieter, darker part of town. Ramona gave him an inquiring look, but when he didn't explain, she sat back, waiting. Not far from Nellis Air Force base he slowed and turned into the large crowded lot of a sprawling building draped in neon. He shut off the engine, rolled down his window. A steel guitar faintly twanged. Far away a siren sounded.

"The High Fliers Club," Ramona said. "I hope you weren't planning to take me dancing in there."

Fats didn't speak, sat still, trancelike.

Ramona shifted in her seat. "If you're looking for a fight, this is the place to come. Hardly a night goes by when somebody doesn't get his head busted."

Fats sighed, as if he'd been holding his breath. "For a while, when I was going to the community college, I worked here, bouncing. There were fights. I. . .liked it."

Ramona said nothing.

"Guys like Boo, Mitch, I know them. I was like them. Getting hit is fun. Busting heads is better. Anger, the cold kind, is good."

"This was after Donna dumped you, you mean?"

"Yeah," he said. "But really, it wasn't her. I'd been angry for a long time."

"Why?" Ramona asked.

"I don't know," Fats said. "I. . .ended up a deputy sheriff, but I could just as well have been a thug. I've never killed anybody, but I could have."

A couple came out of the club, leaning together, and wobbled toward a line of cars.

Ramona said, "What are you trying to tell me, Fats?"

"You need to know," he began, struggled, started over. "If we're going any farther, you need to know what I am."

"I've known that since the day you came into my office," she said. "I think it's you who needs to know who you are."

For a moment his anger thickened in his throat. Fucking psychology.

Then he looked at her and the anger passed. "Maybe so," he said, starting the engine.

He had to ask Ramona for directions back to her house. Other than that, they didn't speak until, as he again shut off the engine at her place, Ramona asked, "So are we going any farther, Fats, you and me?"

He didn't hesitate. "I hope so."

The next morning Fats and Ramona drove separately to Huffman's for breakfast. They said little at the restaurant. On the mountain each had grown comfortable with the other's silence, but this was different, an absence heavily weighted with the unsaid. They attended to their meals and their own thoughts.

Afterward he followed her to the police building. Their parting in the foyer ignored any intimacy. They didn't touch. He told her he'd call. She nodded, smiled. He watched her stride off down the hallway.

He found his way to the homicide division office, where he wrote out and signed a formal statement describing how and why he had come to be in the Clark County morgue identifying the remains of James "Strutter" Martin.

Then he drove back to Ramona's house, hooked up the horse trailer, and set off for Judge Barlow's ranch. Water, damp pools shrinking in the sun or dark stains stiffening into mud, marked the passage of the storm. When he turned off on the graveled road, he saw where the bank had given away. The earth bore the new sharp cuts of a big blade.

Then the road rose up onto the flat. Rain had darkened the white-washed adobe walls of the Barlow hacienda. No vehicles stood before them. As Fats pulled up, an elderly, bow-legged Latino came out, waving him down the passageway to the stables.

Judge Barlow was tied up in meetings, Jorge said. With his help, Fats loaded Omar into the trailer, all the while assuring the old horse that he'd be well taken care of and would be happy with his new home and new pals. But he was concerned. In the daylight Omar looked worn out, all ribs and joints, his coat dull.

"You think he's up to the trip?"

Jorge shrugged. "Don't know. Vet said so."

"We'll see, I guess," Fats said, climbing into the cab.

Fats drove carefully into the city, through it, out into the desert. Here, among the Joshua trees and sage, the storm had done no real damage. The emptiness had absorbed its force. What the water washed away, what new pattern it left on the land, was of no real consequence. In the desert, natural changes changed nothing.

Desert people don't change either, not without strife. As Fats drove, he thought of what he'd tried to tell Ramona the night before, about what he used to be, still might be. But the truth was that she was right. He didn't really know who or what he was.

He'd been born into a world that was disappearing even as he learned its rules and ways. So he knew why so many of his neighbors wore weapons on their hips. He knew too how empty the gesture was: what they wanted to protect with their guns was long lost. That made them, and him, angry. But more and more the anger was futile.

Things were changing, he knew, and he was changing too. He just didn't know what he was changing into.

9

Omar was enjoying a roll in the pasture grass.

"He's real old, Fats," Bill said. "Not in great shape."

"He's had an infection," Fats said. "Maybe we can get him to feeling better."

"Maybe," Bill said dubiously. He scuffed dust. "About Strutter..."

"Inside," Fats said. "I don't want to do this more than once."

They mucked out and washed down the horse trailer, Bill all the while talking about the storm that here had hardly happened: a couple of light showers, barely enough rain to dampen down the dust. The desert air, like the land, had already dried out. The late-afternoon sun seemed especially large in the August sky.

The brothers went into the house and sat at the kitchen table while at the stove Mary tended a pot of venison chili. Much as he had with Ramona Clare, Fats said what he had to say, again as he did so stiffening with anger. Putrefaction.

When he finished, Mary spoke. "The two the other day, that's who you think did it? Killed him?"

"Them, or guys just like them."

"So what do we do now?"

"Nothing's changed," Fats said, "Abel Lasky still wants that briefcase full of money."

Bill grinned. "Broke that asshole's jaw, did you? Sorry I missed that."

Fats rose. "They ain't done with us, Bill. Maybe for a while I'll be packing. You might want to carry yourself. And check with Alec Duggar."

Mary frowned, concerned. "What about the kids? School starts next week. They can't take guns to class."

"Lasky ain't about to bother the family," Fats said. "His important friends wouldn't much like it. It'll be just me. Maybe Bill."

"I'll watch the kids," Bill said. "Haul and fetch when necessary. They'll be all right."

After a bit, Fats went back to his little house, showered and changed. He put in a call to Dale Zahn but got a busy signal. He was just replacing his phone in his pocket when it shivered. A throaty-voiced woman calling from the main office of Deseret Construction told him that David Mohr would be in Gull Valley the next day and would like to stop by briefly at mid-morning, if that was convenient. Fats, curious, agreed to be available.

He put his phone away. Then from the bedside table drawer he took out his old Colt and cleaning kit. He'd worked over the revolver only a few days before, and he hadn't fired it since, yet this seemed to him somehow the right thing to do. A ritual of sorts. He wiped and swabbed and oiled. Then he laid the holstered weapon on the table beside his bed, where he could get at it quickly in the night.

He called Dale Zahn again. The sheriff had just spoken with Sergeant Clare, who had passed on what she knew about Strutter's death. Fats was relieved not to have to go over it all himself. He was tired of talking of rot and corruption, tired of his impotent anger.

They agreed that Edna Kachuba might show up in Blue Lake and that deputies ought to keep an eye on Alec Duggar's place.

Then the sheriff said that they should have a sit-down about Fats going back on active duty. Because Fats had officially taken early retirement, there would be a pile of paperwork, and maybe a couple of not-quite-kosher deals to cut, iffy requests to oblige, which Zahn wanted to get a start on. He'd be out of town for a couple of days, he said, but he'd leave a stack of forms for Fats with Caroline Sam in the office.

After the call, Fats walked back to the big house. Mary stirred chili as he passed through the kitchen to the small, closetlike space she used for an office. He got the computer up and running, then started searching.

Deseret Construction had for fifty years built and repaired roads and bridges and water storage and delivery systems around the West. Recently the corporation had taken up real estate speculation, ventured into oil and mineral lease trading, and invested in large-scale agriculture projects. The firm, financial experts said, was in solid shape: earning projections were positive, the stock price was steadily rising. The firm's founder was a man named Harlen Mohr, the CEO his son David. In official photos they looked much alike: the same flinty gaze, small hard smile, stiff jaw. The father had built the company on shrewd judgement, sound engineering, and aggressive salesmanship, or so the website claimed. The son had urged the corporation into wider concerns, at the same time establishing effective working relations with political, financial, and educational institutions.

How much of this was PR BS Fats couldn't tell. But he knew that the sort of thing he was reading was filled with falsehoods large and small. Not that it mattered much. Everybody lies.

Mary called all to the table. Fats enjoyed the meal, the food, the family—everyone was present but Buddy, who was guiding a pair of watercolorists on an exploration of the Turquoise Range. Fats said little until they had finished and the twins were off to their own affairs. Then he told Mary and Bill about the impending visit of David Mohr.

Bill grinned. "You suppose he wants to offer you a job again?"

"He wants something," Fats said. "You can put money on that."

Fats returned to his house, undressed, and lay in the evening heat. He dozed, awoke, dozed again. At last he took up his phone.

She didn't answer. He left a brief message. Twenty minutes later, Ramona called him back. She'd been in the shower, she said. She'd been thinking of him, she said.

Distance seemed to have dissolved the awkwardness of their parting. Uncertainty, she confessed, had restrained her. What were they doing? Was this just a bump in the night? It felt like more, but how could they tell? Where were they going, and were they going there together? Experiencing rather than worrying over life and love was fine, up to a point, but at that point a person as far down the road as she was needed to know where it was headed.

Fats listened. He understood. He told her that he was lying on his bed, naked, aroused.

She laughed.

They talked, then, of how they might get together, what they might do. She wanted to return to the desert. He said there were several ways they might manage that. They talked about his family. They talked about horses. They talked about Splash, and then, because they had to, about Strutter and money. She asked, "Are you going to keep looking for it?"

"I never was," Fats said. "I was looking for Strutter."

"It's a lot of money, Fats," she said slowly. "It would solve a lot of problems."

"Make a bunch too, seeing as how it belongs to somebody else," he said.

"You think if you found it and kept it, it would be stealing?"

"Yeah. But that doesn't bother me much," Fats said. "It's all the crap it'd bring with it."

"I guess," she said with what might have been regret.

Fats let the silence deepen. Finally he said, "Things could look different tomorrow."

He told her about the phone call from Deseret Construction.

"Fats," she said quietly, "what the hell is going on?"

"I don't have a clue," he lied.

The white limousine slowly tugged a tail of dust across the ranch yard and up to the house. After a moment, the two large bodyguards, again in jeans and poplin jackets, climbed out of the front seats. One opened a back door, out of which slid David Mohr, holding a bottle of water. Hatless, he wore shorts and a UNLV T-shirt still damp from, seemingly, a run. He hid his hard-eyed stare behind green-tinted Ray-Bans.

Fats stepped from the porch, giving the interior of the vehicle a glance. Along with a seat that apparently reclined into a cot, there was a PC, a small writing desk, and a mini-fridge.

"I don't fly. This setup helps me stay in touch." David Mohr still spoke as if through gritted teeth. He adjusted his sunglasses and offered Fats his hand. "Thank you for making the time to see me."

Fats shook hands. "What can I do for you?"

Mohr let his head swivel, swinging his gaze over stables and barn, pond and pastures. "Nice place. Could you show it to me, while we talk?"

Fats felt an angry urge to resist. Too many people already knew too much of the Rangle brothers' business. But curiosity overwhelmed the impulse.

Fats gave his visitor a tour, introduced him to Bill, in the stable, and Mary, who regarded David Mohr with a contemplative eye. The two men in light jackets, now having donned tinted glasses identical to those of their boss, managed to stay just out of earshot.

David Mohr, taking small swallows from his water bottle, nudging with a knuckle his shades, looked and listened carefully, asked the right questions, nodded at the right times. He gave the pastured horses, which included Omar standing still and alone, an appreciative look. But as the men moved from the stable into the barn, he began to speak, in his clamp-jawed manner, of his own business.

Deseret Construction had recently bought a number of Nevada properties—over-extended ranches, worked-out mines, abandoned homesteads—and planned to acquire more, some eventually to resell but others to develop in one way or another, agriculture or energy being the most likely enterprises. What David Mohr wanted at this point was to establish a widely recognized corporate presence in the state, to build up and run a business in such a way as to demonstrate not only that Deseret Construction was an important part of the economy but also that it appreciated all and shared many of the concerns of locals, that it was in fact a good neighbor. It was a public relations ploy, obviously, with significant political implications, but if handled properly could benefit not only Deseret Construction but the affected Nevada citizenry as well.

He had his eye on the Rocking W, which inept business practices had sunk into debt. Careful investment and sound management could return the ranch to profitability. David Mohr had just been there, jogged around the property, gotten a good idea of what needed to be done so that it could support a cattle operation of some size. The rescue of the ranch would have a positive effect on both the Pinenut County economy and the reputation of Deseret Construction.

"To do this, we'll need friends in Gull Valley," Mohr said. "I hope you will be one of them."

Fats didn't know what that meant.

They were back at the limo. Mary had invited David Mohr in for coffee, but with a tight smile he'd declined. He had an appointment in town. But he didn't leave immediately.

Instead he stood in the sun and said to Frats, "You didn't call about a job."

"No," Fats said.

"If we buy the Rocking W, we'll need a man to oversee the project."

"He'll have to know a whole lot more about ranching than I do."

"And he won't lie to us."

For a moment Fats stayed silent. Then he said, slowly, "Everybody lies."

"Everybody in Nevada, maybe," Mohr said. He took the last swallow from his water bottle. "Everybody lies. And everybody needs to stay hydrated. The only truths that never change around here."

Fats watched him.

David Mohr tightened his little smile. "It's too much of a coincidence. You find the plane, then you go looking for your missing cousin—what do you call him, Strutter?—whom you hadn't thought about for a month. Because he stole something. That could be the only reason he didn't tell anyone about the plane. And then from Carroll Coyle you learn what he took."

Maybe Mohr had figured it out. Maybe he'd been told. Fats would worry about that later.

"He's the one who took our money," Mohr went on. "That's why you were looking for him, because you knew he had it." Nothing in his tone changed. His lips still barely moved as he spoke. Small beads of sweat appeared at his temple.

"You're right about Strutter," Fats said calmly. "He found the plane. He probably stole the briefcase. But you're wrong about me. I was looking for him because he was missing, and because we have his horse."

"And now he's dead."

"And I'm not looking for him anymore."

"And the money?"

"It's not my money," Fats said. "So I'm not looking for it."

"Not even for a reward?"

"First I've heard about a reward," Fats said.

"You need to learn to listen more carefully." David Mohr stood silent in the sun. Then he said, "Even though you're an admitted liar, Ex-Deputy, I'm going to take you at your word. You're not looking for my money. But I'd like to offer you a small contract, a commission, if you will."

"What kind of contract?"

"As I said when we met, you're the resourceful sort. Should your sense of things happen to lead you to a briefcase with a lot of money and some business papers in it, however this might come about, I'd ask you to keep our interests in mind."

"What interests? The $240,000?"

"The money, of course, yes," Mohr said. Sunlight flashed on his glasses as he gave Fats a long steady look. "But the papers, too. They lay out some of our political plans. Nothing earth-shattering, but they'd cause us a bit of embarrassment if they got in the wrong hands."

Fats nodded. "Carroll Coyle asked me to look out for your interests too."

"Forget Coyle," David Mohr said sharply. "We're dispensing with the middleman."

Fats nodded. "And this contract—what do I get out of it?"

"You'll be amply rewarded," Mohr said. "As you will be for climbing that mountain and finding bodies. We're still in your debt."

"Just being a good neighbor," Fats said.

David Mohr made a sound that might have been a laugh.

As if at a secret signal, one of the big men got in behind the wheel of the limo while the other opened a rear door for David Mohr. The door shut, the engine came to quiet life, and the long white vehicle swung around the ranch yard and raised dust as it drove off.

Fats went back to work.

That afternoon, he was in the barn securing a shoe on the front hoof of Pard, one of the pack horses they'd soon put up to auction, when Mary came in. She watched until he was finished. Then she asked, "What does the CEO of Deseret Construction want with us?"

"He knows Strutter beat me to the plane. He wants me to find his money."

"That's it?"

He told her what David Mohr had said about the Rocking W.

"He was offering you a job?"

"Sounded like it."

"Why, Fats? What's going on?"

Fats sighed. "I don't know."

Mary looked pained. "I just got a call from the bank."

Fats squared his shoulders as if preparing to suffer an assault. "How bad is it?"

"They changed their mind, Fats," she said steadily. "We get the loan at prime rate. It'll save us a carload of money."

Fats nodded. "That'd be Mohr. It's a reward for finding their vice president. I wouldn't take their job, so he did it this way."

"Even though he knows Strutter got there first."

Fats shrugged. "Like I say, he wants me to find his money. That's all I can figure."

"Can you? Find it, I mean?"

"No," Fats said. "Especially since I ain't looking for it."

"How does he know that about Strutter, though? Who told him?"

"He could of worked it out himself," Fats said.

"Or?" Mary tried to grin.

"Or not."

Fats spent the next day on the phone, dealing with death and those who made it official. Almost immediately frustrated by the blanks in the bureaucratic mind, he kept his temper only through a major effort and after a couple of calming conversations with Sergeant Ramona Clare, who herself made inquiries on his behalf. The working day was nearly done by the time he'd persuaded Clark County authorities that Strutter almost certainly had died intestate and that he was the dead man's next of kin, had exacted a promise of haste in issuing a death certificate, and had agreed to the protocols of cremation. He would drive to Las Vegas and pick up Strutter's ashes when they were available. He told Ramona that he would probably want to stay a couple of days. She told him that accommodations could be arranged.

The next morning he visited the Pinenut County Courthouse, locating documents that established ownership of what little of value

Strutter had possessed: an old single-wide mobile home and the lot it sat slumped on, a rough-running pickup and a beat-up horse trailer, and a sound, good-looking pinto. Tack, tools, and personal effects Fats would take for safekeeping from the mess at Blackpool Estates.

Finished with the records, he stopped in at the sheriff's office and picked up the forms Dale Zahn had left for him. Caroline Sam, in charge in the sheriff's absence, gave him and his .38 Colt a knowing nod. "You think you need that?"

"Never know," Fats said.

She smiled. "I understand you may be coming back."

"Never know," he said again.

"I hope so," she said.

"Yeah," he said. He knew she meant it. He almost smiled as he left.

The sun was high in the sky. Fats let its heat briefly bake his shoulders. Then he climbed in his pickup and drove out to the desert pond.

A Three Bar M pickup idled before the open door of Jenny Jones's trailer. As Fats pulled to a stop, Donna Zahn stepped out of the cab. She adjusted the Beretta on her hip. "I thought you were the ME."

The settling dust couldn't mask the foulness that drifted out of the single-wide. Fats clamped down on a small shudder. "She gone?"

"A couple of days now, from the stink." Donna tugged at her hat brim. She seemed distressed, but distantly, not quite present.

Fats checked the urge to look at the body. They wouldn't want him going inside, the deputies, the ME. And he'd had enough of death lately. "Anything to see?"

"Not really," Donna said. "It looks like she died in her sleep." When he didn't speak, she nibbled at her lip and asked, almost anxiously, "What brings you out here?"

"Thought I'd check Strutter's place for a will."

"Dale told me about him, Strutter." She stepped back, leaned against the fender of her pickup, increasing the distance between them. In the bright sunlight her cheeks and chin looked clawed. "I . . . he was some sort of relative, wasn't he? I . . . I'm sorry."

But she didn't seem sorry. She seemed anxious, edgy. She was unsettled, maybe by the passing of the demented old woman, maybe by something else. She patted her pistol, as if to assure her safety.

Fats asked, "Expecting trouble?"

She nodded at his Colt, said nervously. "Are you?"

Fats told her what he'd just told Caroline Sam. "Never know."

"His. . . Strutter's property, horse, effects—they're yours now?"

"Legally, the county has custody," Fats said. "It'll take them a long time to sort it out. I might gather up some things for safekeeping. But we're taking care of Splash, that's all that matters."

"I suppose so," she said. She looked past him, toward the black pool. Then she said rigidly, "I'm glad we ran into each other, Fats. I wanted to talk to you. To tell you, really. . ." She gnawed at her lip. "I'm divorcing Dale."

Fats found that he didn't care what Donna Zahn might do.

"He doesn't know it yet. . ." She stopped, gave him a look that was nearly a plea. "I've hired detectives. . . In Las Vegas and elsewhere, he's got. . . women."

"No news there," Fats said, and immediately regretted it. He hadn't wanted to say that. He hadn't wanted to say anything.

She watched him, warily now. "I wouldn't be telling you this, Norman—I mean, our marriage is our business, the divorce has nothing to do with you. Except. . ."

He knew then what she was going to say. Not the words, not exactly. But the substance, the gist, the truth.

"One of the women he sleeps with is Ramona Clare."

Fats looked out over her shoulder into the distant desert haze.

As if he had challenged her charge, she scowled angrily. "It's true. He's with her now."

Fats said nothing.

Donna gnawed again at her lip. "It's just that. . . when I saw the two of you in Safeway, together, you looked so, well, I don't know if happy is the right word. Maybe. . . satisfied. I mean, I just thought how years ago we'd. . . hurt you, and now it looked like we were about to do it again."

She talked into his silence. She had names, dates, places, she said—evidence of adultery, which might or might not become public, depending on how he chose to respond, which would turn on his political plans. Messy divorces weren't usually a problem for aspirants to office in Nevada, but Donna was willing to keep private matters private, as long as Dale gave her what she wanted. Which was all they had, purportedly. Which was, it turned out, not a lot—the ranch was pretty much it. But the outfit had been her family's, pieced together and built up by her forebearers, and she wasn't about to split it up or share it. There were, she suspected, accumulations of cash, fruits of the kind of corruption that law enforcement officers of a certain sort could with little risk of exposure engage in. Her lawyers, she was sure, would see that she got her due portion.

As for Ramona Clare, Dale had been sleeping with her off and on since they worked together years before. What each actually felt for the other Donna didn't know—probably nothing very deep, at least on Dale's part. Nor did she know what Ramona might have told Fats, except that it almost certainly wasn't the truth.

Dust boiled up out by the highway. Fats watched as a sheriff's rig slewed and bounced across the desert toward them.

"I'm sorry, Norman," Donna said again. Fats said nothing.

Donna spoke briefly with the deputies, then with the just-arrived assistant ME, before she drove off. The county functionaries took Fats's statement, after which they ignored him.

While they were busy, Fats slowly, carefully searched Strutter's trailer, tidying a little as he went, stuffing rot and refuse into black garbage bags he took from the horse shed. The air in the rooms was thick, as if here too something was dead and decaying.

In a concealed storage space he found weapons, a .410 shotgun and an old 30.30, as well as a machete and a set of skinning knives. Out in the horse shelter he gathered up camping and fishing gear, saddles and tack. All he settled into the bed of his pickup. Everything else—clothes, utensils, dry foodstuffs—he left where he found it.

He came across no will. Young men like Strutter didn't make wills. It struck him then that he hadn't made a will either.

Neither did he find a briefcase filled with nearly a quarter of a million dollars.

After an hour, sweaty, dusty, discouraged, Fats sat at Strutter's small kitchen table, sipping from a warm bottle of water. He looked out at the pond, the illusory black water, the green-black reeds, the soggy rotting brace and plank of what had been a pier. It seemed to him then not a pond, not water at all, but instead a portal into elemental darkness.

And then, finally, looking out at the dark water, Fats felt the reality of Strutter's death. He felt it physically, a force pressing against his chest, his lungs. His breath came painfully, with difficulty. His throat clogged with ache. And anger.

Goddamn Strutter. He didn't need to die. To putrefy.

Goddamn Ramona Clare. Not because she'd been sleeping with Dale Zahn, no—oddly, Fats didn't care who she'd slept with. It was, like Donna Zahn's marriage, none of his business. But she'd made him, for a few brief days, feel that he might actually be able to have a life. Goddamn her.

Fats drove home. The rest of the day he spent tending to the weapons and gear he'd taken from Strutter's. He soaped tack, oiled guns, sharpened knives. Then he stowed all Strutter's stuff in a corner of the outfitting shed in the barn.

That night Ramona phoned. Their conversation was different, pocked with small silences. When she asked him if something was wrong, Fats lied and said no.

The next morning, Fats, with Mary and Bill, the two men armed, drove into town to the bank and signed papers. The loan would become final when approved at the next week's board meeting. The loan manager didn't say what had prompted the decision to offer Cherry Creek Stables a better interest rate.

As Bill headed off on errands, Fats took Mary to lunch at the Wagon Wheel Café. She was at ease, as she hadn't been for some time—months, he thought, even more. She talked about the preliminary drawings she'd made of an extension to the stable. She thought they would be able to double the number of horses they boarded. Given that the twins were starting high school the next day, she thought the business might need another hand. With a slow smile she said she might know someone who'd be interested in the job.

On their way home, Fats detoured past Alec Duggar's place. His lawn was freshly mowed, his roses carefully tended to, his house in good shape, looking snug.

As they crept by, Mary said, "You really think she'd come back here, the dancer?"

He could only shrug. He didn't know where she was. He didn't really know anything.

That evening he called Doc Wills. Word was, the PI wheezed, that Abel Lasky had held off dealing with Boo and Mitch—an accounting was inevitable, they'd stolen $9,000 that Lasky perversely believed belonged to him, but he was giving them a break: if they could find the money Strutter had bragged about, all would be forgiven. They were beating and battering their way through Salome's friends and fellow dancers, looking for a lead, a hint, a clue as to where she might have gone.

They hadn't learned anything helpful. They'd be coming out to Gull Valley soon, Fats thought. They had nowhere else to go.

Fats thanked him. Doc Wills said he'd send Carroll Coyle a bill.

Fats took off his clothes and lay in the heat. He was suddenly very tired of not knowing. What he was sure of, though, was that he didn't want Lasky's thugs stomping around Cherry Creek Stables.

He phoned Ramona Clare and asked if she could put him up for a couple of days. She was pleased, until he told her what he planned to do. Caution crept into her voice. "Are you sure, Fats? There are other ways to deal with this."

"I'm sure," he said, even though he wasn't.

They said good night. He was just dozing off when his phone buzzed. It was Alec Duggar. "She's here," he said. "She wants to see you."

Yellow light outlined the draped window of Alec Duggar's front room. Fats parked at the edge of the lawn, quietly got out, and crossed the grass. The door swung open, and then, as Fats stepped past the old man, quickly shut behind him.

In the dim light of a single table lamp, Salome sat on the edge of the sofa, heels and hot pants and crop top a costume, heavy makeup a mask. "Took you long enough."

He ignored that, sat. "Where you been?"

"Traveling," she sneered. "A blow job's better than a bus ticket."

Alec Duggar groaned. "Don't, Edna."

"Yeah," she said to herself. She took a deep breath. "I've got a deal for you."

Alec Duggar smoothed his hands over his paunch. "I don't think I want to hear what you two have to talk about. I'll be in the kitchen, making coffee."

When he'd left the room, Salome started to speak. Her plan was simple enough. She thought she could find the money Strutter stole. But she had two problems. The first was that she didn't drive, had no way of getting to the money and then safely away. The second was that, should Abel Lasky's goons catch up with her, she had no defense. Fats was the solution to both. If he would get her to the money and then to Salt Lake City, where she could lose herself, she'd give him $40,000.

"That's too much," she insisted. "You probably won't have to do anything, really, just haul me around, unless Boo and his buddies show up. Then if that happens, you'll have fun, won't you, busting heads, maybe even get to use that thing on your hip."

Instinctively, Fats patted the holstered Colt. "Where do we go?"

She hesitated. Her back arched, her breasts jutted aggressively, but the message of her body was at odds with the anxiety rasping in her voice. "Blackpool."

That figured. The money had to be somewhere close so Strutter could get at it quick if he had to. Someplace he knew well. But Fats had searched carefully. So, he assumed, had Dale Zahn.

"You know where the money is?" Fats frowned. "You know for sure?"

"I know," she insisted, "where it has to be."

"You knew when you and Boo searched his trailer."

"But I wasn't going to tell him, was I? I just let it alone, let some time go by, waiting for a chance to get back here. Then you came along."

"Why me now? Why can't Mr. Duggar haul you around?"

"No." She shook her head. "What good would he be against Boo? Besides..." She looked around the room, cheaply furnished, deeply shadowed. "He tried to be nice to me when I was here. I don't want him involved in this. I wouldn't even have come here tonight if I'd had anyplace else to go. But he took me right in."

Fats thought about it. "Once we got the money, what's to keep me from taking it all?"

Her face became even more masklike. "You wouldn't."

"Why not?" he asked, and discovered that he was interested in her answer.

"You're a dildo, Fats," she said, "but you aren't that kind of dildo. All you want is people to beat up."

"Maybe I'll beat you up," he said, not smiling.

"I been beat up by experts," she said. "But you're the sort that only goes after guys you figure have it coming."

Again he was interested. "What makes you think that?"

She looked down at her hands. They were folded almost formally in her lap. "Some of us were in the park one night, smoking dope, when these two drunk cowboys drove their pickup onto the lawn, tearing up the grass and flowers and stuff, hollering and honking their horn and all that. You came along and dragged the driver out of the cab. Maybe. . . he might have resisted. You hit him a couple times."

Fats remembered that night, the dope smokers, the drunks.

"You started after the other guy," she said. "But he'd climbed out, just stood there with his hands up. And you stopped. You really wanted to pound the asshole, that was for sure, but you didn't."

Fats shifted on the sofa. "Doesn't mean much, that little fracas."

"Yeah, well, how about this? If you took all the money, I'd know, and I might tell somebody, so you'd have to shut me up. You'd have to kill me. And I don't think you'd do that."

Fats did smile then. "Got it all worked out, don't you? But what if I just give the money back to the people it belongs to?"

"Come on, Fats," she said with a grin, and the grin changed her face. For a moment she looked real, not the caricature she'd created. "Be serious."

Fats watched her. "What happens after we get the money?"

"You drive me up to Salt Lake City," she said. "I know people there. If I can get to them, I'll be all right."

Fats looked at her. She was lying, he knew, but he didn't know about what. Maybe everything.

"And when do we do this?"

"Now," she said, "today. I mean, in the morning, as soon as it gets light."

Fats shook his head, explained: Jenny Jones's death would have county authorities swarming over her trailer, taping up and searching. They might also have gotten word from Las Vegas about Strutter and put his place off limits too. "Anyhow," Fats said, getting up, "I'm off to Vegas to see if I can't persuade your friend Boo to back off. You'll have to lie low for a couple of days, just to be safe."

"Here, with Uncle Alec?" She shook her head. "I don't like that, Fats. I don't want him involved."

"He already is," Fats said. "Just stay in the house, don't move around, while I take care of the bouncers. Then, with Boo and his buddies out of the picture, Mr. Duggar can drive you where you want to go."

She didn't like it, but she saw how it would work. She stood. "Yeah. Let's see if it's okay with Uncle Alec."

She disappeared into the back of the house. Then she returned. "In a couple of days, then?"

"That," Fats said, "is the plan."

"Are you gonna kill him? Boo?"

Fats didn't know the answer to her question.

10

Fats got a few hours' sleep. Risen, he packed a small bag of toiletries and a change of clothes and, unholstered, his Colt Trooper .38 Special. He left in darkness, drove to and slowly through Blue Lake, into and out of Coldwater Canyon. The black softened to gray, the day dawned, the desert began to collect rather than to give off heat.

He reached Las Vegas at mid-morning. After a short stint on the interstate, he exited to contest traffic to the Strip. He found a side-street parking spot, tucked his Colt in his belt and under his shirttail, and walked back to the Dolly's mini-casino of Doc Wills.

Click, clack, mutter, groan. What might have been the same grim gamers punched the video poker machines. At the same spot in the back sat the retired cop. He wore the same straw fedora and dark glasses and a similar shirt, this one lime green with orange flamingos. He was still pale and pasty, stick thin. His chest swelled as he took in air. He showed no surprise at seeing Fats Rangle.

The two drank coffee. Doc Wills played one hand of poker after another as he talked. There had been developments.

About the time Fats and the PI were on the phone, Boo and Mitch had caught up with Terry Blume in the parking garage of his condo. They beat him savagely, might have killed him if they hadn't been interrupted by a patrolling security man. Terry was in the hospital, ribs broken, face ruined. "They thought he might know something about that money everybody's after. It was payback, too, for some fuss out your way, I hear. Him being a faggot didn't help."

Fats choked back his anger.

The two goons had made a big mistake, Wills went on. Terry Blume had friends, among them Carroll Coyle, whose personal assistant and boy toy he was, as well as Judge Vi Barlow, who often expressed fondness for the young man. These were people Abel Lasky worked to be photographed with, to become a crony of, and when he heard what the bouncers had done, he went into a rage. Word quickly buzzed about town: he would generously reward whoever might bring him the heads of the two goons. A pair of local skip tracers had caught Mitch packing his car for a long trip. He hadn't been seen since, nor was it thought likely that he would be ever again. Boo, meanwhile, had gone to ground.

Fats listened as, between gasps for air, Doc Wills gave him the news, finishing with a question. "You after a piece of Lasky's action, are you?"

"All I care about is making sure no harm comes to my family."

"You plan to do that with the piece there in your pants?"

Fats had already noted where Doc Wills's own pistol disturbed the fall of his shirttail. "If it comes to that."

"You've got a permit for it, I'd guess."

"I do," Fats said. Then he said, "But I'm thinking I made a mistake coming down here. If Boo's running, he wouldn't hang around Vegas, would he? Not where everybody knows his haunts."

"He won't run," Wills said. "He sure as hell won't go to the desert. He'll stay here, where at least he knows his way around. But somebody'll nail him pretty quick, I'd guess."

Something in the set of the sick man's jaw put Fats on alert. "You know where he is, don't you?"

Wills bunched his thin shoulders in a shrug.

"How 'bout we go cahoots?" Fats said. "You tell me where he is, I get him and give him to you?"

Doc Wills stopped punching keys. "You sound pretty sure of yourself. What if you can't take him?"

Fats scowled. "I will. I have to."

Wills hesitated. Then he said, "I don't know where he is, not for sure. But word gets around. I can try to set up a meet. You got anything to attract his interest?"

"How about $240,000?"

That got Doc Wills's attention. "The money Lasky's after, you found it?"

"Nope."

Doc Wills shook his head, smiling. He dealt another hand. Nothing.

Fats rose. "How long will this take?"

"If it works," Wills said, "it'll be fast. He probably already knows you're here."

"How could he?"

Doc Wills grinned. "This is Las Vegas."

The sun arced overhead. Fats stood on the sidewalk, letting the heat weigh on his shoulders and back. The pistol at his waist pressed pleasantly against his abdominal muscles. Tourists, thronging, ignored him.

After a minute, he called the ME's office. Strutter's ashes could be picked up any time after noon. Fats said he'd be by.

He called Ramona Clare, told her he was in town, asked her if she could find out where Terry Blume was. Ten minutes later she called back with directions to UMC Trauma Center. She suggested, with an almost offhand air, that they have lunch at Huffman's. He agreed. He didn't want to meet in a setting that allowed intimacy, and it seemed neither did she.

He found the medical facility on West Charleston without difficulty. The hallways shone; the cool air smelled of chemicals. White-clad men and women, silent or speaking softly, scurried in and out of rooms.

The door to Terry Blume's private room was open. Through it Fats saw machines and tubes and a bed and the shape of a body under sheets and a face obliterated by bandages. Then he noticed the man standing before a window.

Carroll Coyle, elegantly attired as always, ugly as ever, gave Fats a look he couldn't read. "He's out. He will be for a while." Coyle's voice was choked with feeling. "The doctors worked on him for hours, doing what they could. For now. There's more to do, but it will have to wait. His system has had about all it can take."

Fats hardly heard him. His hand were fists.

Carroll Coyle looked at Fats, fell silent, and cautiously stepped back, away from him.

After a silent struggle Fats finally got control of himself.

Coyle slowly released the breath he'd been holding. "Why are you here?"

"I'm not sure," Fats said.

Coyle's expression changed. "Do you know who did this?"

"Yes," Fats said. Tersely, biting down on his anger, he told him what he could.

Coyle, listening, seemed to get uglier, his scarred and lumpy features distorted by feelings—sorrow, guilt, rage. "Name your price, Deputy." Coyle said. "I want him dead, this Boo fuck."

Fats stayed silent. Then, at last, he said, his voice a raspy hiss, "I don't kill people for money."

Something in Fats's voice, his face, his gaze, caused Coyle to quail. "Yeah, well. . .no, I mean. . . ."

Anger scraped at Fats's throat. "Abel Lasky's already put a price on Boo's head. If anybody gets him, they'll kill him, probably. Easier that way. If I get him, I'll turn him over to Wills. All I want is to make sure he stays away from my family. That's my only interest."

Coyle nodded. "Yes, all right. I. . . ." He looked at the figure in the bed, sheeted and swaddled. "He won't be attractive anymore. Somebody should pay for that."

"One way or another," Fats said, "somebody will."

The two men walked out. In the parking lot, Coyle stopped. "It was nothing serious, Terry and me. He was bright and beautiful; I'm a rung on the ladder he's climbing. Still. . .it hurts. Turns out I cared more than I knew."

Fats wasn't sure why Coyle had told him this. Maybe because he had to tell somebody.

Fats's anger stayed with him. Driving through the heat and congestion, he seethed. He managed to keep within himself, but barely.

Huffman's lunch crowd was subdued, a few street cops but mostly, by the look of their crisp uniforms or neat conservative civies, administrative and clerical officers. Ramona Clare waited in a corner booth. Big, bright-eyed, she seemed almost to command the room. Her smile, as he approached, at once asserted confidence and asked a question.

Fats told her where he'd been and what he'd learned. As he started on his meat loaf, she told him what she knew, which wasn't much more. Boo and Mitch had roughed up one of Lasky's dancers, who was brave enough or afraid enough to call the cops. So the two were being chased by Las Vegas Metro even before the assault on Terry Blume. She was sure they'd find Boo soon. Somebody would give him up for a price.

Fats listened. When she finished, he stayed silent.

She gave him a small, tentative smile. "Everybody in the room knows you've got a piece under your shirt."

"I've got a permit for it," he said.

"You're upset," she said then. Her smile widened but lost force. She stabbed a fork at her salad. "I hope you're not going to take it out on me."

Fats felt his anger swelling again. He swallowed it. "He—Coyle—he thought I was a hired killer."

She smiled again. "You get a look sometimes, Fats. When you're angry. Like now. You get, well, not evil, but. . . stormy. Very stormy."

When he stayed silent, she went on: "We talked about this, Fats. You get angry. You get that look like you want to smash something or somebody, and people. . . they're afraid of you."

Now it was her turn to go silent. The sounds of the diners around them drifted in the room, meaninglessly. Fats put down his fork, pushed his half-eaten meat loaf aside. "I get angry when people lie to me."

She stilled.

"You probably don't know, since Dale Zahn himself doesn't know yet," he said, "but Donna's divorcing him. She's hired private investigators. She's got names, dates, photographs."

Ramona Clare said nothing, but Fats sensed her anger.

"The thing is," Fats said, "it wasn't necessary. Lying, I mean. Who you sleep with is none of my business. Nobody's made any promises yet."

In a single sudden movement she was up and out of the booth. She looked down at him. "You really are an asshole, aren't you, Fats?" Then she walked out.

Fats checked the impulse to go after her. Even though she was right. But he was too angry. He didn't know why. Everybody lies.

A half an hour later, he left the ME's office carrying a container the size and shape of a quart of Jim Beam. He'd been surprised at how little Strutter reduced to, a couple of pounds of ash and bits of bone. The cause of death was registered as "probable myocardial infarction."

He wasn't quite back to his pickup when his phone buzzed. Judge

Barlow had heard he was in town. She'd like to discuss a couple of matters with him, if they could meet at her late husband's firm in, say, forty-five minutes. Fats said he'd be there.

Barlow, Wright, and O'Leary had offices downtown, not far from the railway station, a walkable way from the Manx Club, where Fats decided to park. He sat for a while, but no one came out to check on or to challenge him.

He didn't much like the idea of packing a pistol to a meeting with Judge Barlow, but he couldn't leave the Colt in the pickup with Strutter's ashes. He got out, readjusted the piece to smooth away any bulge beneath his shirttail, and set off.

Heat rose from the sidewalk up through the soles of his boots. Distant music disturbed the afternoon. Shadows gathered in the open ditch where Strutter's snagged body had hung, rotting.

The law firm occupied the top third floor of an old art deco stone and stucco building. Exiting the elevator, Fats found himself in a large room with slowly churning ceiling fans, dark wall panels, heavy leather furniture, and glossy, rug-strewn hardwood floors, all of it suggesting substance, masculine and monied. The perfectly presented middle-aged receptionist picked up and spoke into a phone, and almost immediately Judge Barlow appeared, her skirt suit a conservatively cut pale lavender, her smile and handshake warm.

She led him down a hallway to a bright, tidy office. A small window let in light onto mahogany and fabric and a few plants. Diplomas and large desertscapes adorned the walls. Judge Barlow directed Fats to a seat at a small table and sat across from him.

Concern furrowed her brow as she asked about Terry Blume— Carroll Coyle had called her, but all she knew was that the young man had been beaten and was hospitalized. Fats filled her in, choking back his anger. She listened and grew still. She would call the hospital, she said, visit Terry when he was awake and up to it.

She asked about Omar. He told her the old horse had settled in. She said that she understood that Fats would soon no longer be an ex-deputy. He was surprised, and irked: everybody in Nevada seemed to know his business.

She noticed, offered an apologetic smile. "Dale Zahn told me.

We've been...communicating. It seems that he'll have a role in my next campaign."

Fats nodded, wondering. Judge Barlow hadn't run for reelection after her second term. Political gossip had her setting up for a state-wide race, but she was said not to have determined which office she'd seek. How the sheriff of Pinenut County might fit into her plans Fats had no idea. Neither did he know what she might mean by "communicating."

"I think I mentioned that Dale and I went to law school together. We took the same tax class from E. B., in fact."

E. B. Barlow had been twenty-five years her senior, wealthy and politically active. They married the day after her graduation, and he'd died of a massive coronary two weeks after she was elected to the bench. The foremost tax attorney in Las Vegas, he was among the law school's first faculty, but he'd made a reputation and a for-tune representing gaming companies, among them a couple owned by questionable characters—not mobsters, exactly, or at least never proved to be.

"I met him once, E. B.," Fats said. "I delivered an envelope to him."

She smiled. "Ah, yes. The envelopes."

A local federal prosecutor had once tried to persuade a grand jury that the envelopes E. B. Barlow regularly received from the hands of young messengers of little consequence like Norman "Fats" Rangle must be illicit. Las Vegas had a good laugh. Corruption was com-monplace, assumed.

"In fact," Judge Barlow said, "I never knew what was in those envelopes. By design. E. B. insisted that I remain above the fray, as it were. Plausible deniability and all that."

Her hands were small, delicate, her fingers bare. She folded them carefully. "Nevada politics can be a dirty business. It's difficult sometimes to avoid smears and stains. The best one can do is make sure they are small and not indelible."

She paused, as if giving him time to process what she was saying. "So I'm concerned for my reputation, Fats. I tend it carefully. I'm now financially independent and have no business interests. My personal life is boring. I'm forthright about my ambition. I'm honest.

If those who are working to prepare my candidacy for higher office are engaged in some. . .shadiness, I'm not aware of it."

Fats thought he knew where this was going. "But. . ."

"But," she said, frowning now, "that airplane you found. There was money in it—gray money, I'm given to understand. Some of it might have been intended for my campaign. This sort of thing is not quite aboveboard, but it's not actually illegal. If it got out that I was to be the recipient of these funds, well, the damage wouldn't be beyond repair."

All this seemed a preamble. Fats waited.

"What troubles me is how to account for the fuss about it. I mean, a quarter of a million dollars is a lot of money, but not to a firm like Deseret Construction. And why is David Mohr taking a personal interest in the affair?"

"I don't know," Fats said. "Is this what you and Dale Zahn have been communicating about?"

"Among other things," she said. "He suggested I talk to you."

Fats looked at her. It was her wholeness, he thought, that made her appear trustworthy: she seemed complete in herself, she needed nothing and nothing could touch her. He told her what he could about Strutter and the plane and the search for a missing briefcase.

Judge Barlow listened to him. Then she said, "Hunches?"

"No," he lied.

"Something's going on, Fats," she said quietly. "It isn't just the money, it's something else, something bigger. I think I need to know what it is. Staying above the fray is one thing, but sometimes what you don't know can ruin you."

"And you want me to. . . ?"

She smiled then. "David Mohr told me how you play your cards close to your vest, Fats. You don't commit, don't promise. But you're right, I do want something. I want to know."

"Yes," he said.

As if an understanding had been reached, she sat back in her chair. "If you don't mind my inquiring, Fats, why did you decide to go back to the sheriff's office?"

Had anyone else asked him that question, he would have walked out. But he gave Vi Barlow an answer. "It just makes sense econom-ically. It lets us do more with the stable."

"You and your brother."

"And sister-in-law, Mary. She's the brains of the outfit."

She smiled again. "Is there anything happening in Gull Valley that troubles you, that you can't account for or explain?"

"Nothing shady, no more than usual," he said. "There's a lot of money floating around. People like yourself are interested in property out there. And an outfit called Hydroneva is buying up water rights."

"I've heard the name," she said. "Speculators, would they be?"

"I don't know," Fats said.

"It's big business these days, water," she said. "There's still a lot of pipeline talk. And that lithium mine they're proposing up north of Winnemucca, it will pump over a billion gallons a year. Demand is going up. So is the price. Ultimately, we're talking a lot of money, Fats."

"I tried to get a line on Hydroneva," he said. "Ran into a maze of holding companies."

"Nothing unusual about that." Judge Barlow smiled again, now a bit wanly. "And there may be no connection." She pursed her lips. "It's just that I have this feeling, Fats, that I'm being. . .manipulated. Used. Lied to."

"Don't we all."

From a small holder on her desk she took an embossed card. "This is my private number. Use it for any message you want to keep confidential."

They talked for a few more minutes, about Omar, about the plan to expand Cherry Creek Stables, about Judge Barlow's interest in the Carsten place. She thought she might try to get out to Gull Valley to take a look at the property. She also said again that she'd see Terry Blume as soon as his doctors allowed visitors.

Fats let her lead him back to the outer office, accepted her thanks and her hand. He rode the elevator down and stepped into the late-afternoon heat, the glare of the sunlight, the murmur and rustle of the city. After a moment, he took out his phone and texted a message: "Sorry."

Almost immediately he received a reply: "This evening, my place."
He started back to his pickup. Coming again to the brief break
in the drainage tunnel where Strutter's moldering body had been
entangled with flood-gathered debris, he stopped. A dusty path led
down to the fifty feet of open channel. The three-foot retaining walls
and both concrete entrances to the tunnel were smeared with graffiti,
some crude, some accomplished. Only damp stains indicated that
water had recently run over the silted floor. Now it was just a drying
ditch with darkness at either end. He walked on.

Once back in his pickup, Fats took the Colt out of his belt and
laid it at his hip. He sipped warm water from a plastic bottle. Then,
because he could think of nothing else to do, nowhere else to go, he
sat. In the heat of the cab, he began to sweat. Leaning back, in his
mind he traced the trickles down his ribs, felt his body was being
emptied of toxins, oozing unpleasantness into a flow bearing Strutter's
body down the dark tunnel, in the muddy water, tossing, swirling...

His phone whirred and shivered. Immediately he was awake, if
not wholly aware. Time had passed, he realized: an hour, from the
slant of the sun, maybe more. Groggy, he answered.

Doc Wills wheezed. "He'll be where he dumped the body."

Fats went blank. Then his mind engaged. "Strutter's body? The
drainage ditch, you mean?"

"That's what he said."

"I'm practically there right now," Fats said slowly. "He—this
sounds like a setup."

"That it does," Wills scoffed. Or laughed. "But if you want him,
that's where he'll be."

That's where Boo was already, Fats was certain. Waiting, probably
with a weapon.

Fats took a flashlight from the glove compartment. Climbing from
the cab, he stuffed the Colt in the waistband of his jeans. Then he
walked out of the parking lot, to the street, back to the downstream
open section of storm drain. He carefully slid down the path and off
the low wall into the ditch.

He pulled out the Colt. He might meet tunnel people, as they were
called, those already returned to make a camp out of the heat. They
were homeless, most of them addicts of one sort or another. Few,

he knew, were dangerous, but he wasn't about to take chances. He flicked on the flashlight and stepped into the darkness.

The air was noticeably cooler, heavy, dank. As the sounds of the city muted, his footsteps echoed faintly. The beam of his flashlight glistened on water that pooled and puddled in low spots but didn't move. The flood would have swept away the often-elaborate campsites constructed in the dark, but it had left litter: a swollen paperback, a wad of blankets, a sequined slipper.

Fats moved carefully, quietly, in the utter black. His flash found graffiti that had once decorated camp walls. The tunnel widened into a chamber, where an eddy had left a mess of paper and cartons and cloth and plastic, tree limbs and broken wooden boxes, a sodden mattress. Farther up the passageway a smaller tunnel branched off. Then came another chamber, this feebly lighted by a ceiling grate. He heard the soft hiss of tires on hot asphalt, in the faint light made out a spread of cardboard and a sleeping bag and the shiny stare of a gaunt figure sitting cross-legged in the dimness, wielding a length of rebar. Fats passed by. Not far down the dark he caught a scent he knew. He regripped the Colt. He let his flashlight search until it found fur, a large drowned and decaying cat.

After another black silent stretch, he reached another ceiling grate, heard voices, understood that he was beneath the Manx Club's parking lot. He slowed, softened his step, breathed quietly, listened.

The underground air began to change subtly, become drier, warmer. Far ahead the darkness paled. Fats stopped, flicked off the flashlight, moved toward what became an archway of light. Soon he could see the entrance and the empty glare beyond.

He stopped again. All was still. Then a shiver moved through a sheen of shallow water spreading from a small alcove just inside the tunnel.

Fats took a few silent steps forward. Then he stopped, cocked the Colt, aimed at the different darkness that identified the recess, and squeezed the trigger.

The big boom of the gunshot echoed down the tunnel. Fats waited for quiet, then fired again.

When the sound had stilled, he called out, lying, "I've got enough ammo to play with you all day, Boo."

His words dimmed to mere sound as they reverberated through the darkness.

"Eventually, a ricochet will nail you. But I don't want you dead. I don't even want whatever Abel Lasky's offering for your head. I just want to talk."

The watery sheen stirred again.

"Toss out your piece," Fats called. "Then come on out, hands first."

Silence. Fats fired again.

After a moment, a pistol came skidding out of the alcove, riling the water on the concrete floor. Then, fingers spread, palms up and empty, the big bald man offered his hands as he stepped into sight. Against the light beyond the entrance, he made a slowly moving silhouette, a perfect target.

"Out," Fats ordered.

With the toe of his boot, he found Boo's weapon in a pool of water. He kicked it down the tunnel. Then he too stepped out into the sun and the heat and the sounds of the city. He laid the flashlight on the top of the low retaining wall, at the same time poking his Colt into the ex-bouncer's ribs. "Assume the position."

Boo wore another muscle T-shirt, this one a pale yellow, too close-fitting to conceal a pistol, and tight black jeans, and he probably wouldn't have had two weapons, but Fats still searched him carefully. Then he backed away. "Why'd you kill Strutter?"

Boo turned to face him. He was watchful, Fats saw, not particularly afraid but wary. The way he'd set himself, balanced, steady, said that he would know what to do when it came time for fists.

"Didn't plan to," Boo said. "Didn't want to, even. It just . . . happened."

"How?"

Boo shrugged. "We was trying to get him to tell us about the big money he was bragging up to the broad. Figured to rough him up some is all. But I give him a little pop in the chest, a nothing punch, you know, he just gets this funny look on his face and falls down dead."

"And you dumped him here, left him to rot, stink."

Suddenly, Fats was finished. He'd been bounced and banged by anger all day, and he was tired of it, wanted to end it, wanted to hit somebody. It was time. He shifted his shoulders, loosening his muscles. He'd go for the gut first, organs, kidneys and liver.

Boo still didn't seem especially concerned. "Couldn't leave him there in the fucking parking lot, could we?"

Adrenalin, anticipation, had Fats rocking on the balls of his feet. "And Terry Blume?"

Boo's grin was laced with menace. "That was for fun."

Fats gave the area a glance: dirt slopes to the retaining walls, in the narrow ditch room enough to move some, but not much. Just the way he liked it. There'd be nothing cute or clever, just fists and will.

He rocked. He quivered, abdomen, chest. "How about we have a little fun, you and me."

Boo grinned again. "I wouldn't mind. Except like out in the boonies, you got the gun."

"Yeah, I do," Fats said, pointing the barrel skyward. It was shaking. So was the hand that held it. It seemed somehow far away.

"But that ain't why we're here," Boo snorted, suddenly angry himself. "Word is you want a deal. Word is you got a line on that money the runt blabbed about."

"There isn't any money," Fats heard himself lie. "That was a lie, just to get you here."

"So I'm here," Boo said, even more angry now. "What the fuck you want?"

Fats heard a voice, realized after a moment that it was his. "I want to bust you up."

Boo took a deep breath, made his hands fists. "I'd like you to try. But why would you be so stupid? You got a gun. Why don't you use it? Anybody with any brains would. Lasky wants me dead, and won't care who or how."

Fats was ready now. "No fun that way."

"Toss it, then, and I'll beat your fucking head in."

Fats smiled. He took off his hat and laid it on the level top of the retaining wall. Then beside the Stetson he placed the Colt. He stepped aside. "Come and get it."

Boo grinned. "You're fucking crazy."

Suddenly calm, sure, Fats lifted his fists with urgent intent. Boo was bigger, heavier, he could cause pain, but Fats didn't care. Getting hit was part of the fun. Getting hurt made it all mean.

But before he could move, a long shadow passed across the ditch. A voice from above sounded like someone being strangled. "Hold it, gents."

Doc Wills looked down at them. He was still wearing his tourist outfit, straw hat, shades, silly shirt, but now he gestured with a snub-nosed revolver. "Step away from the weapon."

Boo paled. Holding out his hands in a silent plea, he backed to the tunnel entrance.

"You too, Deputy," Wills wheezed, jerking the pistol. In the sunlight, his hands looked scaly, his bare arms thin, frail.

Fats, confused, didn't move. He'd been about to hurl all that he was at the big muscled goon. Stopped, he was for the moment lost to himself.

"Move it, Rangle."

Fats finally took his meaning. He sidled over beside Boo, then watched Wills ease cautiously down the steep dirt path, sit carefully on the retaining wall, take up the Colt, and stuff the snub-nose into the holster under his shirttail. He moved slowly, as if infirm. Behind his dark glasses, he looked old and worn out. He struggled for breath.

Boo broke the silence, his voice strange. "What's going on, Doc?"

Wills waited until he had regained wind. Then he held up the Colt and spun the chamber, checking it for bullets. "You finally got to be worth something, Boo."

The big man looked sick. Sweat beaded on his forehead. His mouth worked. He managed to speak then. "You said we was in this together."

"I lied."

As if in genuine wonder, Boo asked, "You about to shoot me, Doc?"

"Yep," the dying man said as he pointed the Colt and squeezed the trigger.

Out in the open air, the sound of the gunshot was just one more bit of the Las Vegas blare.

The big man stumbled back a step. He fell heavily. Blood oozed from a casino chip–sized hole in his chest. He seemed, in the moment before his eyes glazed over, outraged.

Fats stood stunned. He knew what had happened but he didn't know what was going on.

"Stuff him out of sight," Doc Wills said.

Fats looked down at the body. Blood slowly spread on the yellow shirt, the stain now the size of a big fist. Fats's fist.

He was shaking again, now violently. All that anger and adrenalin had no outlet. Once more he had no one to hit.

"Drag him out of the sun," Doc Wills said shortly. "Now."

Fats did as he was told. The effort was awkward, but he managed to get the big, heavy body hidden, more or less, in the alcove. Then he stepped back into the sun.

Doc Wills still sat on the retaining wall. He gestured with the Colt. "You too."

Calmed by the exertion, Fats finally understood. "Why?"

"I never leave witnesses." Again he jerked the pistol.

Fats watched him. Then he said, "As soon as you talk to Abel Lasky, everybody in town will know you killed Boo. Nobody'll care."

"You never know," Wills said. "Why should I chance it?"

"Hey, this is Las Vegas," Fats said. "Chancing it makes this town go."

The Colt quivered. It almost seemed too heavy for Wills's spotted, high-veined hand.

"Besides," Fats said then, "you're about done for."

After a moment, Doc Wills removed his dark glasses. His eyes were rheumy, red-rimmed, darkly ringed. He didn't look like a killer. He looked like a dying old man.

Hatless, in the hot sun, Fats was getting a headache. Now it all—the ditch, the tunnel, the body—seemed unreal.

"You know I'm not going to rat you out, Doc," Fats said wearily. "If you're going to shoot me, shoot me. Otherwise, give me my hat and flashlight and pistol, and I'll help you out of this ditch, and you can go collect from Abel Lasky and I'll go apologize to a woman I mistreated."

Doc Wills replaced his sunglasses. He looked, Fats saw then, almost reptilian. He watched. Finally he said, "I'll keep the pistol."

Fats realized then that he wasn't going to die. Somehow that made the murder he'd witnessed seem imagined, part of a show the city put on for suckers. He took up his hat and flash.

"I like that Colt, Doc," Fats said, settling into the shade of his hat brim.

Doc shook his head. The body in the tunnel had a bullet in it. The bullet was fired from the gun licensed to Fats. If the pistol somehow came into the possession of the cops, they'd know who to come after. But for now, at least, Doc would keep the Colt. In case.

Fats didn't like it, but there wasn't anything he could do about it.

"Maybe you'll get lucky," Wills said. "I could croak any time now. This little climb I've got here could kill me."

"I'll give you a hand," Fats said.

"This Colt," the dying man said with a grin. "I'll leave it to you in my will."

Fats awoke at midnight, still damp from sex. Beside him Ramona slept heavily. They had coupled brutishly, purging. For Fats the slap and gasp drove away his anger. What Ramona Clare was getting rid of he could not have said.

They had reconciled quickly. He shouldn't have accused her of lying, should have only asked her to explain. But everybody lies, so he didn't really have any right to be upset. Besides, she hadn't lied, actually. Well, all right, she hadn't told the whole truth. Yes, she'd slept with Dale Zahn, and recently. She didn't know why. They'd go for months without meeting. Then he'd knock on her door and she'd let him in. But it wasn't serious. Not like things were with Fats. Or at least like they could be.

They had eaten supermarket lasagna and drunk merlot. They'd talked, quietly, calmly, seeming, without actually saying so, to assume a future. A desert future.

Then, finally, he'd told her what had happened in the storm drain in the middle of the day in the glare and groan and heat of the Las Vegas afternoon.

For a while she'd looked at him silently. Then she'd said, "I'm a cop, Fats. I'm supposed to report anything I learn about a crime."

"I know," he said.

"You're corrupting me."

"Yes."

Then they'd gone to bed.

Then they'd slept. Then Fats awoke and lay in the dark, still astonished at murder.

11

Fats was in no hurry to head home. He didn't much want to leave Ramona. On the other hand, he wanted out of Las Vegas. And he had matters to attend to in Gull Valley.

It was mid-morning before he left. After breakfasting in Huffman's, he took Ramona's suggestion and reported his Colt stolen from his pickup overnight. Then he drove downtown and made his way to the storm drain ditch. The body was still there. Fats followed his flashlight beam a bit farther into the darkness. Eventually, he found Boo's pistol, a .38 Glock automatic. He stuffed it in his belt and climbed back up to his pickup.

On the road to Blue Lake, for long stretches he was alone, until a dusty ranch or mining or government vehicle materialized out of the heat waves. The press of the Glock against his abdomen had him edgy. For perhaps the first time, he found no solace in desert solitude.

He was approaching the wide mouth of Coldwater Canyon when his phone shivered. Dale Zahn wanted to talk. He was at the Three Bar M, where, he suggested, they could have coffee.

A mile or so from the ranch, Fats met a white pickup. Donna Zahn lifted a hand in greeting. He waved, relieved that she wouldn't be at the house.

Loose planking rattled as Fats passed over the bridge across Coldwater Creek. In the ranch yard, nothing moved. A cat watched from the shade of the sheriff's cruiser.

Fats knew the place well: ranch house, barn, outbuildings, pens and chutes, fences and corrals. It had once been a carefully kept-up operation. Now it showed subtle signs of decline: gap, lean, sag.

Dale Zahn, carrying two dark bottles of Coors, stepped out the kitchen door, nodded toward an old cottonwood that shaded a flagstone patio. "Too hot for coffee."

Settled at a wicker table, Dale inquired after Strutter's ashes and effects, including his pinto, Splash. He'd heard about Terry Blume and asked for the whole story. He also wanted to know about the young woman at Alec Duggar's. Fats told him what he could about all of it.

Dale assumed his pondering pose. "I hear you talked to the head honcho of Deseret Construction. Can you tell me what he wanted?"

"He wanted me to find his money," Fats said, "and he asked about the Rocking W."

"Did he now?" Dale studied his beer bottle.

"He talked about buying the property," Fats said. "Some PR scheme, as I understand it."

"It'll be pricey, especially with the water rights," the sheriff said. "It's a wonder that Hydroneva outfit hasn't got ahold of them."

Fats took a small swallow of beer.

"I've been doing some checking," Dale Zahn went on. "Like you said, whose money is behind that outfit is hard to pin down. I don't know why that would be. Do you?"

Fats heard what the sheriff hadn't quite said. "Doesn't necessarily mean they're up to something crooked."

"I suppose they've got a right to stay anonymous, yeah. One name did come up a couple of times, though. Carroll Coyle."

Fats nodded. "It might not mean anything. I'd guess he's got lots of clients. He's a middleman."

"Or a front," Dale Zahn said. "He's connected to Deseret Construction. And to David Mohr. And to Vi Barlow."

Fats hadn't seen that coming. "The judge? You think something dicey is going on and she's part of it?"

"No," Dale said. "That is, yeah, I think something's going on, but no, I don't think she's involved. I just want to make sure that she isn't politically. . .contaminated."

"Contaminated," Fats repeated. "She used the word 'stain.' That was right after she told me you'd be part of her next campaign."

The sheriff smiled his politician's smile. "Just setting up options, Fats."

Fats nodded. "What would you guess is going on?"

Coldwater Creek shushed and gurgled in the silence. Then Dale

Zahn said, "I don't know. But the CEO of Deseret Construction is nosing around out here for some reason. Why him? You'd think he'd have people to do that. Meanwhile, Hydroneva is buying up all the water in Gull Valley, who knows what for. Maybe there's a plan. Maybe it's just speculation—Nevada's favorite pastime."

Fats considered it. "There's a good-sized aquifer in Gull Valley, but the demand is in Vegas. The state watermaster put the kibosh on that Spring Valley pipeline idea, and he ain't about to okay any other attempts to move a lot of water."

"For now, maybe. But we're talking billions of dollars, Fats," Dale Zahn said. "Where there's that much money, there's a way to get things done."

Fats drank more beer. "Judge Barlow thinks the amount of money supposed to be in that briefcase Strutter stole isn't enough to explain why everybody's so hot after it."

"I think she's right," the sheriff said. "There's something else involved."

"Maybe we'll find out what," Fats said. "Like I said, the girl, Salome, Edna—she thinks she knows where the money is."

"And now," Dale Zahn said, "there's nobody threatening her?"

Fats let the question hang in the heat for a moment. Dale Zahn, he realized, knew about Boo. There were a couple of ways he could have found out. Fats didn't feel like pursuing the matter. "So I hear."

The two men watched one another. Then Dale Zahn smiled. He was about to speak when, with a clatter of loose planks, a white Three Bar M pickup rolled across the creek bridge.

Donna parked and came over. She gave her husband a dead-eyed stare. But when she spoke it was to Fats. "Norman," she said, stripping off her work gloves, "how are you?"

For a moment he didn't respond. Instead, he watched her stuff her gloves in a hip pocket, then let her hand hover, trembling faintly, over the butt of her holstered Beretta. He found it odd, almost ominous.

"Fine, thanks. And on my way." He finished his beer and rose.

She took off her hat, wiped her sleeve across her brow. "Don't go on my account."

In the harsh desert sunlight, she looked, Fats thought, much like her ranch: poorly tended to. Even with the help she hired, the work was too much for her. The same might be said, Fats thought then, of her marriage. He could almost feel sorry for her. Almost.

"Things to do," he said.

She donned her hat, as if to hide in the shade of its broad brim. "Are you planning to use that thing in your pants?" She seemed suddenly angry.

Fats stood stunned. He looked at her, then at her husband. It was Dale's grin that finally brought him back to the moment. The Glock, she meant.

"Never know," he said, and started for his pickup.

"Let me know what goes with the girl," the sheriff said. "And we've still got paperwork to do."

Fats left them, husband and wife, to swelter in the heat.

He drove to town, to Alec Duggar's rose-rimmed bungalow. The old retired railroader showed him in. Edna Kachuba—Salome—perched anxiously on the edge of the sofa. "You fix it?"

"Somebody did," Fats said. "Or so I hear. Boo won't be any more trouble. But Abel Lasky could send somebody else after you. Let's hang on as we are for at least the rest of the day. If everything's clear, we can look around Strutter's tomorrow morning."

"No, let's do it now," she said, rising, her preposterous breasts bouncing in her halter top.

"Give the county time to finish up with Jenny's place," Fats said. "If the money's there, it ain't goin' anywhere."

"Hey, let's go now, at least to check. Maybe they're done."

"I've got things to do," Fats said.

She smiled a hustler's sexual smile. "Nothing as fun was what I could do for you."

Alec Duggar spoke, his voice gone gravelly, his expression pained. "You don't need to talk that talk, girl."

She looked at the big-bellied old man. Then she shrugged. "Yeah, you keep saying."

Duggar's face folded in dismay. He left the room.

She looked at Fats. "Tomorrow morning. Early."

"Early," Fats agreed.

He drove back to Cherry Creek. There nothing moved. Fats put a hand on the butt of the Glock, suddenly alert. Then Bill stepped from the barn and waved, and Fats spoke to himself: "Easy. Easy."

But he wouldn't be easy. Not till whatever was coming was come and done.

He placed Strutter's ashes on his bedside table. He thought he might spread them at Shoshone Springs the next time he was up there.

The afternoon heat abated, the evening air began to stir. Fats skipped dinner, had a beer with Bill and Mary, and went to bed early. Just after midnight, he awoke to noisy blasts of wind. Some hours later dawn broke, breezy and cooler. Fats breakfasted with the family, saw to a few chores, gave the twins a ride to school, and then drove over to Alec Duggar's.

As Fats crossed the grass, the old man appeared in the doorway. "She ain't here."

Fats didn't say anything.

Duggar eyed him anxiously. "She—she was afraid of you."

When Fats stayed silent, Duggar went on in a rush: "She said you'd try to take the money from her. Beat her up. Kill her, maybe. Said you'd probably killed that muscle-bound bastard from Las Vegas."

Fats spoke quietly. "You believe all that, Mr. Duggar?"

"I—" Duggar rubbed the back of his hand against his stubbled chin. "I don't know. I don't know what to think. But she didn't want you around, that's for sure. The money—she says Strutter told her it was right there, he could watch over it from his kitchen table. You think she really knows where it is?"

"She must think so," Fats said. "Otherwise, none of what she's doing makes any sense."

"Maybe not even then."

She didn't really have a plan, Alec Duggar said, just impulses. She'd hemmed and hawed, then decided she couldn't wait till morning, she had to go before it got dark. She persuaded him to take her out to Blackpool Estates and leave her there.

"She didn't want you to stay with her?"

"I guess she figured I'd attract attention, or my truck would, something like that. I think she didn't want anybody to know what she was doing. Maybe she just wanted to get shuck of me. But I don't really know. I didn't like leaving her, it's a spooky place out there, even in the daytime, but she. . ."

She had a phone, she'd call him to come get her when she'd found the briefcase, the old man said. If she didn't, she'd sleep in Strutter's trailer and start looking again in the morning. He was supposed to tell Fats he could forget about helping her. "She said to say she didn't need you. Nobody's after her now. She ain't scared no more."

"Except of me," Fats said angrily. "So you're going out there now?"

Duggar didn't answer for a moment. Then he said, worry weighting his words, "She hasn't called me. And she ain't answering her phone."

"We can be there in a few minutes, Mr. Duggar," Fats said. He preferred not to go out to Strutter's alone. He didn't want help. He wanted a witness.

The old man shuffled uncertainly in the doorway. Then he said, "Let me lock up."

Small squalls of wind whipped up dust as they drove. Fats's pickup bucked gusts on Main Street. When they passed the Dirt Plant, Alec Duggar suddenly sighed heavily, giving Fats a bleak, silent look.

Fats too was worried. There might be several reasons Salome wasn't answering her phone, but none eased his concern.

Wind bent the blackish reeds that lined the wave-wrinkled blackish water. The door to Strutter's trailer banged. Torn public administrator's tape across Jenny Jones's door fluttered and snapped.

"She ain't here," Duggar said.

"Let's see," Fats said.

In Strutter's kitchen, an empty Coke can stood on the tiny table. Fats sat for a moment. From here Strutter had watched over the briefcase, or so he said. Fats looked out the small window: patch of reeds, wreck of dock, dark water.

Alec Duggar came in out of the wind. "That Coke—she was drinking it when we got here."

Fats rose. "She's been and gone, looks like."

They stepped outside. Fats looked around carefully. The wind had blurred the prints of feet and tires. The reeds around the pool could be searched, but neither he nor Duggar had brought waders. The rotting pier shivered in the wind.

There was nothing to indicate that a crime had been committed, and it was too soon to file a missing person report. Alec Duggar, hearing that, looked out onto the pond with dismay. "That mean we can't call the sheriff?"

"Nope," Fats said, taking out his cell.

In a minute he had Dale Zahn on the line. In ten minutes, Dale's cruiser was churning dust into the wind as it approached. A few minutes after that, both Alec Duggar and Fats Rangle had told the sheriff what they had to tell him.

Soon two other sheriff's vehicles arrived. Caroline Sam started a search, directing two young male deputies. One donned waders and stepped into the reeds. The other moved out into the desert in a carefully calibrated circle.

"No point in worrying, Mr. Duggar," the sheriff said. "She might have found what she was looking for, walked over to the highway, and caught a ride out of here."

"She'd of come home," Duggar said.

"Not necessarily," Dale Zahn said. "Not with a briefcase full of money."

The old man sagged, nearly fell onto the fender of Fats's pickup. "I never should of let her talk me into bringing her out here."

Dale Zahn spat in the dust. "Blame enough to go around. Maybe you remember we passed each other on the road by the Dirt Plant. It was pretty obvious where you were going. If I'd been doing my job, I'd have come and shooed you off. This is still a restricted area."

Alec Duggar seemed dazed. "So now what do we do?"

"Nothing, for a while," the sheriff said. "Fats can run you home. We'll look around here some more, but I don't imagine we'll find anything. This afternoon you can come in and make an official MP report. Then we can send word to other agencies to keep a lookout."

Caroline Sam came up. "We're short waders. Can I borrow yours?"

The sheriff went to his cruiser, opened the trunk, and removed a pair of waders stuffed neatly behind a large, locked, steel evidence box. He gave the old man one of his reassuring smiles. "Who knows—maybe when you get home she'll be sitting in the sun on the front steps."

She wasn't.

The rest of the day, Fats kept busy. He gave the auctioneer a tentative list of items and machines they were selling. He called the vet, who said she could come out the next day and look over the animals. He and Bill and Buddy cleaned tack and hardware. At noon they ate chicken salad sandwiches with Mary, who was smiling. Word of their expansion plans was out. She'd already had inquiries about the new facilities. "The bank loan will put us in good shape," she said. Then she grinned. "Even able to afford galivantings to Las Vegas, if there aren't too many of them."

"Yeah," Fats said. "We'll see how that goes."

The wind died down. The temperature rose. Bill and Buddy went into town, while Fats spent the afternoon with the horses, checking, chatting. Omar concerned him, seemed lethargic, the rasp in his respiration more noticeable. Fats determined to see that the vet gave the old guy a good looking over.

When the twins got home from school, Fats called Alec Duggar. He'd heard nothing from no one. He'd filed a missing person report. He sounded both frustrated and depressed.

After dinner Fats called Dale Zahn. The search of the Blackpool reeds hadn't turned up anything. Neither had inquiries at the bus station and the truck stop. Still, the sheriff thought Salome had probably found what she was looking for and was gone. "Whatever's happening," he mused, "she's on her own. It's pretty clear Duggar is telling the truth, and nobody else knew she was out there."

"Except you," Fats said.

The sheriff went silent for a moment. Then he said, "Yeah, I should have figured it. I wasn't thinking. I had my mind on other things. But she's probably lit out. Easy enough walk to the highway. Some trucker or buckaroo probably came along and picked her up—we'll know who in a few days. That sort of thing, somebody says something eventually."

Fats didn't respond.

"If not, there's only one place she could be."

Fats had been thinking that too. "We'll know when? Tomorrow?"

"I'd guess. That's quick, but there isn't much to her, other than the boobs. Tits on a stick."

Decomposition. Gases. She'd soon float to the surface. Putrefaction. Tits on a stick. Right enough. So why, Fats wondered, did it trouble him?

"I'll have deputies keep checking," Dale Zahn went on. "Meanwhile, we're getting the word out, missing person protocol and all that. People will be watching out for her. She'll try to lose herself, but all that money will throw her. She'll make a mistake, somebody'll spot her."

"Maybe," Fats said doubtfully.

He expressed the same doubt when he talked later to Ramona. She too was dubious. "She's not stupid, it sounds like."

They talked too about Boo. His body had been found after an anonymous tip. "That would be your pal Doc Wills," she said.

"He'll stay my pal," Fats said, "as long as he's got my Colt."

They agreed to get together.

The vet showed up right after breakfast. She checked over Omar carefully, pronouncing him without disease or injury but faltering. Fats was hearing in the horse's breathing the catarrh that comes with aging, the inevitable degeneration. The old horse was in no distress, but he wouldn't live much longer. He shouldn't be ridden anymore.

"Put out to pasture," Bill said. "Like a death sentence, ain't it?"

Fats, with Buddy and Bill, trailed the vet as she worked her way through the stable. But his mind was on Vi Barlow and how he was going to tell her about Omar. He didn't want to do it by phone, but he couldn't really justify another trip to Las Vegas so soon. He was about to stroll over to the house to talk to Mary about it when his phone burred.

Dale Zahn was in his office with Carroll Coyle, who'd just flown in. He wanted to meet. Fats didn't, especially, but to distract himself from his dilemma he agreed to come into town.

He didn't hurry. He talked more with the vet, asked her to write up an assessment of Omar that he could give to Judge Barlow. He waited while Mary made up a list of groceries for him to bring back. He gassed up at the truck stop. So it was some time before he parked his pickup in front of the courthouse annex.

The only other vehicle at the curb was a rented Jeep Cherokee, its engine running. From it climbed a blond, sharp-featured young man who hid his gaze behind green-tinted Ray-Bans. He was of decent size, hatless, slim in tan jeans and pale brown polo shirt. He moved with an athletic, almost feline ease. His face was expressionless.

His silence was for show, Fats knew. Still, he guessed the guy would have skills. Fats nodded and made for the sheriff's office.

Inside, the air-conditioner hummed. Caroline cocked an eyebrow and smiled. He rapped on Dale Zahn's door and went in.

The sheriff lounged behind his desk. Carroll Coyle rose quickly from a chair. "Took your own sweet time, didn't you, Rangle?"

"Things to do," Fats said.

"You wanted privacy, Mr. Coyle," the sheriff said. "The interview room's available."

Fats showed Carroll Coyle out into a narrow hallway, through another door into a room with a table, precast chairs, and an assortment of electronic devices. On a small box fitted into one corner of the ceiling a tiny red light blinked.

Coyle sat at the table. Today he was in sage-colored linen and a silk shirt the blue of the desert sky. His face was slick and red. "You're playing a dangerous game, Rangle."

"No game," Fats said. "What can I do for you?"

"You had her and let her go," Coyle spat. "You knew where she was and didn't tell us. Now she's gone again."

Coyle seemed to know almost everything. Where he got his information was the question.

"And maybe this was by design. Maybe she found the briefcase and got you to give her transportation out of here. Or maybe you've got her stashed in some desert shack somewhere. Or maybe you took it from her and throttled her and hauled the body to some godforsaken spot and dumped it in a hole. Maybe . . ." He leaned forward, tried to look fierce. "There's lots of maybes, Rangle, possibilities. Another one is that it's been you all along—you found the briefcase, you've got the money, you're just waiting for things to die down before you spend it."

This last came almost a question. Fats ignored it.

Coyle sat back. "But what actually happened doesn't matter. Because now it's all on you."

His cadences were the sort that come with rehearsal. He'd been practicing his little speech.

"You understand, Ex-Fucking-Deputy? They've had enough. They want that briefcase and they don't have it and they blame you. So far they've been nice, but they're through with that. You won't like what's coming."

Fats didn't bother to ask who Coyle was talking about.

Coyle grinned grimly. "They're going to. . .encourage you. The lot of you."

Fats gave him a new attention. "What does that mean?"

"Up to now, you haven't had a reason to want the briefcase returned," Coyle said, grinning more widely now. "Not a compelling reason, that is. So they're going to give you one. Maybe more."

"Meaning. . ."

"It might mean that the county commissioners find that they can't approve your, um, unretirement, that you don't become an ex–ex-deputy. It might mean that lawyers and accountants get involved in your loan application and choke it to death. Or that inspectors from every government agency known to mankind descend on Cherry Creek Stables, or that a rumor spreads that the Rangles are abusing the horses they board. . ."

Fats felt his fists go heavy, his gut muscles hard. The flesh on his chest and back began to quiver. Only the blinking red light in the corner of the ceiling kept him in his chair.

They could do all that, he knew. They were corrupt and the system was corrupt and they could manipulate it to get done, one way or another, anything they wanted.

And there was nothing he could do about it.

Carroll Coyle rose, shot his gold-linked cuffs. "I flew all the way up here this morning, Ex-Deputy, to tell you all this personally, face-to-face, so there's no misunderstanding."

Fats said nothing.

"Do you understand?"

He got out the word. "Yes."

Carroll Coyle smiled nastily. "Do you have any questions, Rangle? Any questions at all?"

Fats couldn't trust himself to move, to rise, for fear that his body would take control and get to battering. So he stayed in his chair as he said quietly, "Still blue about Terry Blume?"

Coyle flushed angrily, jerked open the door. "Fuck you, Rangle. Just. . . fuck you."

Alone, Fats sat for several minutes. Finally, after a violent shudder, the tension began to seep from his muscles. By the time he got back to the sheriff's inner office he was nearly under control again.

Dale Zahn went to the small refrigerator. "Coyle isn't happy. Not too bright, either. Says he wants privacy, then goes into a wired room. But maybe he was just worried about his new young man, waiting out there in the sun." He handed Fats a bottle of water, opened his own. "Horst, the guy's name. Not as pretty as the other one, is he? What do you make of him?"

"He's not a personal assistant."

"Not a bodyguard either. More a keeper?"

"Could be."

"He's under pressure, Coyle?" Dale Zahn grinned. "Then he's stupid enough to go and threaten you."

"Not just me," Fats said, clenching his jaws. "My family. Their livelihood."

"What I heard was enough to make it my business, Fats. Pinenut County business." His grin faded. "This briefcase bullshit. Anything more you can tell me?"

Fats drank half the water in the bottle. He was angry again. "What briefcase? I don't have anybody's briefcase. I haven't seen anybody's briefcase. I don't even know if there *is* a fucking briefcase, and neither does anyone else, not for sure. Bullshit is the word, all right."

The two men sat silently for a while. Then Dale Zahn said, "It all hangs on the girl, doesn't it? Salome, Edna, whatever her name is. Strutter told her he had big money, that he'd hidden it, where—in plain sight?"

"Maybe he did," Fats said, "or maybe he was just feeding her a line of talk."

"If so, she bought it. The question is, do we?"

Fats didn't know. That evening, he asked Ramona. She agreed that the dancer's behavior could be explained only by a conviction that the money was hidden at Strutter's place. She told him too that the authorities weren't especially interested in who might have put a bullet in a bald bouncer's heart. In Las Vegas, which saw two hundred-plus murders a year, what was one more?

He didn't tell her about Carroll Coyle's threats. He didn't tell Bill and Mary either. He wasn't going to tell anyone until he'd decided what he was going to do.

The next morning, once chores were done and the twins were off to school, unease took him to the desert and Blackpool Estates.

Vehicles were gathered before Strutter's trailer. The sheriff stood at the ruined pier, looking out over the water. He didn't turn as Fats joined him. "I was about to call you."

Fifty yards out, fabric floated. And flesh.

"Come up tits first," said the sheriff. "Figures."

Fats stood silent, suddenly stricken.

Tits on a stick, Dale had said the day before. But how would he know?

A Search and Rescue team paddled a rubber raft out to retrieve the body. As they lifted the remains from the boat, Fats saw the features blurred by bloat, the swell and sag of the flesh.

The sheriff took a quick but careful look. "No obvious sign of assault."

"Accident? Slip on the slick pier, bang her head, and fall in, something like that?"

"I don't think so." Dale Zahn looked down at the old wooden platform, rotting posts, two-by-four braces, planks slicked with slime. "This is a suspicious death, at least."

"Part of the briefcase bullshit?"

"Say she found it," Dale Zahn said, nodding. "And somebody killed her for it."

Fats now said nothing.

The sheriff went on, in a different tone, "Just to make it official, where were you when this happened?"

"Home," Fats snarled. "Cherry Creek. Bill and Mary will confirm. Why don't you give them a call right now, before I have a chance to tell them what to say?"

"Easy there," Dale smiled. "It's all routine, you know that."

His anger ebbing, Fats nodded. "Yeah, okay. But how about you?"

"Where was I?" The sheriff's smile became a grin.

When he'd seen Alec Duggar and the girl on the road by the Dirt Plant, the sheriff said, he was on his way to his office, where he spent the next several hours working up a tentative budget to present at the upcoming county commissioners' meeting. Two deputies could vouch for him. He left about midnight. Donna was home when he arrived a few minutes later.

"The problem is," Fats said, "other than Alec Duggar, there's no one else involved in this. Nobody except the bunch in Vegas."

"There's somebody else. We just don't know who."

"Or why," Fats said.

"To sum it up, we don't know squat."

Fats followed Dale Zahn over to their vehicles. The sheriff was off to see Alec Duggar, to give him the bad news and ask him to come in to formally identify the body. Once he got the report from the medical examiner, he'd decide what to do.

Fats nodded, suddenly sure. "But I don't have to wait, do I?"

The sheriff frowned. "I don't want you mucking around in this, Fats. You could screw up the whole investigation. You don't have any authority."

"Probably just as well," Fats said.

The sheriff's gaze hardened. His jaw set. "This is my county, Fats. It's my job to handle this, and I will."

"And it's my family that's being threatened," Fats said.

"I'm telling you officially. I'll use the law on you if I have to. Just stay out of it."

"Yeah, all right," Fats said. But they both knew he was lying.

12

Fats knew he need do nothing. The next move was not his.

At Cherry Creek, waiting, he busied himself with the Glock .38 that had belonged to the dead bouncer Boo. He brushed and lubricated and polished, taking an odd comfort from the pistol's heft and balance. Like the men and women carrying firearms in Blue Lake, he didn't really expect to use the weapon. But he wanted all to know he had one near to hand.

At midday, he had lunch with Bill and Mary. He still hadn't told them about Carroll Coyle's threats. He would if it became necessary and when the time was right.

That afternoon he drove through the heat of the day into town. Alec Duggar was out in his yard, on his knees as if praying to his roses. He seemed dazed, heat-stricken. Fats offered condolences but wasn't sure Duggar actually heard him.

He drove over to the veterinarian's compound and picked up the report on Omar. The old gray could pass on anytime now. All anyone could do was keep him contented.

Fats was back at Cherry Creek, out in the pasture with a trenching tool clearing clogs from the narrow irrigation channels when the phone call came. He listened to the burr, felt the quiver of his telephone. Caller ID showed him what he didn't want to see. At last he answered, listened.

She wanted him to come back down to Las Vegas. They needed to talk. Face-to-face. Something had come up. It was important—no, more than that, for them it was critical, crucial, complicated. She didn't want to try to explain over the phone. She asked him to trust her. She said that if he cared for her he'd come.

He worked to keep out of his voice his distress, and his anger. He offered a couple of objections, so that when he agreed he would seem to have been persuaded. He had business to take care of in Blue Lake, he lied at last, but he could be at her house about midnight. She said she'd be waiting.

A half hour later, Glock on the seat beside him, he was on his way to Las Vegas. He didn't really see the desert he drove through. He could only silently repeat her words, testing them for truth, and search his memory of her voice for some signal that her phone call didn't mean what it must.

The sun settled, the day darkened. Las Vegas lights contested the night. The interstate carried him through the neon clamor to an exit and, soon, a dimly lit suburban stillness. He found and then coasted along a curving lane until he saw, two blocks ahead, Ramona's SUV parked in her drive. Her garage was closed. Her living room window was tightly draped.

Fats turned at a corner, circled back to a high-rise apartment building he'd passed, and parked inconspicuously in its lot. He took up the Glock, eased himself out into the night, slipped the pistol under his shirttail, and set off.

Downtown neon paled the city sky. In the faint light of neighborhood street lamps, sprinklers sprayed grass, washed sidewalks, dampened gutters. Little else moved—a passenger jet climbed steeply away from the airport, a slow sedan braked at a cross street, a man in his open garage smoked a cigarette. From far off came the *ack-ack* of a deaccelerating motorcycle engine. Nearer, air-conditioners whirred and hummed. Murmurs that might have been voices, sounds that might have been music, seeped from houses out into the silence.

Fats took it all in. Nothing seemed, to his sense of things, out of place. He made his way around Ramona's block, getting a good look at her small backyard and patio and draped French doors. When he could again see her front entrance, he found and stepped into a patch of darkness. He watched for movement, shifts of shadows, and listened for sounds of stir. He attended to the night.

Several houses down, a mountain lion emerged from a shadow. Not large, apparently young, no doubt hungry, alert but easy, the cat padded down the street. In his own shadow, Fats got a grip on the Glock, even as he understood there was no danger. The lion was looking for something to kill, but not Fats. Its graceful stride said that, at the moment at least, it didn't mind sharing the silence with another hunter. Fats watched until the lion turned and disappeared into the darkness.

For a long while, Fats looked and listened. The lion didn't return. No vehicles passed by. The man in the open garage came out, lit and smoked another cigarette, flipped the butt into the street, and rolled shut the door.

Finally, Fats slipped out of the shadow, walked quietly to his pickup, drove back to Ramona's house, and parked at the curb. He cautiously approached the house and pressed her doorbell.

She opened the door. She was still in uniform. Her eyes seemed especially large. "Fats," she said with a warmth her eyes belied, "I'm so glad you could come."

She showed him into her empty living room, then stepped into an embrace, one arm encircling his shoulders. She pressed her body to his, whispered, "Trust me."

Something in the feel of her, her animal existence, persuaded him.

The push of her pelvis pressed against the Glock. Then her free hand found it. Fats tensed. She lifted the automatic from his belt, moved back, and aimed the pistol at his abdomen. "Against the wall," she ordered, her voice now loud, edged with anxiety.

He watched her watch him move. Her eyes were speaking to him, but he didn't know what they were saying.

"It's all right," she called out then. "I've got his gun."

In the silence, Fats had the sense, as once before, that the house was unoccupied. Then footfalls scuffed the kitchen linoleum, a deep wheeze disturbed the air, and into the room, the .38 Colt Special in his clawlike hand, came Doc Wills. He was bent nearly double, after air. His eyes were wet, the skin under them sagging and dark. He smiled sourly. He leveled the Colt at Fats. "I had a hunch, when you walked into my place, it might come to this."

Fats watched him, a dying old sociopath dressed like a tourist with a gun in his hand.

"Done by your own weapon," Wills panted. "Is that what they call irony?"

Fats had only one possible move, a sudden rush, but his chances were thinner than slim. There was too much space between them.

Hoping to distract or at least stall Wills, Fats said, "You can't be doing this for money."

"Why else?" Wills said. He grinned, his eyes never leaving Fats even as he said to Ramona, "I hope this ex-deputy ain't important to you."

"He is some, yes," she said. She raised the Glock, as if to hand it to him. Fats saw that Doc Wills didn't see that she had her finger on the trigger.

The pistol's report cracked sharply but didn't resound. The Colt Special slipped from Wills's fingers. He gaped, gasped as he sank to his knees and folded onto the floor. He lay clutching his abdomen. Blood seeped between his fingers. He looked at Fats, at Ramona. His mouth moved. He seemed to want to say something. Instead, he died.

Ramona Clare kept the pistol aimed at him, but her hand holding the weapon quivered. Then her whole body began to tremble. She looked at the Glock, then at Fats, helplessly.

Fats took her in his arms, pressed his solid flesh against her shock. He held her silently, securely, until her body stilled. He led her to the sofa, sat her down, took the Glock and stuffed it in his waistband. She looked at him, but her eyes were empty. She was absent, much as Alec Duggar had seemed at his roses.

Fats too was not wholly present. It had all taken place so suddenly. He was still uncertain what, in fact, had just happened.

He left her to give the corpse a quick check. There wasn't a lot of blood. The entry wound was small, and the bullet was still in the body, which lay on an old solid shag rug. Fats fingered the dead man's wallet, which contained a few twenties, credit cards, and identification as a licensed investigator and retired Las Vegas Metro sergeant. A front pants pocket held a set of keys. His other pockets were empty. Clipped to his belt was a turned-off cell phone.

Fats took most of the money. With his shirttail he wiped what he'd touched, then got everything back into the appropriate pockets. He left the phone on the dead man's belt. He put the Glock in Wills's hip holster and stuffed the Colt in his own waistband.

He went back to the sofa, sat again beside Ramona, and spoke softly, much as he did to horses. He told her what he was going to do. She didn't seem to take it in.

"I didn't . . ." She seemed dazed, as if powerfully struck. "I thought I was tougher than this."

"Tough enough."

She nodded at the Colt. "Are you going to shoot me?"

He didn't answer.

"You should," she said.

"Shut up," he said.

She told him then that she hadn't planned to kill Doc Wills. She hadn't planned anything. Maybe she'd be able to distract him, give Fats an edge—that was as far as she'd gotten. She couldn't think, all she'd known was that Fats was walking into a death trap. When he appeared, she'd acted on impulse.

Fats wasn't sure he believed everything she said, but for the moment it didn't matter.

He didn't really plan now either. All he could think of to do was to create confusion. He rolled up the body in the rug, and carried it out to his pickup, and slid it into the bed. The old ex-cop was husklike, so wizened that Fats, lifting, hardly felt his weight, for a moment feared that the body wasn't there. He thought of Strutter's ashes, so little left of him. He remembered the drainage ditch. Putrefaction.

He didn't like leaving Ramona, but he had to get done what he was doing. He got in the pickup and drove off.

The city was beginning to still, the heat to subside. Streets were less traveled, sidewalks less crowded. Along the Strip, lost-looking partyers and homeless scavengers shuffled and weaved, trucks and vans at casinos brought supplies in or hauled waste out, water splashed pointlessly, neon flickered and flashed. Downtown, the few figures still on the streets seemed stunned, survivors of an assault. Fats drove with the AC off and his window rolled down, listening to the hum and hiss of the city, smelling the faint rot that a desert breeze would scour from the night.

Near the train station, Fats passed a police car that pulled out and followed him. And at last he realized how utterly stupid what he was doing was, hauling a body in an open pickup bed through a city full of police officers and CCTV cameras. But there wasn't much he could do but keep on going. When the police car pulled off, Fats, absurdly angry, laughed out loud.

At the drainage ditch, he got out, tugged the rug-wrapped body from the pickup bed, carefully slid it down the incline to the ditch, and dragged it into the tunnel, where it couldn't be seen from the street. He unrolled the body, tugged the rug deeper into the dark, and left it.

His movements echoed into silence. The darkness seemed complete. The damp air clung to his skin. Again he thought of Strutter, putrid. Again, suddenly, he was angry.

Stepping back into the open, he saw someone looking down at him. In the shadowed night the man was mostly face, hollowed out, gouged. He didn't move as Fats slowly climbed to the street. He smiled a toothless smile. "Got a find?"

He looked much like Doc Wills, years younger but long ruined, by methamphetamines, most likely, gaunt, in a baggy Raiders T-shirt and droopy jeans, strands of greasy dark hair, face torn at. Fats thought of the mountain lion. This derelict would hardly make the cat a meal.

"A dead body," Fats said.

The dark absence that was the man's smile grew larger. "Gonna share?"

Fats reached in his pocket and took out two of the $20 bills he'd lifted from Doc Wills's wallet. He held out the money. "Have fun."

The man swiped at the cash. His smile disappeared. "Can I see him?"

"He ain't going anywhere," Fats said. "But you probably better light out. Cops find you anywhere around here, they'll give you a hard time about the money."

"Yeah," the man said. He stuffed the bills in his pocket. "You won't tell, will you?"

"No," Fats said. He watched the man scuttle down the street. Then he got in his pickup and drove back to Ramona.

She was in her terrycloth robe, showered and sipping bourbon. She was upset. At him. "Everything you did was wrong."

The body would be found and identified. The police would do the forensics and study CCTV footage and, more than likely, show up at her door. Did he wipe away fingerprints? What about DNA, his on the body, hers on the rug? Doc had come by taxi, so his car wouldn't figure in any investigation, but his phone records would lead them to Fats. And once the police were asking him, and her, questions, what sort of story could they tell that would explain both the killing and the dumping of the body? "We should have reported it, told them the truth."

"Not necessarily," Fats said. He'd wiped away his fingerprints. The authorities would have the DNA they found on the body, and on the rug if they made the connection, but nothing to compare it to. He could account for the phone calls Doc Wills had made to him. The PI's phone had been off, so it couldn't be traced. There was no reason for the cops to suspect them of anything.

"A good detective could get to us eventually." She half filled her glass from a bottle of Jim Beam on the coffee table and handed it to him.

Fats drank bourbon. "But maybe they won't look for us that hard."

He worked it out as he talked. Normally, the suspicious death of a retired officer would bring the police out in force, after vengeance for one of their own. If that happened, as she said, they were in trouble.

"On the other hand," Fats considered, "Doc Wills was a killer, a man all honest cops, and even some corrupt ones, won't be sorry to see gone. Some might figure he was overdue a bullet in the gut and not much care who put it there."

Sergeant Clare again shook her head, slowly, silently.

"He was talking about irony," Fats said. "Finding the lethal weapon in the dead man's holster ought to qualify. The police might even figure it for a mob or gang hit."

"Or they might not," she said. "It's fifty-fifty at best, Fats."

"Maybe we can improve the odds," he said. He held out the empty glass for a refill.

If they were to tell the authorities the truth, they'd have to tell it all, including the story about a search for a briefcase full of gray money, and of the deaths of a muscle-bound bouncer, a young buckaroo, and the exotic dancer he bragged to. That story involved the social-climbing owner of a strip club, a powerful political agent, the CEO of a billion-dollar company, a cow county sheriff, and maybe even a former judge touted as a future governor or senator.

Ramona had seen where he was going, was shaking her head even before he finished. "You think you can lose a murder investigation because it would threaten reputations?"

Fats shrugged. "Used to happen all the time around here. Nobody thought corruption. It was just the Las Vegas way of doing business."

"Things have changed, Fats," she urged.

"Not a lot, I'd bet," he said. "But let's see, shall we?"

They talked it through, eventually devising something resembling a plan. Or at least the start of one. And a simple story. As far as anyone was concerned, Fats had had truck trouble in the desert and got into Las Vegas barely in time to take Ramona to breakfast. Neither of them had seen Doc Wills.

They had a couple of hours. Ramona lay down. Fats cleaned away the few blood spatters he could find, picked up the shell casing, took a shower, and lay down beside her. Neither spoke.

At last, in the pre-dawn dimness she said, "I'm sorry, Fats."

"Later," he said.

They didn't speak again of death and dying until they were settled in a small booth in Huffman's, surrounded by loud, laughing police officers and their weapons and paraphernalia, and by silent television screens flashing images and ads. In the din, Fats went over the plan, such as it was. She would go to work as usual, where she would keep an ear out for any reports of a body found in the storm drain system. He would phone for an appointment to see Judge Barlow about the vet's report on Omar. He would also try to get in touch with Carroll Coyle.

Fats didn't like involving Coyle, but he wasn't about to call around after David Mohr, who might not even be in Nevada, and he wasn't going to let Vi Barlow anywhere near this. It was Coyle or no one. Fats wouldn't tell him the truth, of course. He'd keep Ramona out of it, and he'd give Coyle just enough to make him believe that a serious investigation of Doc Wills's death could place in jeopardy important plans and careers.

"It's iffy," she said. "How can..."

She trailed off, her attention attracted by a TV shot of a young mountain lion ambling down an empty afternoon suburban street. The restaurant momentarily quieted. The cat continued nonchalantly on as closed captioning explained its presence: drought, loss of habitat, territorial needs.

"I saw him last night," Fats said. "That lion. He walked right past your house."

She pushed her breakfast aside. "They come into town once in a while. Kill raccoons that live in the sewer, sometimes a pet animal. Just enough to remind us they're around."

Fats nodded. The clatter of plates resumed, the hum and growl of voices.

"He knocks at my door, I let him in." Ramona looked at Fats, looked away. "He calls, says come, I come. Do this, I do it." She shook her head in disbelief. "It's always been that way."

It took him a moment: she wasn't talking about a mountain lion.

"I don't know why, Fats," she said. "I've never known. I mean, he's just..." She pursed her lips, tried to speak, gave it up. She took up her coffee cup, then put it down. "He used me to set you up for Doc Wills?"

"That's how it figures," Fats said.

A brawny two-striper came up, slowed, offered Ramona a leer. "Big night, Sarge?"

She glared until he was gone. Then she said, "I didn't know that's what it was. I mean, I worked it out, but not until after Doc showed up, when I couldn't call to warn you."

Fats said nothing.

"I would have, warned you, I mean. If I could have," she said. "If you don't believe anything else I've ever told you, Fats, believe that."

Fats believed only that everybody lied. Even so, in this case he was prepared to take her at her word. Not because he was persuaded that she was being truthful—her version had a couple of convenient omissions—but because it really didn't matter one way of the other.

"Besides, it didn't make any sense," she said, "Why would he want you dead?"

Fats tried to read her face but couldn't. He paused as a waitress silently filled their coffee cups.

"Ask him," he said.

"Fats, goddamn it—"

"I'm serious," he said. "In an hour or so, give him a call. Tell him I'm still alive, see what he says."

They parted with an awkward embrace. Her body brushed the Colt, again secure behind his waistband. He was taking a chance, carrying a weapon he'd reported missing, but in Las Vegas he had come to find comfort in the feel of it against his groin.

Fats walked to his pickup, feeling the heat of the day gathering on tarmac and concrete. Sitting in the cab, he made phone calls. He got Vi Barlow on her private line. She'd be home for the next hour. He told her he was on his way.

After his phone rang a long time, Carroll Coyle answered it himself. He'd been adjusting, Fats guessed: caller ID would have told him that Fats was still alive. He now agreed to meet at Judge Barlow's.

Mary said that everything at Cherry Creek was fine. She asked when he'd be home. He said soon. She said to say hey to Ramona.

To Fats, driving, the city seemed stained and muddied by the flood. Not so the desert, when he reached it. The narrow arroyo leading to Judge Barlow's was, but for isolated pools and a damp spot or two, dry. The collapse of the bank looked old and inevitable. The Barlow hacienda stood solid and white in the sun.

Water bubbled in the courtyard fountain. As he passed it, vet's report in hand, Judge Barlow appeared in the elm-shaded front doorway. She was dressed for serious business—pinstripes and silk scarves—but her smile was friendly. She showed him into a big, cool room, furnished with glazed tiles and large pots and leafy plants and colorful rugs, standard Southwest decor. One wall was dominated by a huge, smoke-blackened fireplace, the one Fats had seen Dale Zahn leaning against as he spoke with Carroll Coyle.

He declined the judge's offer of coffee. As they sat on a sofa, he handed her the report. "I won't take up much of your time," he told her. "But I wanted to give this to you in person."

He watched her read, watched her accept the vet's verdict. "I guess I knew," she said. "The doctor here, well, he was more positive, maybe he was just trying to ease my anxiety, but. . . I could tell. That's one of the reasons I was so eager to put him with other horses—I thought maybe it might keep him alive a little longer."

Fats nodded. "Maybe it will."

She sighed. "Thank you for bringing this to me yourself, Fats. It would have been all right if you'd just mailed it, but this...helps."

The small silence that followed signaled, Fats thought, that it was time for him to leave. But before he could stand, Judge Barlow said, "How are things in Gull Valley?"

She hadn't heard about Salome's death. He told her.

She sat very still until he finished. "But what could it be, Fats? What's important enough to kill for? Why this young woman?"

The question hung between them. Fats remembered: tits on a stick.

His phone buzzed, receiving a text message. He ignored it.

From outside came the sound of an arriving automobile. Now Fats did stand. "Carroll Coyle said he'd meet me here."

She walked him to the door, offered her hand. "Thanks again, Ex-Deputy."

Fats stepped into and then out of the shade of the elm tree.

Coyle came up. He, like the judge, wore pinstripes, beautifully fitted. Beyond the courtyard entry, parked next to Fats's pickup, was the Bentley convertible. Leaning on a fender was Coyle's new companion.

Coyle scowled, edgy, angry. "Don't go anywhere."

Fats said nothing.

Coyle stepped past him, stopped, turned. "You haven't heard, have you? He's dead."

"Who..." Then Fats connected. "Terry Blume, you mean? How...?"

Fats's reaction seemed to deepen Coyle's sneer. "Wait for me," he said, and strode off toward the front door.

After a stunned moment, Fats crossed to the fountain. From a hook screwed into the stone dangled a battered old tin cup. As Fats filled it, the blond man, still hatless, wearing green-tinted sunglasses, came over. He was older than Fats had thought, late thirties or thereabouts. "They call you Fats. How come?"

"I used to be," Fats said. He drank. Then he refilled the cup and handed it to, he remembered, Horst.

"Not lately, I'd guess." Horst drank and gave back the cup. Then he nodded at Fats's middle. "Risky place to keep a pistol. Mind if I take a look at it?"

Fats studied him. "What if I say no?"

Horst smiled, with a knuckle nudged up his Ray-Bans. "I could take it from you."

Fats withdrew the Colt, pointed it deliberately at the dirt. "Or I could shoot you with it."

Horst still smiled.

Fats handed him the Colt.

"Don't see many of these old guys around these days."

"You know guns?" Fats asked.

"I know them," he said, getting the fit and feel of the weapon. "I don't have a need for them, mostly."

"The Pinenut County sheriff," Fats said, "he thinks you don't really work for Coyle."

Horst turned the pistol back and forth. "Does he, now? What do you think?"

"You don't strike me as the personal assistant type. Keeper, the sheriff thinks."

"Quite a thinker, that sheriff," Horst said.

Fats nodded. "Did you ever notice how all you Deseret Construction guys wear the same Ray-Bans?"

"Ex-deputy, they told me you were," Horst said, handing back the Colt. "They said you were smart enough. Could be a nasty bastard, though."

"I'm a pussycat," Fats said. He stuffed the Colt in his waistband. "You know what happened to your predecessor? I thought he just got beat up."

"Subdural hematoma, they say," Horst said. "Bleeding on the brain. They missed it at first, then they knew it was there but couldn't find it, and while they were looking for it, they lost him. That's what I heard, anyway."

Fats nodded, although he didn't quite understand.

"You a particular friend of his?" Horst's eyebrow arched.

"Not really," Fats said. "Seemed a decent sort. Not many of those around these parts."

The two men stood silent in the sun. Then Fats said, "You're gonna get your brains scrambled. You need a hat."

Horst shrugged. "I've got one in the car if I need it. But I don't imagine we'll be here much longer. In fact. . ."

Even as he spoke, the front door had swung open. Carroll Coyle stood in the doorway, talking to Vi Barlow.

"I've got a couple of things to tell Coyle," Fats said quietly, "but not in your hearing. You can beat it out of him later, if you're a mind to. I just don't want you to get it from me."

"I suppose if I don't go along with this, you just won't tell him. And then I'd have to beat it out of you."

"I suppose," Fats said.

"Except that's not what I was hired to do," Horst said, and stepped away, heading for the Bentley.

Fats quickly checked his phone text. Doc Wills's body had been found.

Carroll Coyle came up, looking unhappy. In the glare of the late morning's sun, his forehead glistened. "What are you doing, talking to the judge without going through me?"

Fats remembered what David Mohr had said. "Dispensing with the middleman."

"Listen, asshole," Coyle fumed. "I've had about enough of your bullshit. Maybe it's time Horst teaches you a few manners."

"I don't think that's in his job description."

Coyle flushed. Frustration scraped at his voice. "Goddamn it, where's Wills? Is he dead?"

Fats held up his phone to show the text message. Coyle made a sound like a moan. "Did you kill him?"

"I don't go around killing people," Fats said. "I don't know why you keep thinking otherwise."

Before Coyle could respond, Fats had his say, tersely but specifically. Wills was dead. The police would want to go hard after his killer. But any serious inquiry would lead to other recent deaths and destroy the political plans of powerful parties. Those parties would not want that kind of investigation to take place.

Coyle understood immediately. "You think you can get a murder inquiry quashed?"

"Me, no. But some people you represent, yeah," Fats said.

"No way," Coyle said, shaking his head. "Not a chance."

"For you, though, it doesn't matter. You'll need to pass on the message. If they can bury the case, they will. If not, well, they're not going to like what comes."

Coyle made a connection. "But you're the one who doesn't want the police involved. You and whoever you're working for."

Fats said nothing.

"You're just a hired thug, aren't you, Ex-Deputy? Rotten to the core."

Now Fats smiled.

Again Coyle slowly shook his head. "You're finished, Rangle, you and that Cherry Creek bunch. You're dead meat."

Fats said nothing.

"You better hope Horst doesn't decide to deal with you."

Fats smiled. "Oh, I do."

Fats drove back to Ramona's. He parked at the curb, walked around the house, and stretched out in a patio lounger. Then he phoned her.

"What did he say?"

"He lied."

Fats said, "I'm at your place."

"Stay there," she said. "I'm taking the afternoon off."

He clicked off his phone. Then he slid his hat brim over his eyes. Soon he was asleep.

By the sun, three hours passed before he woke up. Ramona sat beside him, wearing shorts and halter, sipping an IPA. When Fats stirred, she rose and got him a beer. Then she sat, silently, waiting.

He told her what he'd told Carroll Coyle.

"So what do we do now?"

"You go about things as usual," Fats said. "I go back to Blue Lake and deal with Dale Zahn."

"Deal with?" She frowned. "What does that mean?"

"It means arrest him for the murder of Salome, née Enid Kachuba."

"Arrest . . . ?"

He laid it out for her: what he knew, what he guessed, what he believed.

Dale Zahn had killed Salome. He had the briefcase that Strutter Martin had stolen from the crashed plane. He knew that Fats knew this and would try to prove it and so had to be dealt with. Dispensed with. Killed. Simple as that. The details didn't much matter. At the center of everything was, as it had been all along, whatever was in that fucking briefcase.

Ramona objected. "You don't have actual evidence to support any of this, do you?"

"So I'll have to get him to confess."

Ramona finished her beer. She looked at him. "What about us, Fats? Is there an 'us' anymore?"

"As far as I'm concerned there is," he said.

"But I. . .I lied to you. I almost got you killed."

"Yeah," he said, "well, everybody lies."

13

When Fats got home at midnight, Bill was sitting on the porch. "Something's got the horses stirred up."

"All kinds of critters about. A lion prowling around in Vegas last night."

"Probably ain't that," Bill said wryly. After a moment he asked, "What's going on, Fats?"

Fats hesitated. Driving through the darkening desert, he had considered what he wanted Bill and Mary to know. Not everything, at least not now. He gave Bill the car trouble story and a more or less straight version of his meeting with Vi Barlow. He told him about Terry Blume.

"Too bad. I liked him," Bill said. "I guess maybe I'll keep on packing for a while."

"Wouldn't hurt."

"That old Colt in your crotch, you'll blow away your business if you ain't careful."

"I'm always careful," Fats said.

The brothers parted. Tired but not ready for sleep, Fats walked to the stables. The horses were calm, made night noises: snort, nicker, fart. Fats spoke to them all softly, soothing.

Nearly twelve hours later, he sat on a bench in Cottonwood Creek Park. In the elm-shaded block of scabby grass, a narrow flow gurgled down the slight incline to a concrete culvert. At an iron picnic table, two middle-aged women, clerks in the recorder's office, chatted over lunch. Fats paid them and the occasional passing vehicle little mind. He was watching the door to the jail annex.

The sheriff came out of his office, posed for a moment, then crossed over to Fats's bench. Again he looked costumed, wearing a stiff new Stetson and an ash-colored suit, a bright badge on his belt. He sauntered, assessing, satisfying himself that Fats was weaponless. "High noon, Fats? You've seen too many cowboy movies." He took a seat, smiled his politician's smile. "You wanted to talk. So talk."

They sat in the shade. Even so, Fats felt the late August heat slick the back of his neck. "You put a hired killer on me," he said angrily, through gritted teeth.

"You don't mean old Doc Wills, do you?" The sheriff nudged back his new hat. "I did ask him to have a talk with you."

"A talk with a pistol."

"Did you kill him?"

"Is he dead?"

"So she says. Sergeant Clare, that is. Ramona. Seems somebody shot him."

"Wasn't me," Fats said. "You still want me dead?"

The sheriff lazily pushed back his coattail, patted the S & W .357 Magnum in the holster on his hip, a theatrical threat. "Why would I want that, Fats?"

Fats clamped down on his anger. "Only you and Alec Duggar knew where she was. Salome. Enid Kachuba. Duggar wouldn't hurt her, so it had to be you."

"Pretty feeble. Somebody else could have come along." Dale Zahn looked amused.

"Tits on a stick, you called her," Fats said. "How would you know? You never seen her. The only time had to have been at Blackpool, when she died."

The sheriff grinned. "I have an alibi, for Christ's sake. I was in my office."

"An office with a frosted window and a back way out."

Dale gave a little laugh. "No one saw me use it."

"Somebody saw something." Fats said. "Somebody always does. You know I'll find out what happened, eventually. So you tried to stop me."

For a moment, the two men sat still, quiet. Around them settled a small-town summer silence, accentuated by the faint splash of the creek. The sheriff's smile, when it came, was different: tight, forced. "Pretty day today, everything quiet, peaceful." He nodded at the two women at the picnic table, now making motions to depart. "Marla and Joleen down there, if they heard such talk, they'd think you been out in the sun too long."

"You killed her for the briefcase," Fats said. "You found it, or she did, and you fought over it. I don't know the details, but it has to be."

The sheriff reset his hat. "The ME says she drowned. There are no signs of recent violence on the body. An accident, probably. You've got nothing that says otherwise."

"Nothing *yet*," Fats said.

Dale Zahn sat silently, looking out through the elms to a dust-dulled sky. Then he said, "I don't want to fuss with you about this, Fats. I've got more important things to take care of."

"Political things," Fats said. "Maybe fewer than you think."

"I'm open to a deal, Fats."

"If you mean splitting the airplane money," Fats said, "I might be interested if I could figure out what to do with it."

"That's the problem with money that officially doesn't exist," Dale agreed. "You try to spend it, people notice, and they wonder where you got it, and pretty soon you're in deep shit. But there's other things beside money." The sheriff was smiling his politician's smile again.

He wasn't going to run for reelection. When Fats returned to work, Dale would designate him chief criminal investigator. Of the deputies, Fats would be senior. Dale would back his candidacy for sheriff. Although Caroline Sam would have some supporters—newcomers, PC types—if Fats could keep from slugging people till then, he'd be the odds-on favorite.

Fats sat silent. Cottonwood Creek burbled. Dale Zahn grinned. "Donna's divorcing me. She thinks I don't know, but I'm halfway out of here already. I've been lining up my ducks in Vegas—people, money. If I play it right, I could end up Clark County sheriff some-day."

The Clark County sheriff was one of the most powerful offices in Las Vegas—in fact in Nevada. And once he reestablished residency, Dale Zahn would make a strong candidate, with a résumé not unlike Vi Barlow's: Nevada native, degrees from both universities, police career, law degree, cow county sheriff. With the right kind of friends, he could make a vigorous run.

But there were other implications, Fats knew. "One of these backers would have to be Deseret Construction. If you want their support, you'd best get their money back to them. Get on their good side."

The sheriff slowly shook his head, his smile widening. "You forget, Fats. We're talking about money that doesn't exist."

Fats was uncertain. "Politically, I'd think the money ain't as important to you as Deseret's good will."

"I know what I'm doing, Fats," the sheriff said.

Fats wasn't sure quite what to make of it all. "And what would you want from me?"

"Nothing. That is, I want you to do nothing. Leave the girl's death to me."

Fats thought about it. He wasn't opposed to taking bribes, it was the way of the world he'd long lived in, but he felt, for no reason that he could explain, a debt, almost a duty, to the young woman dead by drowning in the desert. "There's bodies, Sheriff. No one will waste a tear on thugs like Boo and Doc Wills, and Terry Blume's friends will make sure that that asshole Mitch is in prison for a long, long time, but Salome, she's owed."

Dale Zahn shrugged. "The books don't always get balanced, Fats, you know that."

"Yeah," Fats said. "But then there's Deseret Construction and the threats to my family and our business if they didn't get their fucking briefcase back."

"That's Coyle, I'd guess."

"And if it isn't?"

"Two can play that game," Dale said easily. "David Mohr wants to do business in Pinenut County, wants a business-friendly environment. I can see that he gets it. Or not. I'd guess we could persuade him to leave you folks alone."

Fats looked at him, at his easy smile, his can-do confidence. "You know what else is in that briefcase, don't you?"

"I can guess," Dale Zahn said. "We know the cash is political money. Mohr told you the papers were political. Candidates, contributors, favors, graft. Good old-fashioned corruption."

"That stuff goes on all the time," Fats said. "What makes this so important?"

"I don't know," the sheriff said. "The people involved, maybe. Or the amount of money—it's got to be billions."

Fats thought about it. Then he said, "Water?"

"Could be," Dale Zahn said. "Everything in Nevada depends on it."

Fats sat silent for a long moment. Then he stood. "Can you keep them away from Cherry Creek?"

"Yes," the sheriff said.

"Then," Fats lied, "I'll leave things be."

Fats decided to drop in on Alec Duggar, who was just finishing lunch. He accepted Fats's sympathy, offered him a seat in his living room and a cold Coors. He was doing all right, he said over the hum of the AC. He'd been busy with funeral arrangements, lining up a preacher, settling on a gravesite. "Found a nice plot, not far from my wife, and me when my time comes."

Fats sipped his beer.

"I been thinking about calling you," Duggar said. "I—the ME says it was an accident, probably, Enid drowning. Because she didn't swim—at least she never did when she was here. He, and the sheriff too, they say she must have went out on that old pier, you know how it's all slick with pond scum, and she slipped and fell in."

Fats sipped beer. "Could of been."

Duggar slid to the edge of his seat. "So where's the money? I mean, that's what she went out there for, to get the money. She said she knew where it had to be." His tone had changed. He smoothed a hand over his paunch. "Anybody with the sense God give a goose would know where it is."

Dale Zahn had the briefcase, the money, the papers, Fats knew almost to a certainty. But he decided to let the conversation go where it would. "I gave the property a good going over," Fats said. "So did the sheriff and his crew."

Alec Duggar made a sound like a horse's snort. "She said he told her he could see it from his kitchen, the money. Sitting there, when you look out, what do you see? You see the fucking water!" He seemed surprised, even embarrassed, at the obscenity. He tilted his beer can up, as if to hide behind it.

Fats thought about it. "Why don't we run out there and you can show me?"

Duggar hoisted his bulk up from the chair. "We can take my rig."

His ten-year-old Ram Charger was carefully kept, recently washed and detailed clean. He drove with an old man's caution through town, down the highway toward the Dirt Plant. Passing it, he asked a question. "If the money's there. . . what do we do with it?"

"Couldn't spend it," Fats said. "Best to give it back to Deseret Construction, I'd guess."

"I supposed we'd have to," Duggar said, disappointed. "There a reward? Finder's fee?"

"They might be grateful," Fats said. As they turned off onto the road to Coldwater Canyon, he added, "If we find it out here, any reward we'll split."

"Seems fair."

The old man lapsed into silence. From the highway, he drove slowly over the dirt road to the desolate scene.

Dust fell where it rose. Nothing else stirred. The medical examiner's tape still blocked the door to Jenny Jones's trailer. The door to Strutter's home still hung from a single hinge.

"Come on," Alec Duggar said. "I'll show you."

The air in Strutter's kitchen was still hot, foul, seemed itself rotted. Putrefaction. Duggar sat heavily at the tiny table, faced the small window. "Look."

Fats looked at what he had seen before. In the distance, a section of Jenny Jones's trailer. Closer, a slice of dirt. Reeds. Black water. And the old pier, mostly collapsed.

"If I wanted to hide something out here," Alec Duggar said, "it'd be in the water, deep. But I'd have to tie it to something, else I couldn't get it back up. Some sort of buoy would tell everybody where it was. The only thing to hook it to is the pier."

"I checked that pier, Mr. Duggar," Fats said.

"Why don't we just check it again?"

Fats shrugged, followed him out into the sun and over to the old dock.

Once the structure had been solid, set on sunken posts, cross-braced, the platform planks tightly fitted and screwed down, the safety rails secure. Now planking leaned underwater, posts supported nothing, a few boards were warped, rails gone.

Duggar stepped up onto the platform. "Let's see what we can see." The old wood shuddered under their weight. Wet, slippery planks made movement tricky. Nails and screws caught at their clothes as, on hands and knees, they searched for the briefcase.

They'd been at it nearly an hour when Alec Duggar, up to his elbows in water, raised up with a grunt. "Here," he said.

"Found something?" Fats asked.

"I did," Duggar said, bending over the water. "I found where it ain't anymore."

He showed Fats. A slimy post rose out of the dark water. In the slick, a trail had been scraped by the removal of a rope. The rope had been underwater, out of sight.

"There's a screw eye a couple feet down," Duggar said, tugging down his shirtsleeve. "About as far as a little guy or gal could reach."

Fats didn't bother to confirm it.

"Wrap it in garbage bags," Duggar said, "weigh it down, tie it to a rope, secure it to the post. Nobody'll find it unless they know where to look. Like Edna. She knew all along."

"Real iffy, Mr. Duggar," Fats said.

Duggar backed his bulk away from the water. "It was there. Somebody beat us to it."

"Could be," Fats said as he helped the big old man to his feet.

Alec Duggar eased his way off the pier. Soaked, sweating, he was red-faced with what Fats took for exertion until he realized that the old man was angry. "It's the sheriff, ain't it? He's the only one knew she was out here, him and you."

"There's been a lot of people out here, what with Jenny Jones dying and all." Fats brushed at his wet cuffs. "Could of been anybody— deputy, ME workers, gawkers even."

"No, it was him. Nobody else knew about the money," Duggar said. "Slicker. I wish I'd voted for you."

They drove back to town. As Fats was about to get in his own pickup, Alec Duggar said, "Tomorrow, 4:00. The funeral, graveside service. The heat of the day, I know, but that was the only time the preacher was available."

Fats hadn't thought about a funeral. But now he said, "Yeah, if I can."

Fats spent much of the rest of the afternoon with a curry comb, pleasing himself as much as he did the groomed animals. He gave a great deal of attention to Omar, brushing, talking, as if preparing the old horse for a final parade.

He was just getting ready to shower before dinner when his phone buzzed. Vi Barlow said that she was flying in to Blue Lake early the next morning. Dale Zahn had volunteered to show her some properties in Gull Valley, but before they set off, she hoped she might be able to stop in at Cherry Creek and say hello, and perhaps goodbye, to her horse. Carroll Coyle and his driver would be with them.

Fats couldn't resist. "Driver?"

"Yes, well. . ." She hesitated. "It's complicated, apparently."

Fats told the judge that she and whoever came with her would of course be welcome.

Night was gathering in the shadows when Fats called Ramona Clare. She had little to tell him. Detectives were working the Doc Wills case, but not very hard. The serial number of the Glock in his holster had been filed off, which led them to assume they were dealing with a professional hit. The body having been dumped in the storm drain suggested that Wills's death was somehow connected to that of Marlon "Boo" Enderby, but they didn't know how. Neither, it seemed, did they much care.

Ramona clearly was feeling less stressed. No one had contacted her. She didn't expect anyone to now. "Nobody's actually celebrating, but nobody's much bothered either."

Then Fats gave her the gist of his conversation with Dale Zahn and told her of his afternoon with Alec Duggar at Blackpool Estates. She listened, said little.

Then they talked of other, private things, past and possibly future. Fats had never before spoken so.

Early the next morning, a sheriff's cruiser emerged from the gap in the desert hills and rolled into the Cherry Creek lot. Mary stepped from the porch to greet her guests, and Dale Zahn made introductions—

Horst's family name, it turned out, was Schiller. Coffee was offered to and accepted by the men as Mary and Vi Barlow, after a brief discussion, took themselves off to the stables.

Over an hour passed before the women returned. Judge Barlow smiled her satisfaction that Omar was being well cared for—he acted, she said, tired but content and happy to see her. After their visit with the horse, Mary had given her a tour, much as Fats had shown David Mohr around not that long before. She thoroughly approved of what she saw and heard. Desert bred, she encouraged the plans to use water heretofore wasted.

The judge joked with Bill about his extreme good taste in women. Bill drolly responded that he'd known Mary was the only woman for him as soon as she told him so. A look passed between husband and wife then, and the men standing in the heat and dust went momentarily still, and Judge Vi Barlow smiled warmly, and Fats Rangle understood now how unnecessary he was to what of importance was happening at Cherry Creek.

Then the men began to impatiently shift and shuffle. They were an odd group, Fats thought, all in jeans except Carroll Coyle, whose lilac gray summer suit seemed the uniform of an alien army. What he and Horst, so far silent behind his Ray-Bans, were doing with the judge no one bothered to explain. Nor was it made clear just why the sheriff of Pinenut County would be guiding a group looking at desert real estate.

Now Dale Zahn raised an eyebrow. "We should go."

The judge invited Fats along. "It would be a little crowded, but we could fit you in."

"Sheriff knows Gull Valley better than me," he said, declining. "Besides, I got a funeral to go to this afternoon."

Vi Barlow nodded. "The young woman everyone was searching for, yes. Perhaps if we get back in time. . . ."

She said her goodbyes, and soon the group was gone.

The day went on for the Rangles. Mid-morning, when he and Bill came to the house for coffee, Fats told Mary, "Looks like you made a pal."

"It's easy to see why people are high on her," Mary said. "Nothing artificial there."

"Seems like," Fats agreed.

"But . . . what's happening with her and the sheriff?"

He shrugged. "Old Vegas friends. They got some political deal going, I hear."

Mary paused. "Nothing else?"

Fats took her tone, surprised. He hadn't noticed anything. "She's got too much sense to get tangled up with Dale Zahn."

"You never know about that kind of thing, Fats." She appeared to contemplate for a moment the mystery of men and women. "But I hope you're right. He's given Donna enough grief over the years. I don't imagine she can deal with much more."

Fats didn't tell her that Donna Zahn had already had enough. He went back to the horses.

After a late lunch and a long nap, Fats cleaned himself up, donned a freshly laundered white stiff-collared shirt, slipped on a silver and turquoise bolo tie, and wiped the dust from his good boots. He left his Colt holstered in a drawer.

Mary, dressed for company, waited for him. "Support for Alec Duggar. He's old and pretty much alone."

Neither spoke as he drove to and slowly through Blue Lake. The town seemed empty, left to the heat and the stillness. The highway was mostly untraveled.

At the cemetery, two young Hispanics Fats didn't know waited in an old pickup a discreet distance from the grave they would soon refill. No one else was there yet. Mary stayed in the cab, but Fats got out, reset his hat and, under a sun that seemed to pulse, walked among the dead.

He had no one here. His parents—his father long gone and unlamented, his mother more recently departed and missed—were buried in a small Gull Valley graveyard. He knew many of the names he met now, but they were of no significance to him, just names.

Headstones—shiny dark granite, soapy old marble—stood sentinel over remembered dead. Other stones lay flat, sunk into concrete pads, and metal markers provided by the county identified the several unstoned. A few of the graves showed halfhearted signs of recent care: bottles with withered stems or plastic flowers. The ground was covered with scattered sage and rabbit brush, clumps of stiff, bladelike yellow grass, and white decorative gravel. The drabness was interrupted only by the bright green of the artificial grass absurdly draped over the piled dirt from the freshly dug grave.

Fats drifted along the dusty pathways, going nowhere. He didn't think about the dead. He didn't really think about anything.

Stirring up a pale brown cloud, Alec Duggar turned his Ram Charger from the highway onto the cemetery track. He parked and climbed out, the jacket of his summer suit open to accommodate his girth. He offered Fats a formal hand. "They'll be along," he said. "The others. What there is of them."

Fifteen minutes later, the mourners were gathered graveside. The minister was young, nearly yet a boy, black-suited and sweating in the sun. He tried, not quite successfully, to look and sound solemn, saying what is said on these occasions. Then he read from a large Bible. Two sixtyish women in churchy dress looked on dutifully. The mortuary attendant and driver leaned against the white hearse, while the gravediggers remained in the cab of their pickup. Only Mary and Alec Duggar, heads bowed, attended to the service.

Fats listened, trying to remember the young woman dead in dark desert water, but he couldn't bring her to mind, couldn't see her. The preacher read, and Fats, hatless now in the heat, the glare, let the rhythms of the old, well-worn phrases work against the faint throb of a developing headache.

The preacher was reading a psalm about wind in the grass when Dale Zahn's county vehicle pulled in. Vi Barlow got out and came to stand with Mary and Alec Duggar, laying a small hand on the old man's arm.

Dale Zahn moved to the foot of the grave. The other two men remained by the car, Carroll Coyle squinting into the sun, Horst Schiller concealed behind his Ray-Bans, while the minister finished the psalm, then did the dust-to-dust business, closed the book, and stepped back, finished, looking to Dale Zahn as if for instructions.

Vi Barlow talked quietly with Alec Duggar, Mary with Dale Zahn. Fats, his headache a dull pulsation, his vision fragmented by the relentless shine of the sun, put on his hat and set off toward his pickup. He heard himself hailed but didn't stop.

The second call came loud, snarling, nasty. "Rangle! You!"

Fats Rangle stopped, turned.

Carroll Coyle was hollering—what he was saying didn't matter, his words were just noise, for Fats was suddenly, unaccountably, uncontrollably enraged. He saw Coyle's mouth move and was overwhelmed by the need to smash it. Choked by anger, he couldn't speak, he could only storm forward, all fury and fists.

And was knocked off-stride by a hand shoved into his chest. He swung his fist, hitting nothing, and was hit with three swift hard punches that put him down. "Take it easy, Fatman," Horst Schiller said, looming, lurking behind his sunglasses.

On his hands and knees, tasting blood, riding an adrenalin rush, Fats felt, as if after long restraint, finally free.

He got to his feet, wiped the back of his hand across his bloody mouth, crouched, smiled, and lunged into Horst's fists.

The blows came fast, hard, three, four, five punches, and Fats again was in the dust, this time on his back.

"Stay down, Rangle," Horst said evenly. "I'll chop you up."

Fats could feel torn skin on his cheekbone, his eyebrow, the bridge of his nose. His lungs burned, his back ached. He hadn't landed a punch. He was too clumsy, too old.

Slowly he rolled over and up, struggled again into a crouch. He made as if to stand, but instead he charged, low this time. He took two blows to the top of his head and one to his ear, but he got an arm around Horst's knees, then twisted, reached up and grabbed at his belt and dragged him off his feet.

Fats used his weight to pin Horst, prone, to the ground. The younger man got turned enough to bang his fists on Fats's back and neck, but without leverage the blows had little force. Then Fats got his forearms braced across Horst's shoulders. Horst couldn't move, but Fats couldn't punch.

They had fallen so that Horst's head hung above a corner of the concrete holding a small old granite stone. Fats saw. He reached up and closed his fingers in thick blond hair. He jerked Horst's head back. As Horst clawed frantically at Fats's grip, Fats felt the stiff, slightly sweat-damp hair, the tug and strain of scalp, resisting, the thin rind of skull. As if outside himself Fats understood that he could do serious injury. Lethal. He uncurled his fingers and let his hand slide away.

Feeling the release, Horst hunched his shoulders and with a powerful thrust bucked Fats aside. One leg free, he kicked out from under the other, and forced his way to his knees. Then he waited while Fats too got to his knees. Then he hit Fats again, once.

For Fats Rangle, all became glare, yellow and silver and blinding. Then gray. Then . . .

"You went berserk," Dale Zahn said.

They were in an examination room at the Pinenut County Clinic, Fats and the sheriff, waiting for the nurse to return with an insurance form. Fats was sewn up and plastered over but hurting. As the adrenalin wore off, the pain had begun, in his back from falling, his cheek and nose and forehead from sutured nicks, and his ear, now full of stitches fixing a large tear. But what pained him most was his head. The final blow had struck his temple. He was concussed, the doctor said: Tylenol, rest, no driving.

Fats checked his teeth with his tongue: nothing seriously loose. "I guess so."

He'd been out only briefly, half a minute or so. But he could recall little of what followed. Talk, mostly, most of it to Fats unintelligible. He got the outline from the sheriff.

Mary had seen to him while the others planned. Then Dale had hauled Horst Schiller and Carroll Coyle to the airport without Vi Barlow, who'd decided to stay with Omar for a while. Mary had driven her in Fats's pickup back to Cherry Creek, while Alex Duggar took Fats to the clinic, where the sheriff eventually appeared.

"You picked the wrong guy to go after, though."

"I guess so," Fats said again.

"A real hitter. He didn't even take off his shades." The sheriff grinned. "I'd have stopped it, but it didn't last long enough. Besides, it was a fair fight, looked like to me."

"And if he'd killed me," Fats said, "one of your problems would be gone."

The sheriff laughed. "You really are concussed, Fats."

There had been no thought of charges. If Dale had hauled in anyone, it would have been Fats. He'd thrown the first punch, futile as it had been. Horst Schiller had merely defended himself.

Officially, then, nothing had happened.

"But if anybody's life was in danger, it was his." The sheriff frowned. "You could have hurt him bad, Fats, if you'd smashed his head into that stone. Killed him."

Fats started to speak, then didn't. He could have killed a man and hadn't and now he didn't know what to say.

The sheriff frowned again. "You let him off the hook."

Fats felt again the damp, stiff slickness of Horst's hair, the crust of skull beneath it, the tug of clinging scalp.

"Yeah. Not like me at all," Fats said, as if to himself.

"Why'd you go after Coyle? What the hell did he say to you that set you off?"

Pain stopped Fats from shaking his head. "It wasn't what he said—it wasn't even about him, really. I mean, he was standing there in the middle of a cemetery, hollering at me, and I'm getting a headache, and he's a raging asshole..."

Dale Zahn laughed. "We'll put it down to too much sun."

"I can't explain it, really," Fats said, "even to myself."

And suddenly he wanted to talk to Ramona Clare. She would understand.

"We'll see if Blue Lake can sort it out. The story's likely to be all over town by now."

"I got my butt kicked," Fats said. "So much for getting elected sheriff."

"Are you kidding?" Dale Zahn laughed again. "It'll make the difference, if you run for office. You lost. Blue Lake will see that Fats Rangle is human after all."

Fats slipped off the examination table. "I just wish Judge Barlow hadn't been there, seeing me like that."

"Seeing the real Fats Rangle, you mean?"

14

Omar was down.

Out in the Cherry Creek pasture, the old gray gelding lay on his side, his breathing ragged and harsh, flanks and haunches quivering. From time to time he tried to get up, his efforts only sending stronger spasms rippling through his ineffective muscles. He lifted and shook his head. He rolled his eyes as if searching for something.

Mary and Bill looked on as Vi Barlow knelt beside the dying animal, stroking his muzzle, talking quietly to him. As Fats Rangle and Dale Zahn joined her, she gave them a sorrowing smile.

As she murmured to the horse, Bill filled them in. All had been done that could be. The other horses, unsettled, had been stalled. Bill had called the vet, busy with a difficult foaling on a ranch near Caliente, who told him they could wait for her to get there around midnight, or they could do themselves what needed to be done. Omar was failing, Bill had confirmed, and in some distress, but seemed soothed by the touch of Vi Barlow's hands, the soft tones and steady rhythms of her voice. She could have time with him yet.

They would bury him at the pasture's edge, where it dried into desert. Bill would dig the grave with a rented backhoe he'd arranged to pick up at dawn. Meanwhile, Mary had prepared a huge pasta salad, even though no one but the twins was especially hungry. She also insisted, when Vi Barlow said she wanted to see Omar into the earth, that the judge spend the night at Cherry Creek.

Fats understood all this uncertainly. Sometimes what he saw was blurred, what he heard echoed oddly. The pounding pain in his head had eased to a distracting ache, but even now he remembered little of the events in the Blue Lake Cemetery, which seemed to have happened long past, in a different world, to someone else.

No one remarked on his patched-up appearance or took especial notice when he excused himself and made his unsteady way to his small house and bed.

Evening was edging into night when Dale Zahn woke him. "Vi wants you to be part of the end, if you're up to it. Might bring your old Colt."

The sheriff had his own weapon on his hip. Fats didn't understand why they wouldn't use that.

He still hurt, not so much aching now as sore, and his stitches itched, especially those holding his torn ear in place. His mind wasn't quite clear yet, all that he saw and heard registered as not exactly right, but he was remembering more of the fight and its aftermath. He got out the old pistol.

The heat of the day had diminished, the air softened. The pale lot light cast familiar shadows, and the gloaming was full of desert sounds and scents. Fats and Dale Zahn walked into the pasture, joining the figures surrounding the dying horse. Mary and Bill, solemn, silent. Vi Barlow, standing now.

Fats handed her the Colt.

"I'll do it, if you want," Bill volunteered.

"No. I need to," she said, as if speaking to the dark and the desert. "It only seems right. I helped his foaling, almost twenty-five years ago."

Omar coughed, shuddered. He tried to lift his head.

Judge Vi Barlow cocked the Colt, aimed, and fired.

The old horse stiffened, sighed, died.

Vi Barlow swayed, sagged. Mary enfolded her.

Dale Zahn reached out and took the Colt. He grinned at Fats. "Evidence."

"We can't leave him for the night creatures," the judge said, a quaver in her voice.

"No," Mary agreed, "We'll watch. It's only a few hours."

"I just had a nap," Fats said. "I'll stay with him."

The three men stood silent as Mary led Vi Barlow out of the pasture. Bill squatted to examine the wound in the horse's forehead. "Well-placed shot. Not much mess. She's done this before. Or seen it."

Fats and the sheriff stayed silent.

Bill gave each a long look. Then he rose and headed off after the women.

"Evidence of what?"

The sheriff held up the revolver, spun the chamber. "Evidence of a killing, Fats. In Vegas the other day, I hear, a bunch of muscle was shot with a .38. There's lots of pistols of this caliber around, I know, but you reported this particular handgun stolen, yet here it is, in your possession. Las Vegas Metro would find that curious enough to want to take a look at it, you can be sure of that."

The stillness of the night settled around them. Stars had thickened, lowered. "But maybe you just misplaced it, then found it but forgot to report it to the police. Could that be?"

Fats wasn't sure how the sheriff had come to know what he seemed to know.

"So it's evidence of something. I probably won't give it to Vegas, though, not unless they ask me for it, and how could they know I have it if you and I don't tell them?"

When Fats remained silent, Dale Zahn's grin spread. "Then again, I can't give it back to you, can I? I guess I'll have to hang onto it."

Fats finally spoke. "Doc Wills shot that bouncer, Boo."

The sheriff snorted. "Sure he did. With your gun."

"He was doing the same thing you are, threatening me with it."

Dale Zahn laughed softly. "Now when did I threaten you, Fats? What with? I'm just letting you know your old pistol will be locked up for safekeeping like any other evidence of criminal activity I come across."

"So," Fats said, "is that including the briefcase everybody's after? It's evidence too?"

"It would be if I had it," the sheriff said. "Your cousin Strutter stole it from that plane. That means it was involved in a crime committed in my county. But I told you I didn't have it."

"Everybody lies," Fats said.

The sheriff grinned.

Fats touched his fingers gently to his bandaged ear. "You ever figure out what all the fuss is about? What's in the briefcase besides money?"

"Evidence," Dale Zahn grinned again. "Evidence of corruption."

"That's what got Salome—Edna—that's what killed her? Corruption?"

"The rot killed her, Fats. The rot we all live in," the sheriff said, his grin gone. "It'll get you too, if you're not careful"

If that actually meant anything, Fats didn't know what it was. But it turned his thoughts elsewhere. "My pistol," he said. "Did Ramona tell you about it?"

"Interagency cooperation. Always ready to help a fellow law enforcement agent." Dale Zahn gave the old Colt Special a twirl on his finger. "I'm going to find a bed. Enjoy your. . . vigil."

The sheriff ambled out of the pasture, now and then giving the Colt a mocking whirl. At his cruiser, he lifted the hatch, took out a key ring, unlocked the steel evidence box, and stowed away Fats's pistol. He relocked the box, shut the hatch, turned, lifted his hand in a lazy wave.

Fats watched the red taillights disappear into the dark.

He looked down at the dead horse, a mere carcass now, meat already rotting. Putrefaction.

Corruption, Dale Zahn had said, that's what the briefcase held. Decay and death just waiting to do what they did. Strange thought, Fats knew. It didn't make sense. But it was true.

The lot light held the dark at bay. Stars glittered. The creek hissed. The desert air seemed almost material, a drapery concealing another, a more real, reality.

Fats knew he wasn't thinking right. He sat beside Omar and stopped thinking and was absorbed by the night.

Later, how much later he couldn't tell, a shadow moved across the pasture toward him. He tried to rise as Vi Barlow came up, but his stiff legs wouldn't work right. Then she was sitting in the grass beside him. "Thank you for staying with him, Fats," she said quietly. The bones of her face caught what little light the night admitted. "I'm not sure it's really necessary."

"You never know," Fats shrugged. "Critters. Coyotes. Cats."

After a moment, she said, "How are you feeling? Earlier I was so wrapped up in myself I didn't think to ask. I'm sorry."

"I'm fine," Fats said.

"In Pioche, growing up, I saw fistfights," she said. "Nasty affairs."

"Not much of a fight, this one," Fats said.

"You were very angry."

"Yes," he said.

"Was it Carroll Coyle, something he said," she asked, "or just about the way things are? Lots of folks out here are angry, packing pistols and screaming from bumper stickers."

"Both, I guess," Fats said. "Tell the truth, I don't really know." She stroked the muzzle of her dead horse. "He—Horst—seemed... professional." She paused. "What does it say about Carroll Coyle that he would hire a man like that? Hire him to replace Terry Blume?"

"If he did," Fats said. "Dale Zahn thinks Horst might be on David Mohr's payroll."

She looked out into the darkness. "At the funeral, Mr. Duggar was eager to talk to me. He seems to think that Dale is responsible for the young woman's death. She drowned... is that right? In the desert?"

"In maybe the only worthless body of water in the state of Nevada."

"Mr. Duggar thinks that Dale killed her." She shivered slightly. "Did he, Fats?"

"There's no evidence that says so," Fats said, "but yeah."

The silence grew. Finally Judge Barlow said, "We talked, that time in my office, about stains. But a better word is *taint*. It suggests an ongoing corruption. A stain can spread only so far, but tainted meat goes bad, as we say, and the rot keeps advancing. It can ruin everything eventually."

"Me and the sheriff were just discussing rot."

"You can wash away a stain," she said. "Or if it isn't too big, cover it, live with it. But taint has to be cut out."

Fats was suddenly on alert, listening carefully.

Vi Barlow sighed. "I've made an ally of Dale, politically. He's stained, what with his womanizing and some of the things he was into when he was with Las Vegas Metro, but not seriously. If he's involved in this young woman's death, though, that would taint him. I need to know for sure."

"All I've got are guesses," Fats said. "We were discussing evidence too. That's just what I don't have. And he knows it."

"What kind of evidence do you need?"

"I need that briefcase everybody's after, the one that belongs to David Mohr and Deseret Construction."

"But Alec Duggar told me she—Edna, he called her—was killed for the quarter of a million dollars that was supposedly stolen. I don't think David Mohr would kill anybody, and certainly not for that amount of money. Neither would Dale Zahn, as far as that goes."

"Dale says it's not about the money," Fats said. "He thinks there's papers that Mohr doesn't want anyone to see. Political papers."

After a silence, she said carefully, "I suppose that could be. Deseret Construction backs a number of Nevada politicians. Maybe there are questionable . . . arrangements. All I can say is that my relationship with David Mohr is strictly aboveboard. I haven't promised him anything. We haven't made any secret deals, Fats. I don't make deals like that."

Fats didn't know why she would tell him this or if it was the truth. Everybody lies, he believed, even Judge Vi Barlow, no doubt, when it suited. But he chose to believe her, maybe out of relief that she hadn't asked him, as for a moment he feared she would, to kill Dale Zahn. Why he had feared that he couldn't, at the moment, say.

The night deepened. Fats Rangle and Vi Barlow sat in the darkness beside the dead horse, talking softly. The subject shifted, and he found himself giving her a brief history of his family's efforts on Cherry Creek, exercises in frustration with cattle and alcohol until his father drank himself to death. The Rangle boys and their mother managed to keep the place, just, until Mary arrived with her grit and smarts.

Vi told him about Omar, a gift from her husband, about the gray's breeding and birth and breaking, about the pleasure both took in their rides through the desert, and about the comfort she found in his presence when her husband died.

Then, into a small silence he inserted a question. "Why did you really want to bring him out here?"

She didn't immediately answer. When she did, she again chose her words carefully. "What I told you at the time, Fats, was true. There are good stables around Las Vegas, but none better than yours. I knew Omar would be well taken care of. But of course you're right, there was something else. There was you Rangles."

Fats gingerly patted his bandaged ear. "Us? How?"

She smiled. "My political associates want to establish a Gull Valley presence. We want someone local to represent our interests."

David Mohr had said much the same. "You have Dale Zahn."

"He won't be sheriff, or even a resident, of Pinenut County after the next election. We need someone long term." Pale light shadowed her mouth. "If fact, it was Dale who suggested that you and Bill and especially Mary would be better choices."

"Why all this interest in Gull Valley?"

"It's a gamble, Fats," she said. "Some people think Gull Valley is going to boom, maybe not immediately, but soon. People with money will be moving in. You're already seeing the vanguard, with their airplanes and expensive automobiles and well-bred horses. And people with money have power, economic and political. My advisors are betting it will happen."

A sudden animal scream ruptured the silence. Then all went quiet again.

Fats spoke then: "You said, in your office, that you sensed someone trying to manipulate you. Me too." Fats looked at her, her face pale patches and shadow. "People have been after me almost from the moment I found that plane, offering me things—favors, jobs, sex. They want that briefcase. And nobody believes me when I tell them I don't have it.

Judge Barlow frowned. "And what do you think it's all about, finally?"

"I don't know," Fats said. Rot. Putrefaction. "Water?"

She rubbed her small white hands together, washing. "Hydroneva?"

"What else in the desert is worth anything?"

At the house, light appeared as the front door opened. Mary stepped out and made her way toward the pasture. Fats and Vi Barlow watched her approach.

Then the judge said, "The sex stuff. I hope you don't mean Sergeant Clare. I like her."

"Me too," Fats said.

Fats, returned to his bed, drifted in and out of sleep. He was vaguely aware that Mary and Vi Barlow had left the pasture for the porch.

He caught the aroma of freshly brewed coffee. He heard Bill start his pickup and drive off.

In the pre-dawn dimness, he rose, showered, and dressed. His headache lingered, but lightly. Tape and stitches, ugly though they were, were now minor irritants. He took more Tylenol and went out.

Mary, on the porch, greeted him with a cup of coffee. The judge, she said, was showering. Neither had slept much.

"Maybe you can sneak in a nap later," he said, sitting.

"Not hardly," she said. "Work doesn't do itself."

"She's tangled up with Dale Zahn," Fats said then. "Don't seem to be able to work her way out of it."

Mary followed his leap. "Ramona. Yes. Maybe she needs somebody to give her a real good reason to try harder."

"Yeah," Fats said again. "Maybe."

They drank coffee. The day dawned as Vi Barlow joined them on the porch. A bit later, the twins made kitchen noises before they came out and headed for the barn and chores. Fats went with them.

They'd just finished seeing to the horses when Bill drove in, towing a bright red backhoe. Fats opened the gate, and Bill pulled the machine to the far edge of the pasture. Soon he had it unhooked, situated, and leveled, the engine and hydraulics tested. His grin was big and boyish as he began to dig.

He was skilled and meticulous. The grave he cut into the desert was tidy, angles sharp and sides smooth, the removed earth a neat mound. The two women watched him work with approval, which broadened his grin.

At the same time, Fats, with rope and chain, carefully tied the dead horse to the pickup's trailer hitch and slowly, almost gently, tugged the animal across the grass. Then the brothers used both pickup and backhoe to arrange Omar's body at the edge of the grave. As Vi Barlow looked on, with chain and rope and machine they lowered the remains into the earth.

When Dale Zahn's cruiser rolled into sight, no one at the grave showed any interest in his arrival. Bill shut off the backhoe's engine and got out of the seat to join his wife and Vi Barlow. Silently they looked into the grave.

Fats crossed the pasture and met the sheriff at the porch. Wordlessly they sat and watched as Vi Barlow ceremoniously took up a handful of dirt and let it stream through her fingers.

"Dust to dust," the sheriff said. "This seems more like a funeral than what we had yesterday in the cemetery, doesn't it?"

Fats didn't disagree. The early-morning still and silence gave the burial a ritualistic air.

"You look like shit, by the way," the sheriff said. "You need new bandages, and something for the swelling."

Dale Zahn didn't look all that great himself. Under the brim of his Stetson, the flesh of his face sagged. His eyes were red-rimmed and sore-looking, his clothes wrinkled, slept in. "Spend the night in a cell, did you?"

"Donna heard I'd been out all day with Vi Barlow," the sheriff said. "She ignored the fact that Coyle and his shadow were along. She decided I've been sleeping with the judge for years."

Fats remembered Mary's remark. He put it out of his mind.

"She gets wound up," the sheriff said soberly. "There's always been a lot of screaming. She. . .well, you don't know how lucky you are you got out of it."

The three mourners turned from the grave and started across the pasture. When they got to the house, the sheriff, rising, said, "I'm a bit early, Judge, but we can head off to the airport whenever you're ready."

"I'm sorry, Dale. I should have called you. I've made other arrangements." She didn't sound especially apologetic. "I'm going to ride back with David Mohr. He'll be here shortly."

As she spoke, another vehicle seemed to erupt from the desert. The white pickup raced recklessly at them, then slued to a sudden, jerking stop. Donna Zahn leaped out into the cloud of dust, yelling. "You lying son of a bitch!"

She stood shuddering in the early-morning sun. Anger darkened, twisted her features. To Fats she looked somehow unreal, a mocking caricature of herself.

"Donna," Dale Zahn said firmly, "this isn't the time or—"

"Not in front of your slut?" Her voice rose, thinned, took on a tremolo. "Not while you've still got the stink of her on you."

"I slept in the jail last night," he said with husbandly weariness.

"Another lie! Look where I find you! Look who I find you with!"

Vi Barlow said softly, "There's nothing between Dale and me, Donna. There never has been. And last night I slept in the Rangles' spare room. Mary can tell you."

"Don't lie to me, bitch," Donna hissed. "You and your dainty little ways, you...you, you know...."

Rage flooded, washed away thought. She shook herself violently, an animal trying to rid herself of pain. She scrunched her eyes closed, gave out a sudden mindless screech.

Mary reached out a hand. "Donna, you probably haven't eaten. Or slept. Come in and let me fix you—"

"Get away! You're part of it, aren't you, you Rangles? Getting back at me for. . ." She turned suddenly to Fats. "Oh. What did they do to you, Norman? You're all. . .hurt."

"I'm fine," Fats said. "Why don't you let Mary—"

"Help me, Norman." She sagged into herself. "Why don't you help me?"

"Come on, Donna," Dale Zahn, moving toward her. "Let's go home."

"Fuck you," she said, again stiff, furious. "Just. . .fuck you."

He took a step toward her. "We'll go home. You can have a nap. Then we'll—"

"No!" She stepped back, almost stumbling. She put her hand on the grip of the Beretta holstered on her hip. "Stay away from me."

And everything changed.

"Easy," the sheriff said in a different voice, quiet now, calming. "You don't need a weapon, Donna. Nobody's going to hurt you."

She stared at him: angry, fearful, lost. Then she looked at Fats Rangle, asked again, pleading now, "Aren't you going to help me, Norman?"

Before Fats could speak, the sheriff said, "Give me the pistol, Donna." He held out his hand. Again he took a step forward.

"Stay away!"

"The pistol, Donna. You don't need it," the sheriff said, advancing, hand outstretched. "You know you aren't going to hurt anyone with it."

Donna Zahn screamed like the lion on the mountain and drew

the Beretta from its holster and raised it and shot her husband in his forehead.

He flopped back, twisting, into the dust, face down, blood and brain matter spattering the inside crown of his tilted Stetson.

Still screaming, Donna stepped forward and fired again. And again. The brass shell casings cartwheeled into the sunlight. Bloody rosettes blossomed on his shirt. She fired until the clip was empty. Then she dropped the automatic into the dust. Her scream became a wail, softened into keening.

The others stood stunned. Blood spread, soaked into Dale Zahn's shirtfront.

"Jesus," Bill said.

Then Mary moved, spoke quietly, led Donna like an invalid up onto the screened porch and into the house. Bill followed. Vi Barlow and Fats Rangle stayed with the body.

"I thought I'd seen rage yesterday, when you went after Carroll Coyle," the judge said. "But this . . ."

"She's had it hard," Fats said, and found himself, finally, after all these years, feeling something for Donna Zahn.

The judge looked at him closely. "Was she a friend of yours, Fats?"

"Once," he said. "A long time ago."

"She'll need all the friends she can get now," she mused. "Although who knows what they'll charge her with. A good lawyer might get her off. Emptying a pistol into a dead body, screaming all the while—a sane woman probably wouldn't do that."

"Probably not," Fats said.

She nodded at Donna Zahn's Beretta, dull with dust beside the body. "Strange nobody saw this coming."

"Didn't want to, I guess," Fats said. Then he added, "You should get out of the sun, Judge."

Fats watched her step up onto the porch and into the house. Then he looked down at the body lying on its side, eyes open and drying in the sun. Dead meat, already rotting. He looked at the head wound. The back of the sheriff's skull was smeared with blood bearing bits of bone and brain. The bullet sat almost innocently in his hat.

And Fats knew what to do.

He squatted, slid his fingers into Dale Zahn's pocket, and withdrew a ring of keys. Then he moved to the rear of the sheriff's cruiser and opened the hatch. He found the key to the lock on the steel evidence box. In a few seconds he was hefting his Colt Special.

There was something else in the box. Something wrapped in a black garbage bag. Something the size and shape of a briefcase.

For a moment Fats Rangle stood very still, letting it register. Then despite himself he smiled. The arrogant son of a bitch.

He wasn't angry. No reason. He just wasn't.

He stuffed the pistol into his waistband. He carried the garbage bag to his pickup and dropped it into the bed. He slid the dead man's car key into the cruiser's ignition. He took out his phone and called the Pinenut County Sheriff's Office.

While the phone rang, Bill came out of the house. Fats handed him the Colt. "Bury it with the horse."

Bill cocked an eyebrow but said nothing.

Finished phoning, Fats stepped up onto the porch. Vi Barlow came out of the house. They sat silently together, watching Bill start up the backhoe and shovel dirt into the grave.

Then above the crease in the desert hills, dust rose in a thin swirl. Judge Barlow smiled grimly. "Now it starts, Fats."

Caroline Sam arrived and directed gathering officers and agents of authority as they taped off the crime scene, flagged shell casings, took photographs, collected witness statements. That of Judge Vi Barlow seemed to certify the accuracy of the others.

Vi Barlow and Mary Rangle were in the house with Donna when a white limo came in sight, slowly approached, and stopped besides Fats's pickup. David Mohr, again in shades and jogging togs, got out. A state police trooper spoke to him. Then Caroline Sam joined them. Mohr sipped from a water bottle as he listened. After a brief exchange, he got back into the limo.

Fats stood, stretched, and left the porch. He took the black garbage bag from the bed of his pickup. Holding it, he stood silently before the idling limo's rear door.

The window descended, releasing a gust of cool air. David Mohr looked out. "Ex-Deputy? You tried your fists with the wrong man, I hear. You look it."

"I think this belongs to you," Fats said, holding up the bag.

Mohr smiled stiffly. "You don't know for sure?"

"Haven't looked."

Mohr's smile went cold. "As we agreed, Ex-Deputy—everybody lies."

"But not all the time," Fats said.

Mohr slipped off his sunglasses. "Get in."

Once Fats was in and settled, David Mohr took the garbage bag and tugged out a briefcase, leather, with bright brass fittings. The flap lock, bent and scarred, had been forced. Mohr pulled it open, reached in, and withdrew a plain manila folder. He glanced at several sheets of Deseret Construction stationery dark with type before slipping the folder back into the briefcase. "How did you come by it?"

Fats told him.

"So you weren't even looking for it." Mohr considered that, then said. "What was the sheriff going to do with it?"

"He'd of kept the cash," Fats said. "The papers. . .they'd be leverage. Political, I'd guess, knowing Dale."

David Mohr hesitated. Then he retrieved from the briefcase it a neat bundle of worn $100 bills and casually tossed it to Fats Rangle. "For services rendered."

Fats nodded. "I told Alec Duggar that if there was a reward, he'd get half."

Mohr flipped him another packet. "Give him this, for the grief we've caused him."

"Glad to," Fats said.

The AC whispered. David Mohr drank from his water bottle, then fell silent, watching out the window.

Fats turned to see two EMTs, observed by the assistant medical examiner, lift Dale Zahn's body onto a gurney, cover it with a sheet, and wheel it through the dust to their van. They took especial care, as if they were handling something of value.

The cool of the air in the limousine suddenly seemed to Fats artificial, false, part of some elaborate con denying the desert. He recognized the thought as odd. He was concussed, headachy and not quite right—not angry, but he was trying to tell himself something.

Then the CEO of Deseret Construction spoke. "I take it the shoot-
ing of Sheriff Zahn had nothing to do with his having found this?"
"A domestic," Fats said.
"And he didn't tell you what is in this folder?"
Fats hesitated. Death. Putrefaction. "He said there were probably
papers."
"But you haven't actually seen them?" Suspicion edged his voice.
"I said."
"No way, Ex-Deputy." David Mohr, attending to Fat's tone, scoffed.
"You can't have it both ways. You can't insist that everybody lies
and then complain when your own veracity is questioned."
"Fuck my veracity." But he wasn't really angry. "I don't suppose
you'll tell me what this is all about."
"You don't suppose correctly."
"It's water, isn't it? What else is worth something out here?"
David Mohr smiled. "Nothing is worth anything, Ex-Deputy, in
and of itself. It's all a matter of persuasion, convincing people to put
a price on whatever you might happen to have."
"Cons. Scams," Fats said. But he wasn't angry. He didn't know
why or what it meant. "Corruption."
"It's the way things are, Ex-Deputy. You know that." He nodded
at the currency in Fats's hand. "You're part of it."
Fats didn't protest. "Hydroneva. Is that you?"
David Mohr shut the briefcase. "Would it matter?"
"I guess not," Fats said. "It has to be somebody."
"And somebody has to serve as interim sheriff," David Mohr
said. "The county commissioners will make an appointment. You
interested?"
Fats didn't have to think about it. "Dale told me the job was
mostly PR and politics. I'm not real good at either. Caroline Sam
would do the job. I could work for her. Maybe...maybe I'd want
my deputy's badge back."
Mohr smiled again. "That might be arranged."
Fats nodded carefully. "Dale said what was in that briefcase was
rot. Rot and death."
Mohr looked at him. "Everybody dies."
Judge Vi Barlow appeared and opened the door. She glanced at

the two bundles of bills in Fats's hand as he got out. She gave him a longer look but said nothing.

And saying nothing made her part of it.

So now he knew. Not to a certainty, but near enough.

At that moment a trooper and another EMT came out onto the screen porch with Donna Zahn. She wasn't handcuffed. She seemed not to see as the two women helped her to the medical examiner's van.

"She's sedated, mildly," the judge said. "They'll take her to the clinic, not to jail."

To start the process that would end in Donna being treated rather than prosecuted. To Fats that seemed right.

Judge Barlow extended her hand. "Goodbye, Fats. I expect we'll meet again."

"Probably." Because whatever was going on wasn't finished.

She smiled and slid into the cool air and shut the door.

Fats Rangle watched the limo drag dust toward the highway. Then he stood unmoving in the desert heat.

"I didn't want you to hear on the news," he said into the phone. "Dale's dead."

After a while, she said, "Did you kill him?"

"No," he said.

After another while, she said, "We should talk, Fats."

"Yes," he said.

About the Author

BERNARD SCHOPEN was born and raised in Deadwood, South Dakota. He attended Black Hills State College, then earned a BA and MA in English at the University of Washington, and later a PhD at the University of Nevada, Reno. He taught at Truckee Meadows Community College and St. Anselm College before returning to UNR, where he was the recipient of the Alan Bible Teaching Excellence Awaard in 2007. Schopen has published seven novels, including four in the Jack Ross detective series, and was inducted into the Nevada Writers Hall of Fame.